That One Touch

CARRIE ELKS

CHAPTER
One

"DADDY, can you put my hair into a French braid?"

Presley Hartson looked up from his phone, where he was currently tapping out a very annoyed message to a supplier who'd *promised* that the marble tiles he'd ordered three months ago would be at the house he was renovating last week.

Only now were they admitting the tiles were somewhere in customs. But they didn't know where. And he wasn't looking forward to telling his client that.

"Come here." He put his phone down next to him and patted the top of his thighs. Delilah, his six-year-old daughter, jumped onto his lap, holding out her brush and a thick hair band. He took the band and slid it onto his wrist, then started trying to brush her wild hair.

"Ow! That hurts." She turned around to pout at him, and he wanted to laugh. Her expressions were the highlight of his day.

"Sorry." He gave her a rueful look and started brushing again, this time more gently.

"You sure you want a French braid?" he asked once the tangles were all gone. "I do a mean ponytail, you know?"

"I have dance class tonight. Everybody there has braids."

Yeah, but not everybody had a dad with fingers so calloused they could barely feel the strands of hair between them. The tips were thick thanks to years of playing the guitar and construction work, and it took him twice as long as it would anybody else to produce what was – let's face it – a braid that was too thick on one side and veered off just a smidge to the other.

It made him feel bad that he couldn't do this simple thing for her. She wasn't asking for a lot.

Delilah ran off before he could warn her to curb her expectations, her tiny feet pattering in the hallway.

"It's not good, Daddy," she said when she came back from looking in the mirror. "It's wonky."

He bit down a smile. "I know. Sorry, sweetheart."

She appeared back in the kitchen. "It's okay. You'll get there. Let's just stick with a ponytail for now."

That he could do. He undid the braid and brushed her hair again. Her hair was so thick yet so soft – she got that from her mom's side of the family. It smelled of the strawberry shampoo his own mom had bought her.

His phone buzzed as he doubled the hairband to make sure the ponytail was secure. Delilah was clearly already bored, she was trying to pull away from him. "Just one sec," he told her. Sure, it was off center, but at least it wouldn't fall out.

"That's your phone," she said. "Who's the message from."

Another thing that made him smile about his daughter. She was the nosiest kid he knew. "I'll check it later," he told her, kissing the top of her head. "It's time for school. Go grab your things. Your lunch bag is on the counter. We can practice your spelling list in the car."

"Spelling schmelling." Delilah wrinkled her nose. "Uncle Marley says that God invented spellcheck, so we didn't have to learn to spell."

Uncle Marley – Pres' twin brother – had a lot to answer for. The perennial bachelor who lived life to the fullest, but also loved Presley's kid almost as much as he did.

His whole family tried to make up for what Delilah was sure to be missing after her mom had passed. From the day she'd died, they'd formed a protective knot around him and Delilah. He liked that Marley teased his kid. She needed some lightness in her life. God knew, Pres wasn't always able to provide it.

As Delilah grabbed her backpack and slid her feet into the black shiny Mary Janes she'd picked out at the start of the school year, Presley pulled his own boots on and finally read the message.

Yeah, his customer was pissed about the tiles being late. Not that Mrs. Clancy was happy about anything right now. They'd reached the middle of the renovations. The time when all customers seemed to lose it. Being a construction manager sometimes felt like being a psychologist. He could guarantee with a fair amount of accuracy when he'd get the nasty threats like this one.

I'm going to tell all my friends not to use you.

I'm going to call my lawyer.

If you miss the deadline we agreed to I'll be docking your payment accordingly.

Once upon a time he'd have gotten pissed, too, and told the customer where to shove their threats. But he was older now. Wiser. And he had bigger things to worry about than whether Mrs. Clancy's fancy ranch house reno finished a couple of weeks late.

"I can't find my spelling list," Delilah shouted. "Where is it?"

Yeah, a lot bigger things. Like making sure this cute little cupcake of a kid grew into adulthood without him making any more mistakes.

"I took a picture of it on my phone," he told her, walking

into the hallway. "You can use that."

See, he could be a good dad sometimes. When he wasn't working from dusk til dawn and relying on the goodwill of his parents to help him raise his kid. His mom looked after Delilah most afternoons after school, taking her to activities or watching her at their house. He was grateful for it, knowing his daughter was safe and happy while he was trying to keep a roof over their – and everybody else's – heads. But he still felt like he was being pulled seven different ways.

"Thank you." Delilah skipped over to him and took his phone. He opened the front door, the cool rush of springtime air washing over him. Pres loved this time of year. Sunny but not too hot. The summer was a bitch because they'd have to start any outdoor work early to avoid the midday sun.

The sky was a perfect blue dome above them as he pressed the unlock button on his truck, helping Delilah up into the cab because her legs were too little to make the leap between the foot board and seat. He tweaked her ponytail, and she scowled.

Once he'd strapped Delilah safely in and he was in his own seat, he started the engine. "Tell me the words on your list."

"Shouldn't you be reading them off the phone?" Delilah asked over the roar of the engine as he put his foot down on the gas.

"I'll remember them." There were only ten. He at least had the faculties for that. If nothing else, it took his mind off his angry customer.

"Okay then. Copy, Baby, Happy, Study, Lady, Pretty, Empty, Funny, Brother, Sister…"

The way she trailed off made him lift a brow because he knew what was coming next.

"You have brothers, don't you?"

"Yep, they are your uncles." He continued the drive

toward her school.

"But no sisters."

"That's right." Up ahead he could see a couple walking together hand in hand. From behind you couldn't tell their ages, but he knew them to the day without having to see their faces.

"Look, there's Granny and Gramps," Delilah shouted excitedly, even though she saw them multiple times a week.

"Where?" He pretended not to see and Delilah laughed.

"Daddy, they're there. On the sidewalk, see?"

He slowed down and opened his window to call out to his parents. "Enough of the PDA this early in the morning."

His mom just about jumped out of her sneakers. One of the first things he did after Jade died was move closer to his parents. It was that or get a nanny for Delilah and his mom had begged to let them help. Most of the time it was pretty cool living a short walk from them.

Unless his mom was in a nagging mood about him needing a social life, or playing in the band he used to run with his brother, or maybe even meeting somebody new.

Yeah, she especially loved to nag him about that.

No thanks. He had no time for that. And he certainly didn't have time for the complications of dating while trying to raise a kid. His life was too full for relationships.

"Presley!"

Pres bit down a smile because his mom only used his full name when she was telling him off. And he might be almost thirty, but she still did it.

His mom shook her head, but her face softened as she saw Delilah leaning toward the window and waving at her. "Hey cutie pie."

"Hey Granny. I got a ponytail today." Delilah swished her hair around.

"So I see." His mom's eyes crinkled. "And you look cute as a button."

His dad caught Presley's eye. "Still can't do that braid, huh?"

"Nor can you," Presley pointed out.

His dad shrugged. "That's why I had three boys."

"As if you had anything to do with it." His mom rolled her eyes.

"Actually, I did," his dad pointed out. "It's the guy who decides the gender."

Pres cleared his throat because Delilah was listening intently. And he absolutely didn't want to have that kind of discussion with her right now.

"Gray Hartson," his mom said to his dad. "You hush right up."

His dad grinned, like he was enjoying the banter.

It was cool that Pres' dad could walk along the streets unbothered. Anywhere else in the US and fans would surround him, even after all these years post retirement from making music and touring. Gray Hartson had been a big fucking deal in music back in the day.

But somehow he looked more at home walking down the street hand in hand with his wife than he ever had with a guitar up on stage.

"Gotta go," Pres said, winking at his parents. "Be good. Don't get up to anything I wouldn't."

His mom rolled her eyes, but you could tell by the way she looked at him that she loved him fiercely. The way she loved all three of her boys. Presley and Marley had come first – Presley beating his twin by an hour – and then Hendrix a couple of years later.

"Oh, you didn't forget that Dad and I are out-of-town tonight?" his mom asked.

"Yep. I got it." He nodded. "Have a good time."

"You won't forget to pick up Delilah from dance class, will you?" she added, glancing at her granddaughter.

Pres lifted a brow. "Only if she gets her spelling words

wrong."

"Daddy!" Delilah protested. "You can't leave me at dance all night."

"Okay kid." He smiled at her because she was so easy to tease. "Don't worry, I'll be there. When have I ever let you down?"

———

"Okay, that's it for dancing this afternoon. Let's all come sit in a circle and wait for our parents to pick us up." Cassie Simons clapped her hands together, smiling at the troop of little girls all dressed in pink leotards and pale white tights, their tiny feet shining in satin ballet shoes with elastic sewn across the top to keep them from falling off.

She was in a leotard too, but hers was black, with a pair of sheer tights. Her feet were encased in soft ballet shoes. Her long thick hair was twisted neatly into a bun, revealing her heart-shaped face.

This age was her favorite class to teach, she decided, because watching them try so hard to follow her instructions while being giddy that they get to dress up, was a blast.

A few parents had already arrived and were standing against the walls, where they'd watched the last dance of the class – a fun one where Cassie had played the piano and told them to pretend to be birds migrating. Like the dying swan but happier.

Much happier, because they all kept giggling which made her smile.

"Okay, gang," Cassie said, sitting in the middle of the circle with the clipboard full of names she'd been given. "If your parents are here, point them out to me."

Before the words were out of her mouth she knew she'd made a mistake, because ten six-year-old girls started shouting excitedly at once.

"Okay!" she called out. "Let's start again. I'll say your name and you'll tell me if your parents are here. Let's start with Angelina Smith."

Within fifteen minutes all but one of her students had been picked up. Some parents had lingered to introduce themselves to the new teacher at the Forsythe School of Dance, others had asked her questions about how she thought their child was doing and whether she saw any potential in them.

And she'd had to answer honestly. It was too soon and they should be enjoying themselves for now. There was more than enough time for the pain of being over rehearsed and shouted at while your feet bled from being stuffed into pointes when they were older.

She knew that from experience.

"Delilah, isn't it?" she asked the one girl remaining. She was sitting in the corner of the room, holding a giraffe. She was a cute kid. She'd danced enthusiastically for the entire class, and it was clear she had a natural rhythm, as her pony-tail swayed from side to side.

Delilah nodded, suddenly shy, and Cassie's heart clenched, because she knew what it felt like to be forgotten.

"Don't worry, your…" Cassie looked at her sheet, "dad will be here soon. Maybe you can help me clean up while we wait? I could really use your help."

She gave the little girl a warm smile.

"Okay," Delilah said softly, standing up. She walked over to Cassie with her stuffed animal still in one hand. The other reached for Cassie's and Cassie took it, squeezing it reassuringly, because the little girl still looked scared. Maybe she should find something to keep her busy – wasn't that what she used to do when she felt alone? Fill her mind until she didn't think about it any more?

"How good are you at tidying up music?" Cassie asked, leading her to the piano. The sheet music was all over the place. It would probably take Cassie a minute to straighten them up, but she wanted to distract the little girl.

"I'm really good at it," Delilah promised, looking hopeful. She let go of Cassie's hand and reached for the papers. "I'm the best."

Damn, she was cute. She still hadn't let go of the giraffe, though.

"How about we put this little guy on the piano," Cassie murmured. "He can watch you work."

"It's a she. Lola," Delilah told her.

"Of course she is." Cassie looked at the giraffe with a serious expression. "I'm sorry, Miss Lola."

Delilah giggled and damn if that wasn't a good sound.

Ten minutes later and the studio was neat and swept, and Delilah's dad still hadn't arrived. And if she was being honest, Cassie was getting a little furious.

Only a little – not a lot. And not because she was being inconvenienced, she didn't exactly have much to run home for. But because the little girl kept looking hopefully at the door that never opened.

Why was it that some parents always put their kids last?

"I'll tell you what," Cassie said, smiling at Delilah. "Let's grab a couple of drinks from the staff room." And while they did that, she'd ask Gemma, her boss and friend, to call Delilah's dad. Wherever he was, it couldn't be more important than being here to keep his kid from getting upset.

Delilah nodded. "Yes please."

Okay then. Cassie grabbed Lola from the piano and passed her to Delilah before they walked out of the studio and down the hallway to the front of the dance school. A drink, a phone call, and hopefully Delilah would get home before it was time to go to bed.

But before he took her home, Cassie intended to give Delilah's dad a piece of her mind.

CHAPTER
Two

"HEY PRES!" Marley called out from the ground. Presley was on the roof, checking out the areas they'd fixed yesterday. It was due to rain overnight, and he didn't want any leaks. He'd spent half the morning calming Mrs. Clancy down, and he didn't want a repeat of it tomorrow. Good thing he could be a sweet talker if he wanted to be.

All words and no action.

He blinked at the sudden memory of that being screamed at him. He pushed it away and looked down at his brother, who was staring expectantly up at him.

"Yeah?"

"There's a call for you. From Delilah's dance school. You're late picking her up."

Fuck. What time was it? A glance at his watch told him it was half an hour past the time he could be considered a responsible parent.

"Shit." He tried to extricate himself from the short lead he'd clipped to his harness for safety. "Christ, I can't believe it. I set an alarm and everything."

"And left your phone down here," Marley pointed out.

Presley climbed down faster than he should have, unclipping the harness and looking around for his keys. If any of the crew had done that he would've been shouting at them.

"Here." Marley pressed them into his hands. "It's a few minutes, man. Don't look so worried."

"It's half an hour. And you know what Delilah's like about me being late."

She hated it. She always had since the day her mom didn't pick her up from daycare. Yes, she'd had counseling, and they'd had family therapy since then, but some wounds ran deep.

And he'd shoved a damn knife in it to open it up.

"Go. I'll clean up here," his brother urged. "Take her for an ice cream or something. She'll be fine."

Pres nodded at his brother, thankful as always to have Marley on his side. His brother worked with him part time on his days off from the fire house where he was a firefighter.

He was so used to having his brother around. They used to play together in a band, too, before he'd mostly given it up because being a single dad and playing gigs in bars really didn't mix.

It took him a lot less time than it should have to drive to the dance school. And yeah, he might have broken the speed limit but only barely and with a good reason. It was only ten minutes later that he was parking The Beast – Delilah's nickname for his huge truck – in the mostly deserted parking lot of the Forsythe School of Dance and climbing out of the cab in a hurry, his long legs speeding across the blacktop to the building.

When he strode into the reception area he could see that all the lights were off.

And Delilah was sitting on a chair, Lola crushed against her chest, her little legs swinging.

"Daddy." Her entire face lit up as she jumped down from the chair and threw herself at him. He wrapped his arms around her, stroking her silky hair.

"Mr. Hartson?"

He hadn't noticed the woman sitting with her. Was that Delilah's teacher? He had a vague memory of his mom mentioning the old one had left, but he hadn't paid that much attention. His mom did nearly all the pickups from class, so it hadn't been at the top of his mind.

He glanced over at her again. She was wearing a black leotard that clung to her curves, and her legs were encased in white tights that emphasized the tone of her muscles. Not that he should be looking at those.

He swiftly brought his eyes up to her face, hoping she hadn't noticed.

Her lips were pressed together. Her eyes narrow. But damn she was attractive if you were a douchebag who spent too long looking at somebody you shouldn't.

"I'm sorry I'm late," he said. His words were aimed at Delilah, but the teacher nodded.

"Could I have a quick word with you?" the teacher asked. "Alone?"

He glanced at Delilah as if to point out that it was almost impossible to be alone.

"Honey, why don't you grab a couple of those donuts from the staff room for you and your daddy to eat once you get home?" Delilah's teacher suggested, smiling warmly at her.

"Can I?" Delilah breathed, looking excitedly at Pres.

"Sure." He nodded.

Delilah skipped off, clearly happy now that he was here and her world was right again, leaving Pres alone with her teacher.

"Miss…" Damn, he didn't even know her name.

"Cassie Simons." She squared her shoulders but somehow she did it gracefully. It was like watching a bird move across the water. Every part of her seemed fluid. Light.

Such a contrast to his own body. Pres was built for

strength, not grace. Her eyes dipped to his arms, no doubt taking in the tattoos he had inked from his shoulder to his forearm.

All covered in dust from a day working on a construction site.

"I'm sorry I'm late," he said again. "My mom usually picks Delilah up."

"Delilah was very upset when you didn't arrive. She started crying, so I did my best to distract her," Cassie said. She had this soft voice that wrapped itself around you.

But her words felt like a slap.

"Crying?" Pres swallowed hard.

"She thought you weren't coming for her. You can't just leave a six-year-old waiting like that. It's not fair." She lifted a brow at him and he felt like he was being scolded by the teacher.

Annoyance rushed through him. "I didn't mean to. It was a mistake, that's all."

"Yeah, well mistakes to adults can feel like trauma to kids."

She'd just stepped over the line he'd drawn around himself and Delilah, to keep them safe and unhurt. He didn't let anybody that he didn't trust penetrate it. And he was pissed, really pissed that she dove head first into a place she didn't belong.

"How many kids do you have?" he asked her, his voice tight.

She actually blushed. "None."

"Uhuh." He lifted a brow, refusing to break their gaze. She ran the tip of her tongue along her bottom lip, her own eyes unwavering. He felt a tingle of electricity at the base of his spine. Like his muscles were waking up from a deep sleep. He'd be enjoying this, if this woman wasn't making him so mad.

"What's that supposed to mean?" she asked him, tipping

her head to the side. Her eyes were fiery and so damn pretty. His gaze dipped to her mouth.

Then resolutely away.

Her chest rose and fell with her breath. He wasn't going to look at it. He wasn't.

"It means that I'll only be taking advice from someone who knows what they're talking about."

Cassie's mouth dropped open, but she said nothing. And thankfully Delilah came back into the reception area, two iced donuts carefully balanced in her hands. She was walking slowly, like she was afraid they'd fall out of her palms and onto the floor.

"I got pink ones," she said, looking pleased with herself. She lifted her hands – already covered in pink frosting – and licked her thumb.

Okay, it was time to go. He didn't have time to argue with this woman. He had things to do. "Thanks for taking care of her," he said gruffly, taking the donuts from Delilah's sticky hands.

"No problem." Cassie's voice was tight.

"It won't happen again." He'd make sure of that, even if he had to strap an alarm clock on every limb. Being told off by the teacher really wasn't much fun. Especially when he knew she was mostly right, but he was too proud to admit it. He spent most days beating himself up. He didn't really need her help with it right now.

Not even if she had curves he couldn't get out of his mind.

"Can we eat them when we get home?" Delilah asked.

"After dinner. Say goodbye to Miss Cassie."

Delilah did one better. She threw her arms around Cassie's waist, taking her by surprise. "Thank you," she said, still squeezing tight. "You're my favorite teacher."

And when she pulled back, Cassie's cheeks were burning red. "Have a good evening," she said to Delilah as she turned around to grab Lola.

And no, he didn't look at her ass. Or see the sticky residue of Delilah's hand marks on her lower back.

Because somewhere deep down, beneath the tattoos and the dust and the muscles, he was a gentleman. And gentlemen didn't leer at their kid's new dance teacher. No matter how long it had been since their hands had touched another woman. Because his daughter came first, always.

He'd promised himself that from the moment he became a widower.

———

"I can't believe you forgot to pick her up." His mom sighed over the phone. She and his dad were in Washington DC and she'd called to check in before the two of them went out for the night.

"I didn't forget her, I was just a little late, that's all."

"Half an hour late, Presley. I'm surprised they didn't charge you."

He was finishing loading the dishwasher after dinner. Delilah was sitting in the den, fresh from her shower, wearing her favorite pink and white unicorn pajamas while she watched some cartoon he couldn't remember the name of.

She'd fully recovered from him being late, but he hadn't quite gotten there yet. The guilt nagged at him while they ate dinner, and he hadn't wanted to eat the donut Delilah had snagged for him from the dance school. She'd asked if she could have it, but he'd shaken his head and put it in the refrigerator for another day.

Her diet wasn't always the best, but dammit, he was trying.

That was the story of his life. He tried to keep everybody happy. Tried to keep a roof over his kid's head. Tried to help her heal from losing her mom and tried to be both parents to her at the same time.

Tried and failed.

Yeah, he was in that kind of mood. He needed to snap out of it.

"I'll buy her teacher some chocolates or something to say sorry," he murmured, thinking out loud.

"Presley." There she went, telling him off again.

"What? What do you want me to do?"

"I don't know. Not be late." His mom sounded frustrated. And he got it, he did. When Jade died three years ago he'd been a mess. She and his dad had stepped in and taken care of him and Delilah.

But things were better now. They have a house, he has a job, and Delilah's thriving at school. She loved unicorns and giraffes and dance class.

She was a normal little kid, and he was so thankful for that. She laughed, and she cried and she snuggled up to him when they watched movies together.

"I'll sort it out," he promised. "I'll send flowers."

"That's better," his mom said warmly. "You're a good boy at heart."

He laughed at the term boy. He hadn't been that for a long time. By the age of thirteen he and Marley had been taller than their mom. By sixteen they were a full foot higher. Wherever they went, the two of them dominated the room.

The Heartbreak Boys, people in the town would whisper as they walked through the square. As handsome as their daddy, but twice as dangerous.

"You having a good time?" he asked his mom, loading a soap pod into the dishwasher and flicking it on. Once Delilah was in bed, he'd put in a load of laundry and attack some invoices. He had little time to sit around and do nothing, but that was mostly the way he liked it.

He liked being busy. Building things, making things. It beat thinking about how lonely you were in the middle of the night.

His mom was telling him about the party they were about to head to. He listened as he cleaned up the counters, humoring her.

"I guess I'd better go," she finally said. "We'll be home tomorrow to pick Delilah up from school."

"You sure?" he asked. He hated taking advantage of his parents. But they'd had this conversation enough times – they loved having Delilah around. They wouldn't hear of him getting a nanny or putting Delilah in after-school care.

His kid was lucky to have so many people who loved her.

"I'm sure. Now sleep tight. And don't forget to send the flowers."

"I won't." He disconnected the call and slid his phone in his pocket.

"Daddy?" Delilah called out. "Come watch with me."

He dried his hands on a towel and walked into the living room where his daughter was curled up on the sofa, Lola the giraffe wrapped tight in her arms. The stuffie was getting threadbare now, the fur on the ears had been rubbed away by her fingers over the years, and his mom had sewn the poor giraffe's eyes back on.

"Okay." He sat on the sofa next to her and she immediately climbed into his lap. She smelled of flowers and fresh showers and he breathed her in.

"Miss Cassie says I'm good at dancing," Delilah told him, her eyes still glued to the television screen.

"Yeah, you are."

Delilah preened like a cat. "And she says I have pretty hair."

"That's because I put it in such a great pony tail," he teased.

Delilah sighed. "No, she had to re-do it for me. She can do French braids too, but she didn't have time before class."

Of course she could. He got the feeling his kid thought this new teacher was some kind of superhero.

"She's pretty," Delilah continued. "Isn't she?"

Pres blew out a mouthful of air. Yeah, she was, if you liked that kind of thing. Which apparently he did.

Or his libido, if it still existed, did.

His head, not so much. He was still bristling at her words, no matter how close to the truth they were.

She thought he was a bad dad. Yeah, well, he thought that daily, too. She could join the long line of people wanting to join that club.

"Am I pretty?" Delilah asked.

"Yeah, you are. And you're smart and you're funny and I love you very much." He kissed her brow.

"I love you too." She snuggled up against him. "But I'm not that smart. I only got four out of ten on my spelling test."

CHAPTER
Three

THE SUN WAS SHINING as Cassie drove into work, which was a blessing after the overnight rain. She was still getting used to the short commute she now had. When she'd lived in the city, she'd had to catch two trains to get to work. It was one of the reasons she'd agreed to help her friend Gemma out by moving to Hartson's Creek and teaching at the Forsythe Dance Studio.

She'd first met Gemma when she was nine and Gemma was eleven. It had been Cassie's first day at her new school for performing arts and Gemma had been assigned as her buddy. It had been Cassie's mom's dream for Cassie to become a dancer, and Cassie had auditioned three times before she'd been given a place at the school.

They'd spent most of their days dancing, singing, and acting, their academic education second to their physical training. Their classes had been mixed – that's how she and Gemma had become such good friends. They'd sit around after school while they were waiting to be picked up, giggling about the 'trifecta' their teachers were always lecturing them about.

"It's not enough to be great at one thing. You have to be

great at three to make it. Music, dancing, and acting. They're the three legs your careers will rest on."

When Cassie was seventeen, she'd joined the New York Academy of Ballet, and it had almost broken her heart to leave Gemma behind. By nineteen, Gemma had given up on performing and took a gap year to travel the world.

That's where she'd met Riley – her now husband. By twenty they were married and she was pregnant. Soon after they'd moved to Hartson's Creek, Riley's home town, where he had a job at the local bank.

Cassie and Gemma had kept in touch as much as they could. And then when Cassie's career was cut short thanks to her accident, Gemma had offered her a job at the Dance School she'd opened, while Cassie decided what she wanted to do with the rest of her life.

Because it was clear she couldn't dance anymore. Not professionally anyway. Teaching was the best she could manage.

Parking her car outside of the studio, Cassie grabbed her bag before climbing out. She had an hour before her first class – a mommy and me one – so she was planning on doing some exercise. Use it or lose it. And she didn't want to lose it, mostly because dancing filled her soul.

It was the one time she could push everything out of her mind. Forget who she was and any troubles tickling her brain. She'd lose herself in the movement and rhythm of her dance, in the stretching of her feet and the tautness of her muscles.

"Hey!" Gemma greeted her as she walked inside. "I've got a bone to pick with you."

She didn't look annoyed, though. Which was good because Cassie had enough annoyance from Delilah's dad last night. She'd spent the evening trying to work out why she'd reacted so strongly to his anger.

Why she couldn't stop looking at the way his dusty t-shirt clung to his chest, or the inked designs along his arms.

Ugh. He was so not her type. And yet somehow she couldn't get him out of her mind.

"What's wrong?" She stopped at the counter and dropped her bag to the floor.

"These just arrived for you." Gemma pointed at an enormous bouquet behind her. "I put them in some water. They're beautiful."

Cassie stared at them, surprised. "Where did they come from?"

"Only one way to find out." Gemma grinned, passing her a little white envelope – the kind that always seemed to go with flowers. Cassie opened it and unfolded the non-descript card.

The writing was masculine. As though he'd written it himself rather than calling the order through to a shop.

Sorry for being late. It won't happen again.
Presley Hartson

Oh. She looked at it for a moment, like she was trying to read between the lines. Had she really been that much of a bitch last night?

Probably. But then she hated seeing the little girl cry. She'd been there too often herself. Forgotten. Alone.

Ugh, that was history now.

"I take it he came to pick up Delilah eventually, then?" Gemma asked. She'd been the one to call Mr. Hartson at Cassie's request, but she hadn't been able to stay late with Cassie as she had two kids of her own who were hungry for dinner, and there was no way Cassie was going to let them suffer because Presley Hartson worked on his own time frame.

"Yep." Cassie lifted a brow.

"The flowers are a sweet touch. I wish he'd sent me some." Gemma sighed.

"You're married." Cassie smiled because she knew how in love Gemma and Riley were. He was a good guy, and Gemma knew it.

"I know, but a girl can dream. According to Riley, the Hartson brothers were everybody's crush during high school. No other guys had a chance."

For a moment, Cassie imagined Presley Hartson as a teenager, with the kind of swagger he only hinted at yesterday.

Yeah, she probably would have been a fan, too.

"Such a shame though, what happened to his wife," Gemma added, her expression suddenly serious.

Cassie's throat tightened. "What do you mean?"

"You don't know?" Gemma asked. "I suppose you wouldn't. Why would you? You're new." Gemma smiled at her. "We need to write a handbook or something. It could have the history of Hartson's Creek and a brief rundown of Chairs."

"Chairs?" Cassie frowned. "What's that."

Gemma waved her hand. "I'll tell you about that later. But I can't believe I didn't tell you about Presley. His wife died three years ago. He's been raising his little girl alone since then."

Cassie blinked. He was a widower? And she'd given him a hard time about being a bad dad? "Oh." She felt terrible. Worse than terrible.

"He gets help from his parents. His mom is the one who usually does the pick ups from dance class," Gemma continued.

She didn't know whether to be relieved or disappointed that she might not see him again.

Relieved. She was relieved. She didn't need to be mooning after a widowed man. Her life was complicated enough, thank you very much.

She'd only arrived in Hartson's Creek a week ago. She'd barely had time to unpack the boxes the delivery company had left stacked up along the walls in her rented house. Not that she needed most of it. Cassie wasn't really one for too many possessions.

According to the therapist she'd seen after the accident, that came from a lifetime of moving around. After her dad left her mom when Cassie was a baby, they'd moved around a lot. Her mom still did. It was like she was always searching for something she couldn't have.

As for her dad, Cassie barely heard from him. She'd long since accepted he wasn't interested, even if her mom had always pined for him.

Neither of them had visited her at the hospital after her accident. Her dad hadn't even sent a card. Her mom had called from Italy – where she'd been staying with some boyfriend – and that had been it.

When the doctor had explained that her ankle would never heal properly and that she'd never be able to dance en pointe again, she hadn't bothered to tell either of them. Her career was over thanks to a rainy night and a car with balled tires and she'd never felt more alone.

She could teach, though. So when Gemma had visited her – yes visited, even though she'd had to arrange childcare and cover at the dance school – and offered her a job, Cassie had taken it. She'd wanted to get away from New York, the city she'd grown up in. It had felt stupid to stay when she had no job and no prospects for the future.

Moving to West Virginia felt like a good way to take her mind off things while she worked out what she was going to do for the rest of her life.

So here she was. Teaching kids to dance. Living the dream life.

With flowers from a dad she'd misjudged on her first day.

"Is it okay to leave the flowers here?" Cassie asked. "I'll take them home tonight."

"Sure, no problem." Gemma gave her a warm smile.

"Thanks. I'm going to head to the studio and warm up." She picked her bag up, taking one last look at the bouquet. There were lilies. Her favorite. The same flowers her mom always sent her before opening night.

She wasn't sure why that felt significant but somehow it did.

"I'll see you in an hour." She'd buy Gemma a coffee after her first class when she had a break. Maybe this was the main reason she'd taken the job. So she could spend time with her best friend, the way they used to. Gemma felt like the only family she had anymore.

Angry dads aside, she already knew she'd made the right decision in coming here. And if she saw him again, she'd apologize too.

But she probably wouldn't see him again.

———

By Friday, Cassie felt exhausted. She wasn't sure if it was from the mental effort of trying to learn a hundred unfamiliar names or the physical effort of unpacking all the boxes in her house, but either way she was bone tired as she waved off the last children in her class.

She quickly showered in the staff washrooms and pulled on a pair of jeans and a t-shirt, looping her hair into a messy bun before running a slick of gloss over her lips.

By the time she reached the reception area, Gemma had locked the doors. "Ready?" she asked.

She'd invited Cassie to join her and her kids for dinner at the diner. An invitation Cassie had gratefully accepted. Gemma and her children dine there every Friday for dinner –

Riley worked late on Friday nights so it's their little treat for the weekend.

The diner was in the center of Hartson's Creek, flanking the grassy town square where a bandstand stood in the center. Most of the buildings in the center were commercial ones. There was a hair salon – Gemma told her which stylist was the best – along with a realtor, a bank, and a bar. On the other side of the square was a white building with a spire – the First Baptist Church.

Gemma's kids were running ahead of them on the sidewalk. Lucy's the oldest, at seven, and behind her was Andrew, who was five. The kids stopped and waited for them when they arrived at the diner. Gemma reached over their heads and pushed the door open.

The sound of voices and laughter – *and was that a real jukebox?* – hit them as soon as they stepped inside, behind Lucy and Andrew who were already running to the back. "Mom, somebody's in our booth," Lucy complained.

"Honey, it's not ours," Gemma told her. "The seats are first come first serve, remember? There's a table over there. Go grab it."

"But it's not a booth."

Gemma gave her daughter the kind of look that Cassie knew all too well. She used it herself sometimes, when her students were shouting and not listening and she had to clap her hands to be heard.

"Okay." Lucy nodded, looking resigned.

"We're leaving actually, if you want ours," a woman said. She was about Cassie's age, with long dark hair and striking eyes. It was a face that drew a second glance. She slithered across the cracked leather bench seat of the booth, swinging her denim-clad legs to the front to stand.

"Oh, hey Grace," Gemma said, smiling at the woman. "That's so kind of you."

"Not a problem." Grace was the perfect name for her. She

had the kind of innate glamor that you didn't often see in women their age. "I'm just waiting for Pres. Here they are…"

Cassie felt a prickle on the back of her neck as she slowly turned around. Delilah was running out of a door at the back that led to the bathrooms, followed a few feet behind by her father.

Presley Hartson. The man she'd insulted a few days ago.

It was weird how quickly their eyes connected. The impact of his stare made her skin tingle.

She'd thought he was attractive when she'd seen him at the dance school. But that was nothing compared to now. There was no dust, no evidence of a day working hard with his hands. He was wearing a pair of jeans and a gray t-shirt, his hair a little messed up as though he'd been running his hands through it. He had a day's worth of beard growth, too.

It made him look dark and dangerous.

"Miss Cassie," Delilah called out, grinning at her. "What are you doing here?"

Before Cassie could respond, Delilah threw herself against Cassie, her arms circling her waist. It was impossible not to hug her back. She was so full of life and excitement, it made Cassie's heart feel warm.

"I'm just getting some dinner," Cassie told her, smiling at the little girl. "Have you eaten?"

"Yep. I had nuggets. My favorite."

"They were my favorite when I was your age, too," Cassie told her.

"They were?" Delilah's face lit up like Cassie had just told her she'd won a million dollars. "Oh wow." She turned to look at her dad, who'd caught up with them. "Daddy, did you know that Miss Cassie likes nuggets, too?"

Cassie didn't bother to correct her. Anyway, she kind of did still like them. They were comfort food, and she was all for that.

Presley's gaze landed on her again. This time it was cool. Appraising. She parted her lips to take in a breath.

"Hi," he said stiffly.

"Hi." She smiled at him. He didn't smile back. "Thank you for the flowers. You didn't need to."

Delilah had wandered over to Lucy. The two of them started talking rapidly about some TV show they both liked. Grace and Gemma were chatting, and Andrew was standing by his mom's side, looking shy.

Presley shrugged. "No problem."

She took a deep breath, because it had been playing on her mind all week. "I shouldn't have spoken to you the way I did," she told him. "I'm sorry."

He blinked, and she noticed how thick his eyelashes were. Most women would kill for natural lashes like that. Or at least pay a lot of money for them.

"It's fine." His words sounded like a period. No more conversation needed.

And yeah, she wasn't stupid enough to tell him how sorry she was about his wife. But she felt it. Yes, she'd hurt her ankle, but he'd lost his everything. It wasn't comparable, and she felt bad for the way she'd talked to him.

"Delilah, we gotta go," he called out.

"Can't we stay?"

"We have to get ready for Chairs."

"Oh yay!" The little girl clapped her hands together, the diner clearly forgotten. "What are we waiting here for? Let's go."

He gave Cassie a nod and she nodded back. Okay, so he still disliked her, she could live with that.

She didn't have to be friends with everybody. She'd learned that at an early age. But she was a friendly person at heart and hated that she'd gotten off to a poor start with him.

"Bye Miss Cassie!" Delilah waved and ran to the door, Grace and Presley following behind her.

She'd forgotten about Grace. Was she his girlfriend? She was pretty enough. A good match for the stupidly attractive Presley Hartson.

Not that it mattered. It wasn't as though she was interested, anyway. She liked her men to smile now and then.

And not hate her.

"Come on, let's sit down and order," Gemma said, hustling Andrew onto the bench next to Lucy. "I don't know about you guys, but I'm starving."

———

An hour later she and Gemma were laughing about the Trifecta of Performing that was hammered into them at stage school, while the server cleared their plates. They'd spent most of dinner talking about old friends and what they were doing now. Lucy and Andrew were coloring a sheet they'd been given, waiting patiently for the ice cream Gemma had promised them if they behaved well at the table.

"Can I ask you something?" Cassie asked.

"Sure." Gemma smiled.

"Does Presley Hartson's girlfriend dance? She looks like a dancer."

Gemma blinked. "He doesn't have a girlfriend."

Cassie's heart did a weird clench. Ugh. "Who was he with tonight then?"

"Grace?" Gemma asked. "She's his cousin. Her mom and his dad are siblings." Gemma shrugged. "There are a lot of Hartson's in this town. Hence the name."

Cassie blinked, feeling stupid. It was Hartson's Creek. She hadn't put the two together. She had now though. "So the Hartsons are like royalty around here then?"

Gemma shrugged. "Something like that. Maybe they should bring some thrones to Chairs," she chuckled.

Cassie remembered Gemma had mentioned Chairs before,

and never expanded on it. "What is Chairs anyway?" she asked, curious.

Gemma grinned. "Oh I really need to write you that Hartson's Creek manual." She took a sip of her coffee the server had just topped up. "Chairs is when the town gets together on Friday nights. If the weather is good, we all carry our chairs down to a field by the creek and the kids play flag football or hang around and the adults drink lemonade and gossip."

"No way. That's not real. It sounds like something from a TV show," Cassie said. She could picture the *Gilmore Girls* carrying their Chairs to the square to sit around and gossip.

"I'm not lying, I swear," Gemma protested. "I thought it was made up, too, when we first moved here. But it's actually kind of sweet. You get to know everybody really quickly at Chairs." She lifted a brow at Cassie. "Maybe you should come tonight? We're meeting Riley there. He's going straight from work."

"Oh no, I can't. I have to finish my unpacking. But thank you." It was a lie, but only a little one. Fact was, she'd imposed on Gemma enough. She appreciated her friend for showing her around town, but Gemma and her family deserved some family time without her. She was determined not to be a burden on them. She needed to make her own friends.

And then Presley Hartson's face flashed into her mind. She pushed that thought firmly away.

"Maybe next week then?" Gemma asked, reaching for the check, but Cassie grabbed it first.

"For sure," she said. "And this is on me. To say thank you for all you've done."

CHAPTER
Four

PRES SPENT Sunday morning at the construction site, inspecting some work his sub-contractors had done. Luckily, they were building this one from scratch so there were no live-in owners to work around. The Clancys wanted a modern ranch house, with everything built in and future proofed. But their taste for luxury ran a little deeper than their bank balance, so every penny he spent was scrutinized and questioned.

"We've cut back as far as we can," he was telling Mr. Clancy who'd clearly been sent by his wife to check out the progress of the build. "If we need to reduce the budget anymore I can give you a list of things we can remove from the plan, but you said you want everything."

And they wanted it now.

He understood it. The Clancys were living with Mr. Clancy's parents, and that kind of living arrangement rarely suited anybody. Put grown adults of different generations together and there were bound to be problems.

Hell, even his own family had its moments, and they were a close knit tribe.

"Just try not to overrun anymore." Mr. Clancy said,

pressing his lips together. He knew that the budget overrun came from them changing their minds about which rooms they wanted where, and which bricks and windows and kitchen features they preferred.

"I'll do my best," Presley promised. His phone vibrated in his pocket. "I have to go, but we'll be here first thing tomorrow to get back at it." He was due to meet his family at his parents' house. It was Sunday which meant family dinner. A ritual that meant even more to his mom since Jade died.

"Thanks." Mr. Clancy nodded. "We really appreciate your hard work, even if Kate loses it sometimes."

"It's understandable. It's your home, you want it perfect."

They exchanged glances, and that was it. He needed to get home and fast.

His parents had taken Delilah to church that morning the same way they did every Sunday. Most of the Hartson family spent their Sunday mornings there, and between his dad's siblings and spouses, plus their mostly grown-up children, there were a lot of them.

Nowadays, his extended family took up half the pews.

But church just wasn't his thing. It hadn't been growing up, but he'd still trudged along with his parents when he had to. He'd gotten married in a church, had his kid christened in a church and then he'd been to his wife's funeral in a church.

But it was hard to believe in God when he had a little girl without a mom, so he avoided it when he could.

By the time he made it back to his parents' house, their cars were all in the driveway. He parked his truck behind Marley's convertible, climbing out and checking himself in the mirror.

No dirt or dust. Thank God. His mom didn't ask for a lot but she preferred he didn't trudge the construction site into her house on a Sunday.

He walked around to the back of the house, the way he always did. He'd grown up in this house. Spent half of his childhood playing football in the yard with his brothers. Spent the other half in the recording studio at the back of the property, just before the tree line began. First listening to his dad play or produce another band.

Then learning to play himself.

For years playing the guitar was all he wanted to do. Messing around with Marley in the studio, and later with Hendrix as well, had been his idea of heaven. Sure, they'd had to go to school, then college, and finally get a day job.

His parents were well off, but there was no way Pres was going to mooch off them. So he'd started his own company and Marley had joined him. They'd both always been active, hating the idea of sitting behind a desk and taking orders from somebody else. It had been natural for him to want to be the boss, and Marley to work with him when he wasn't at the fire station.

They'd started small. Taking on renovations within their capabilities. Always getting in and dirty while also being project managers. Over the years, their business and their reputation had grown.

Now they were the number one ranked construction company in the surrounding counties.

The glass doors that lined the wall of his parents' kitchen were open, and Presley strolled inside. Delilah was sitting at the counter, furiously coloring away in a book, while his mom was chatting to her, helping his dad make the Sunday pot roast they always preferred.

"Hey." He kissed his daughter's head. She looked up at him grinning. "How was church?" he asked her.

"We learned about another Delilah," she said, her blue crayon between her fingers. "She was very naughty."

He lifted a brow at his mom. She shrugged.

"Good thing you're a good girl then." He looked over at his twin. Marley was peeling potatoes, his thick club of a hand cradling the vegetable in one hand, the other niftily slicing away the skin.

"You not at the station today?" Pres asked him.

"Nope. Got today off. Decided to grace you all with my presence." He flashed a perfect set of white teeth.

"We're honored," their mom drawled. "Now get on with the peeling. I need those potatoes."

"On it, ma'am." Marley touched his fingers to his head in a salute, narrowly avoiding grazing his head with the peeler.

Their mom rolled her eyes and went back to basting the meat.

"Daddy, why don't you come to church with us?" Delilah asked. "The other daddies are there."

He felt his chest tighten. "I have to work, honey."

Not that he was looking, but he felt the warmth of his parents' stares on his face. They knew why he couldn't go. Why he didn't believe in goodness right now.

But he didn't want his kid to know that.

"Another time," he promised. Code word for never.

Delilah nodded as though she understood. "Miss Cassie was there."

And yeah, that band around his chest tightened even more. "That's nice."

"She's so nice, isn't she?"

"Who's nice?" Marley asked.

"Delilah's new dance teacher," his mom said. "I stopped by to say hi after service. And yes, she's very nice."

"She and Daddy argued last week," Delilah added, and Pres rolled his eyes. Great. As if he needed reminding of that.

Hendrix spluttered out a laugh. Pres shot his younger brother a death stare.

"You arguing with nice women, bro?" Hendrix asked. "This is why you're perennially single. You're meant to be nice to them."

"Presley doesn't remember how to be nice." Now Marley was joining in. Though the tone of his voice told Pres he was teasing. "That's why everybody at work calls him the Rottweiler."

"They don't call me the Rottweiler." Pres frowned. "Do they?"

Marley shrugged, looking amused.

"Stop changing the subject," Hendrix said. "I want to hear about Delilah's new dance teacher. What's her name? Is she pretty? Why did nobody introduce me to her?"

"Because you're a neanderthal," Marley said, grabbing Hendrix in a head lock. "We're trying to save the female population of Hartson's Creek from their worst fate."

"Shut the hell up." Hendrix struggled in his brother's grasp. "I'm a catch."

"The kind you should put in a cage," their mom said, rolling her eyes at their mock-fighting. "Now stop fighting. Before I send you both home with no dinner."

Funny how quickly they stepped apart at that threat. A wry smile pulled at Pres' lips. Sometimes his brothers behaved like they were younger than Delilah, who was pointedly ignoring them, deciding her coloring book was more interesting than her uncles beating each other up.

"Seriously though," Hendrix said, reaching over his dad's shoulder to grab a carrot stick. "Hook me up."

"Leave her alone." Pres gave him a pointed glance. "She's Delilah's teacher."

Delilah looked up at her name being said. "Are you talking about me?"

"Ignore us, sweetheart." Marley shot her a wink. "Just uncles behaving badly."

"You should go to church," she said, shaking her head the same way his mom did. Sometimes the similarity between them was striking. "I bet there's a bad Marley and a bad Hendrix in the bible, too. Much worse than the bad Delilah."

Hendrix snorted. Marley shook his head, a smile playing on his lips.

"Yes, they should go to church," his mom said, sending her two younger sons a pointed look. "All three of you should." She lifted a brow at Pres. "Maybe then you'd learn some manners.

———

"All I'm saying is I think it's time," Marley said to Pres later that day, lifting his bottle of beer to his mouth. "It doesn't have to be a big thing, but I miss making music with you. I miss us having fun at gigs together."

Dinner was over, the table had been cleared, and the three brothers had washed the dishes and cleaned up the kitchen while their parents and Delilah sat with their heads almost touching over a jigsaw puzzle.

Pres' daughter was now snoozing, all curled up in his mom's favorite easy chair, her little lips half open as she softly breathed out. The rest of them were watching the sports channel – the sound turned down so that it didn't wake Delilah.

"It won't work," Pres pointed out. "Having a kid is hardly compatible with touring."

It wasn't the first time Marley had suggested they get the band together again. And yeah, Pres got it. He missed playing in front of crowds. Sure, he still played a tune on the guitar when the mood struck, but it was a far cry from the gigs they used to throw back when times were different.

When he wasn't a single dad.

"I'm not talking about touring," Marley said, his eyes catching Pres'. When they were kids it was like looking in a mirror. But Marley didn't have the shadows beneath his eyes that Pres had.

He was lighter. Happy go lucky. Pres loved that for him.

"We can play locally," Marley continued. "There are enough places within driving distance. It doesn't have to be a big deal."

"What am I gonna do, put Delilah in the backseat and tell her to stay there until I come back?" Pres glanced over at her. She hadn't moved at the sound of her name. She really was fast asleep.

"We could watch her," his dad's deep voice intoned. "You know we love her staying with us. And the chances are it'll be on a weekend night, so no school the next day."

"Even if she did have school we could take her," his mom added, her smile soft as she looked over at her granddaughter. "You know she'd love being here with us."

Yeah, she would. Delilah was always asking to spend more time with her grandparents. This house was her second home, after all. But it didn't stop him from feeling guilty. Like he should be able to cope with having a kid but he wasn't.

"See?" Marley said, grinning. "Problem solved."

"So you think Alex and Diana will come back?" Pres asked, playing for time because he hated letting his brother down.

Marley grimaced. "They split up. Diana left town. But Alex would be up for it. I know he would. He hated it when we took the break."

Alex was their bass guitarist, and his girlfriend Diana had played keyboard. Her voice had added a nice tone to the vocals, too.

"We can't play without a keyboardist," Presley pointed out.

Marley shrugged, unfazed. "Then we'll find one. I'll put the word out. Put up some fliers. You don't have to lift a finger. Come on, let's try it. If you hate it, then we'll stop. But it feels like it's time…"

The way his brother said it made Presley feel like he was talking about more than playing in a band.

"Okay. We'll try. But you have to take the lead." He hated auditions. They were awkward and saying no wasn't his thing. He did enough negotiations in his day job.

"Works for me." Marley grinned. "You're a poor judge of character, anyway."

"Thanks." Presley rolled his eyes at him, but Marley's smile widened. The ying to his yang. The light to his darkness. The two of them had been inseparable since the day they were born.

He couldn't help but notice how his mom was squeezing his dad's hand. Or how she was mouthing 'thank you' to Marley when she thought he wasn't looking.

This was clearly part of their '*Operation: Get Pres out of the house for something other than work*' plan.

Maybe they were right. He owed it to them to at least try it. He might not have played much music in the past few years – at least not in public – but he'd written enough songs for them to fill a full set list without trying.

"Did somebody say my name?" Delilah muttered, one eye opening.

Presley bit down a smile. "About half an hour ago."

She blinked, her other eye opening. "Why?"

It was funny how she hated being left out of anything. "We were talking about me and Uncle Marley playing some music together some time."

"Can I play?" she asked.

"You can come watch us rehearse sometime," he promised her. "But if we play in a bar you'd have to stay here with Granny and Gramps."

"We could make pizza and watch movies," his mom said. Delilah's face immediately lit up. "And you could sleep over those nights."

"Can I?" she asked, her gaze sliding back to her dad's. "Can I stay over here and do that?"

So much for feeling guilty for abandoning her. Right now

it felt like she was the one doing the abandoning. And she didn't look guilty at all.

"Yeah, you can stay with them if we have a gig."

"Yes!" She shot her hand into the air, clearly completely awake now. And happy as a clam that she got to spend even more time with her grandparents.

At least somebody was. And he was glad it was her.

CHAPTER
Five

THIS WAS STUPID, Cassie thought a week later, as she sat in her car on a Tuesday evening.

Yes, she was lonely, and yes she needed to find new friends, but maybe this wasn't the way of doing it.

She looked at the crumpled flyer sitting on the empty passenger seat of her car.

Wanted – keyboardist and supporting vocalist. Open Auditions, Moonlight Bar, Tuesday the 25th.

She'd picked the flier up at the coffee shop yesterday, while she was waiting for her cappuccino. And at the time she'd thought maybe this would be a good thing, because she needed friends outside of her best friend and her family.

Cassie could play the keyboard easily. They'd all had to learn an instrument at school and she'd chosen the piano. It had been useful over the years, and after the accident she'd found it mindful to play her favorite tunes while she was stuck at home, recovering from her injuries.

And yeah, she could sing too. Another skill that had been drummed into them as students. And the ad said the vocalist would only be supporting. She assumed it was harmonies rather than having to take the lead.

And she could do that.

It's not as though you're auditioning to be the next Taylor Swift.

Well, that was true. It was just a local band. They'd probably practice once a week and play a gig every now and then. It was a way to meet new people and fill her evenings up.

And if she was being truly honest, part of her missed the buzz of performing on a stage. Sure, it was great teaching little ones.

But sometimes – not too often – she craved that adrenaline rush of knowing she was in the spotlight. That everyone was looking at her.

The door to the bar opened, and a man walked out carrying a black case, looking dejected. She'd been sitting in the lot for ten minutes and this was the first time she'd seen anybody walk in or out.

"Either do it or don't do it, but stop messing around," she muttered to herself.

And then, with a rush of bravado she wasn't expecting, she grabbed the flier from the passenger seat and wrenched her car door open, climbing out before she changed her mind again.

The moon was bright overhead as she walked down the sidewalk toward the bar, illuminating the tall buildings of the town square, stopping short at the entrance under the partly lit illuminated sign. *Moonlight Bar*. The first o kept flickering on and off.

The door to the bar was stiff, and she had to push her shoulder against it to force it open, before stumbling inside gracelessly.

Luckily, she still had a dancer's reactions and regained her footing with ease. The bar was empty, save for three men sitting in the corner all looking at her.

Oh great. They'd caught her embarrassing entrance.

And then her breath caught. Because even in the gloom she recognized one of the men. No. She recognized two.

Presley Hartson had a twin. They looked so similar it took her breath away. Gemma had said there were brothers, but she didn't expect to see a duplicate.

"You okay?" the twin asked. She knew it wasn't Presley because he was smiling.

"Sorry. I..." Dear God no. They weren't the band, were they?

"Are you here for the audition?" the third guy – not Presley or his twin – asked. "Come on in. Did you bring your keyboard?"

"No." It was about all she could say. Was it too late to turn around and leave?

Damn right it was. And anyway, she wouldn't give Presley Hartson the satisfaction of thinking he'd scared her away. She'd audition and then hopefully they wouldn't choose her.

And maybe she'd still have some dignity left.

"No you're not here for the audition or no you didn't bring your keyboard?" Not-Presley asked.

"I didn't bring my keyboard," she told him. She hadn't even unpacked it. And now she felt stupid, because of course she should have.

"She can use the piano," the third guy said. "You can play... right?"

"Yes." She nodded. "I can play."

"Come on over here." He smiled at her and if it was any other time she'd be relieved. But she felt edgy. Stupid. Like she'd made the worst decision of her life by coming here.

Still, she walked toward them anyway, so aware of Presley watching her, unsmiling, as she reached the three of them.

"What's your name?" his twin asked.

"Cassie Simons."

"I'm Marley." He leaned forward to shake her hand. "This is Alex. And the grumpy asshole is Presley."

"We've met," Presley said, his face betraying no expression.

"You have?"

"I teach Delilah's ballet class," Cassie said, taking the seat that Marley was gesturing at.

"You're the dance teacher?" Marley asked. He looked at Presley and raised a brow. Had they been talking about her?

Had Presley complained about her to his brother?

Ugh, he almost certainly had. They had to be close after all.

"You dance as well as play the keyboard?" Alex asked, shifting his chair a little closer to her.

"Give the lady some space," Presley growled.

Well okay then.

This wasn't awkward at all. It wasn't as though she wanted to bolt right out of here and scream.

"I'm sorry. Coming here was a mistake." She went to stand, to walk away.

"Why?" That was Presley again.

"Because…" Because we clashed the moment we met. And I can't stop looking at your arms and wondering if those tattoos continue up past your shoulders and onto your chest.

Because you're grumpy and growly and for some stupid reason it turns me on.

"I'm Delilah's teacher. It's a conflict of interest."

"Her dance teacher," Marley said, looking amused. "I don't think it's a problem. Can you play the keyboard and sing?"

She nodded. "Yes."

"And you understand that this is just a hobby band. We'll practice together, play some gigs…"

"More than a hobby," Alex interjected. "I mean, we almost hit it big once."

Marley shot him a look. Alex shrugged and sat back again.

"I understand. I just thought it would be a nice way to meet new people. Have a little fun."

Presley still wasn't saying anything. She looked at him at exactly the same moment he turned to look back at her. The intensity of his eyes made her breath catch in her throat.

It felt like a minute ticked by before they looked away from each other. It had to be less though.

"Why don't you play us a song," Marley asked. "Do you have something prepared?"

"Yeah."

He inclined his head at the piano. She stood, aware that three sets of eyes were following her as she walked over and pulled out the stool, lifting the lid and taking a deep breath.

Just play the song and leave, she told herself. Don't mess it up.

She wasn't going to give Presley Hartson the satisfaction.

As soon as her fingers touched the keys, she relaxed. She took a deep, cleansing breath, letting her muscles soften. And then her fingers started to move, soft notes echoing through the bar.

It was an oldie. A U2 song one of her roommates used to love back when they danced together in New York. During their free time, they'd all get together. Sing, dance, and perform for each other.

This had always been her favorite. "With Or Without You".

Cassie started to sing, matching the timbre of her voice to the notes, making sure she could be heard clearly over the piano. Her eyes were closed, her fingers moving naturally. She could feel the song.

Feel the pain.

Telling the mythical man she was singing to that she couldn't live with or without him.

She played with passion, her fingers slowly bringing the song to an end. Only when her fingers pressed down on the keys for the last note could she bring herself to look over at the men sitting around the table watching her.

Presley was glaring at her. His eyes were tight. There was a tic in his jaw. Before she could say anything, he stood up.

And walked out.

The door to the bar slammed behind him, and for a moment, she couldn't move. Had she done something wrong? Had she missed a note?

Alex was staring at the door, looking confused. Marley was running his hands through his hair.

Cassie glanced at the closed door. "Did I do something wrong?"

Marley shook his head. "No. You were perfect. Absolutely perfect."

Then what? She pulled the piano lid shut and stood. "Well, thank you for your time."

"It wasn't you. That's not why he ran out," Marley said. He looked annoyed for the first time. The resemblance to his twin was even stronger now.

"He ran out because he's an asshole," Alex muttered.

"That's my brother you're talking about," Marley murmured.

She felt like she was in the middle of something she shouldn't be. And yet she couldn't bring herself to walk away.

"The song was played at his wife's funeral," Marley said. "That's why he walked out."

It was like somebody had thrown a bucket of water over her. She'd chosen his wife's funeral song? Of all the songs she could have chosen, why that one?

She took a deep breath. She didn't know. It wasn't her

fault. There was nothing on the flier to say what songs were off limits.

"You sang it well. Really well." Alex was smiling at her. She got the impression he might even be flirting but she couldn't be sure.

She didn't have a radar for that kind of thing.

"Thank you." She took a deep breath. "I should go."

"We'll be in touch," Marley promised.

"Okay." She was pretty sure they wouldn't be. If accusing Presley of being a neglectful father wasn't bad enough, she'd played the one song guaranteed to rub him the wrong way.

The likelihood of her joining his band was about the same as the likelihood of her hitting number one on the Billboard charts.

And that was fine. Seriously. She didn't even want to be in it.

She walked across the sticky floor of the bar, toward the door Presley had stormed out of. She could hear Alex and Marley talking softly to each other, no doubt dissecting the shit show that she'd just been part of, as she pulled open the door and stepped outside.

Smack bang into the one person she wanted to see the least.

Damn, it was like walking into a cast iron suit of armor. The wind rushed out of her as she tried to keep herself from stumbling back.

With reactions that were faster than hers, Presley's hand shot out to steady her, his fingers closing around hers as he pulled her toward him.

The man was made of pure, thick muscle. The kind you got from a hard days' labor.

What was she supposed to be doing? Oh yeah, breathing. That was it. That would be good.

If she could just remember how.

"Sorry. I was just going back in," he said, frowning down at her. "Are you okay?"

Her lungs finally inflated. The relief was so sweet she wanted to smile. "I didn't see you."

"Ditto."

He let go of her and she felt the cool outside air wrap around her body, replacing the heat of his touch that she'd already started getting used to. He ran the same hand through his hair, pushing it off of his face.

"I'm sorry. For walking out. You were good. Really good."

It was stupid how much his opinion warmed her.

"And for being an ass when you arrived. It's getting to be a habit."

She looked up at him. His face was partially lit by the lamp that hung outside the bar door. She could see the blue of his eyes as they assessed her.

"I didn't know," she told him. "About the song."

The merest hint of a wince pulled at his brow before he smoothed it away. "My brother told you about that?"

"Him or Alex. I can't remember which."

"It was Marley." He sounded certain. "And it doesn't matter. It was an excellent song. Suited your voice."

"Thank you." She didn't know what else to say. Was this the most they'd spoken without one of them raising their voices or pissing the other one off? She thought it was, but she'd analyze it later. When she was home and her mind was clear and not all messed up by the emotional high of the audition and the nearness of this man.

"So are you coming back?" he asked.

"Now?"

A smile ghosted his lips. She wondered what it would be like if he let it grow.

"I meant to rehearsals," he said. "Or did we scare you off?"

"The others said they'd be in touch." She lifted a brow.

"I'm assuming they want to talk to you first. Plus, you must have other auditions."

"We don't. You're the only one we've seen who can hold a note and play the keyboard at the same time." He tipped his head to the side. "So is it a yes?"

"I don't know…" she said honestly, trailing off because his gaze was so intense. Everything about him was. Maybe that's why he was so attractive. There was this energy about him that was impossible to ignore.

Sometimes it was light. Sometimes it was dark. But it was always there.

Always pulsing around her.

He dipped his head, as though trying to catch her eye. "Look, if I made you feel uncomfortable in there…"

"You didn't." It was only half a lie. "I just wonder if it's a good idea. I seem to annoy you whenever we come into contact."

"Annoy me?" he repeated. "You think that?"

"Don't I?"

"No."

She waited for him to expand but he didn't. Instead, he opened the door and turned his head to shout. "You want Cassie to come to rehearsal tomorrow night?"

"Yeah we do," Marley shouted back.

"Hell yeah," Alex agreed.

He pulled the door closed and looked at her, his expression unreadable this time. "If you want to be part of the band, you're in."

CHAPTER
Six

WHEN THEY'D HAD a band before, their rehearsals always took place in the studio at the back of their parents' property, and there was no reason to change that now. Pres, Marley, and Hendrix had practically grown up in the place. Pres had learned how to mix music before he could even write. It felt like home in a way that no other place ever did.

They'd chosen not to have auditions there because it felt wrong to have a troop of unknown people through his parents' backyard when they both preferred their privacy.

Not that there was a troop of people. He hadn't lied to Cassie about that. Hartson's Creek and the surrounding areas weren't exactly full of keyboardists waiting for their big break.

Pres arrived at his parents' house at seven. Delilah was clutching his hand as he walked into the rehearsal room. His mom had offered to watch her, but she'd insisted on coming in to say hello to her Uncle Marley and Alex first.

Although he suspected that the person she actually wanted to see was Cassie.

"Is she here?" Delilah asked, peering around as the door closed behind them.

Marley looked up from where he was adjusting his drum kit. "Who?"

"Cassie, silly." She rolled her eyes. Damn, his daughter was getting sassy. He hated to think what she'd be like once she hit the teenage years.

"You calling me silly?" Marley asked, grinning because everybody knew he had the biggest soft spot for his niece.

Delilah looked at Pres. He lifted a brow at her.

"No," she said.

"That's funny, because I swear I heard you say it." Marley stood and started walking over to her. And then he swooped her up into his arms and she giggled. "Am I silly now?" he asked her, swinging her through the air.

"No!" She was laughing louder, almost hiccupping.

"Am I now?" he asked, throwing her and catching her again.

"You're not silly, you're not silly." Another hiccup laugh. "Put me down."

He winked and swung her down to the floor. "She'll be here in five minutes."

"Can I wait, Daddy? Please?"

"Sure. Just try not to touch anything, okay?"

He was setting up the microphones when the door opened and Cassie walked in. She was wearing jeans and a black tank under a white shirt, but damn she knew how to rock them. The woman was so light on her feet she looked like she was dancing even when she was walking.

The tank was knotted at her midriff, revealing her tanned stomach. Something in him tightened.

He ignored it.

"Miss Cassie!" Delilah ran over to her, a huge smile pulling at her lips. "It's me. Delilah. You're playing with my daddy's band."

Cassie's eyes met his. It felt like a fist was trying to punch his stomach.

"I know. I'm excited," Cassie said to Delilah. "Do you play with the band, too?"

Delilah giggled. "No. I'm just allowed to listen."

"For ten minutes. Then Grammy is taking you home to get ready for bed," Pres reminded her.

"I could stay for the whole thing," Delilah said. "And be your audience. I'll give you my honest poninium."

"Opinion," he corrected, trying not to laugh at her hopeful expression. "And no, you can't. You need your sleep."

Knowing she was defeated, Delilah nodded.

"We set the keyboard up over there," Marley said, nodding at the stand. "Come over and we'll adjust it."

For the next five minutes while they finished setting up, Delilah hung around Cassie, talking incessantly. He was impressed with how patient the woman was. Nodding and smiling at Delilah. Leaning down to let his kid whisper in her ear.

His stomach did that weird thing again. Maybe he just wasn't used to seeing Delilah interacting with women.

Sure. Apart from your mom, your aunts, your cousins, her teachers at school…

Okay then. Maybe he just wasn't used to watching her interact with women he didn't know that well. *Whatever.* It didn't matter. He was here to spend some time with his brother. Time that didn't involve building houses or listening to customers bitch at him.

Quality, damn time.

"I think we're ready." Marley ambled over to the drum kit and settled himself on the seat, twirling his drumsticks between his fingers.

Pres glanced over at Cassie. She looked nervous as she studied the music on the keyboard stand. She ran her tongue along her bottom lip as she concentrated on the notes.

A second later, her gaze lifted, and she caught him looking.

"Okay?" he mouthed, feeling guilty that his daughter was monopolizing her time when she probably wanted to center herself.

She nodded, smiling. Marley had messaged her last night, to confirm everything and to ask what songs she knew best. He thought they'd start with those. Just practice their voices and their instruments together. Find their own beats. After that, they'd introduce her to their songs.

The first one was an easy one. "Shallow" by Lady Gaga. The song was apparently one of her favorites, according to Marley.

And no, he wasn't annoyed that his brother and Cassie had struck up such an easy relationship. One where she freely admitted what music she liked to play and where her vocal range lay.

It was fine. More than fine, it was good. He was doing this for his brother, after all.

Marley counted them in, and Pres formed the chords, his fingers plucking the strings as he reached a rhythm. He was aware of her watching him as he leaned into the microphone, his thick voice rasping out the opening words.

He turned to face her, still singing. Her lips were parted, her eyes soft. Her fingers feathered over the keyboard as she kept time to the beat of his voice. In the background he could hear Alex strumming and Marley softly drumming, but his attention was on her.

He reached the end of the first verse, and she swallowed hard, as his guitar led her in. She took a deep breath, her gaze catching his.

And then she started singing, and he felt fucking tingles throughout his body.

She was good. Really good. Much better than she'd been at the audition. Maybe it was the acoustics of the rehearsal room, or maybe she wasn't as nervous.

He wasn't sure. But whatever it was, it was damn magic.

Everybody in the room was staring at her. Including his kid.

And when she reached the crescendo, she blasted it out. From the corner of his eye, he could see Delilah clap her hands together with delight. He turned to look at Marley, who was grinning from ear to ear.

And Alex was openly staring at her.

It was his turn to join in. He matched his voice to hers, an octave lower. Raspier, more achy. Their lips moved in sync, their eyes connecting again.

He'd forgotten how good this felt. How music made him feel like he was soaring.

The song ended, and the clapping began. He saw his mom standing next to Delilah. He hadn't even noticed her come in.

But she was beaming at him. Delilah was jumping up and down. Marley was laughing.

And Christ, was he smiling? Yeah, he was. Or at least his cheeks were doing something unusual.

"Okay. I think she'll do," Marley said.

Truth was, she was probably too good for them. But that was her choice. If she wanted to slum it with the Hartson boys, so be it.

"Come on," he said, not wanting to think about that too much. "Let's play the next track."

———

Twenty minutes later, Presley's mom took Delilah home, much to the little girl's disappointment. She'd run over to hug Cassie goodbye, and tell her how pretty her voice was, before Presley lifted her up, hugged her tight, and promised her he'd be home soon.

She still felt bad about the way she'd accused him of being a bad dad. Especially when anybody could see how much his daughter adored him.

And how he adored her right back.

It made the back of her neck feel hot as she watched him close his eyes and bury his face in his daughter's hair, like she was the most precious thing in the world.

After another half an hour, Marley called a break. Alex ran out straight away, pulling a packet of cigarettes from his pocket and stuffing one between his lips before he'd even made it out of the door. Marley climbed down from his seat behind the drums and grinned at her.

"Coffee, tea? Or we have beer?"

It turned out the studio had a kitchen that was fully stocked. She ended up getting water as Marley explained that the studio was mostly rented out nowadays. There were accommodations to the rear, and she listened as he reeled off a list of famous bands who'd recorded their albums in this building.

"*Silver Thunder* was made here?" she asked. "I never knew that."

"My dad has a lot of connections. He produced that album."

She hadn't known that either. Sure, she'd worked out that their dad was *THE* Gray Hartson. But she had no idea he'd become a producer when he'd retired from recording and performing.

The door behind her swung open, and she felt a gust of cold air, making her shiver.

"Beer?" Marley asked, looking over her shoulder.

"Sure." Pres nodded, stuffing his phone back into his pocket. "Sorry. Just wanted to check that Mom and the kid are okay."

Marley pulled a beer from the refrigerator, and she stepped back to let Presley pass, but the kitchen was small and he was big so his body still brushed against hers.

Her breath caught in her throat.

Pres glanced down at her. She was wearing sneakers,

needing the comfort tonight, and he towered over her. He took the bottle from Marley, twisting the top off and lifting it to his lips.

His throat undulated as he swallowed a mouthful.

And then she saw the label on the bottle. "Non alcoholic?" she asked.

"Gotta drive, got a kid." He shrugged.

"But he likes the taste of beer," Marley said. "So this has to cut it."

"Don't we all like the taste of beer?" Alex asked, striding back in. She could smell the thick aroma of smoke on him.

Good thing he wasn't a vocalist. His voice would be even raspier than Pres'.

He took his own beer – this one with alcohol in it – and popped the cap. For a moment they all stood there, not talking.

And then she and Presley started at once.

"Is Delilah…" That was her.

"I'm sorry Delilah…" And that one him.

She let out a little laugh. "Sorry. You go first."

"I'm sorry she kept hanging around you. You must get enough of that during the day at work."

Cassie blinked. "Not at all. She's lovely. And so friendly. I imagine she's like that with most people. Naturally outgoing."

"No, not really. She can be pretty shy." He shrugged, picking at the label on his bottle. "But thank you. Apparently she was talking about you the whole way home."

"She's very sweet."

"Yeah, she is." His eyes dropped to her mouth then back to her eyes again. Marley's phone rang. He pulled it out and murmured something to the caller, walking past them and through the doorway, mouthing that he'd be right back.

"So Cassie," Alex said, lifting his beer to his mouth. "Do you have a boyfriend?"

She tried not to laugh at the abrupt change in subject. "No."

"You want one?"

She laughed.

"Leave the woman alone. We can't afford to lose another keyboard player," Presley said gruffly.

Oh, that was interesting. She turned to look at him. "What happened to the other keyboard player?" she asked him.

"Alex happened," he said shortly.

"Hey, it wasn't my fault," Alex protested. "I can't help it if all the women fall for me."

"Yeah, but you could stop being an asshole to them and scaring them off," Presley muttered. He looked at Cassie. "Seriously, avoid him."

"You're the asshole," Alex muttered.

"Yep." Presley didn't look at all perturbed about that. "But I'm not the one trying to get it on with our new keyboard player." He glanced at Cassie, who shifted awkwardly. "Sorry. Just ignore him. And me, for that matter."

"Why should she ignore you?" Marley asked, walking back in. And just like that, the atmosphere lightened.

The three of them had a beat. Presley the gruff one, Alex the flirty one, Marley the peacemaker. She wondered where she fit in. If she fit in at all.

"It doesn't matter." Presley shrugged. "Are we ready to get back to rehearsal? I need to get home soon."

"Sure." Marley shot her a smile, and she smiled back. "Let's go make some music."

CHAPTER
Seven

"I CAN'T BELIEVE you didn't tell me you were auditioning," Gemma said, leaning on the counter of the reception desk. Cassie's last class for the day was over and all her students had been picked up on time. Delilah had groaned when she saw her grandmother standing at the end of the hall with all the other parents and guardians.

"You don't have to pick me up on time, you know," she'd said to Maddie Hartson. "I can stay behind and help Miss Cassie clean up any time."

It was a far cry from the tearful little girl who'd been almost inconsolable when her dad had been late picking her up.

But now it was just her and Gemma, and her friend was looking at her proudly. "Look at you, being all grown up and making friends."

Cassie wrinkled her nose. She wasn't sure she exactly made friends. But she'd gotten out of the house without having to rely on Gemma to be there, so it was a start.

"So…." Gemma said, lifting a brow. "How was it? When's your first gig? I'll need extra notice because babysitters are like gold dust around here."

"We're not at the gig stage yet," Cassie told her. She wasn't even sure if she'd could call them a band yet. Sure, her and Pres' voices meshed together well, and the keyboard arrangements were easy to keep up with.

But last night had been... intense.

"It must be weird being the only girl in the band. Even Fleetwood Mac had two women," Gemma mused. "And obviously when I say weird I mean nice. All that male attention."

"I wasn't getting a lot of that," Cassie said. "Although Alex asked me if I wanted to be his girlfriend."

Gemma's eyes widened as she laughed. "What?"

"I think he was kidding." Cassie's brows knitted. "At least, I hope so. He's not my type."

Folding her arms, Gemma leaned forward on the counter. "Well we all know what your type is. Miserable dancers who treat you like shit."

Cassie sighed, because Gemma wasn't too far off the mark. Truth was, when she was dancing for the New York Ballet she had little time for dating. Relationships with male dancers who understood her schedule were easier.

And a lot messier, too, when they ended. Which they always did.

She shook her head. There was no need to feel melancholy. She was fine. She had Gemma and rehearsals with the band to look forward to.

"Are you interested in Alex?" Gemma asked, leaning forward.

"No." Cassie wrinkled her nose. "Not at all." And the smell of smoke was offputting, if she was being honest. He was funny, and he made her laugh, but that was it. "Anyway, relationships and bands don't mix. Give me one example where it works out long term."

Gemma tipped her head to the side, looking deep in thought.

"Um…"

"Well, I can tell you who it didn't work out for," Cassie said. "Either couple in Abba. Lindsey and Stevie in Fleetwood Mac. And then there was Stevie and Mick? Christine and John. I know, how about Sonny and Cher? Are they still together?"

Gemma grinned. "I'm getting the picture. They all split up. Boo hoo."

"And Meg and Jack White?" Cassie was on a roll now. Almost enjoying herself. "How's that relationship going?"

"Eww. Weren't they brother and sister?" Gemma asked.

"No. They were married. It was just weird." Cassie shook her head. "But you get my point."

"I do." Gemma sighed. "But it would be kind of romantic though. Maybe you and Marley…"

"Nope. He's a nice guy, but that's it." It was weird how she didn't feel that undeniable pull to him the way she did to Presley. Maybe if she'd reamed him out the first time they met it would be different.

But she didn't think so. She hadn't met many twins in her life. There were one set of girl twins she'd danced with as a kid, but that was it. And she'd constantly gotten them mixed up.

But now she could tell the difference between Presley and Marley easily. It wasn't only that they wore their hair differently, or that Presley had tattoos where Marley had none. It was in their demeanor. Their expressions.

The way her heart skipped a beat every time her eyes met Pres'.

"The thing about band romances," Gemma said, her voice soft and faraway. "Is that even if they end, they're amazing while they happen. All that chemistry, that longing. The music." She sighed and looked at Cassie again. "You sure you can't give Alex a little try?"

———

They'd been rehearsing for a couple of weeks, and everything about them was gelling. They'd even added a weekend rehearsal to the mix and used it to jam and try out new songs. Pres was impressed by how quickly Cassie had picked everything up.

He hated to admit it, but Marley had been right. It was good to be playing again. Good to be spending some leisure time with adults, even though Pres still felt guilty every time his mom came to pick up Delilah from the studio and take her back to his house to put her to bed.

Yet Delilah was loving it. Every rehearsal day she would run to the studio to wait for Cassie to arrive, then hang around her until Marley counted them in.

Cassie was sweet with her, and he appreciated that. Not every twenty-something woman without children would be the same.

That was why he hadn't bothered dating after they'd lost Jade. That and the fact he just wasn't ready. He had to protect Delilah, and that wasn't compatible with putting his own needs first.

It was hot in the studio tonight. The room had air conditioning, but the door kept opening and shutting, mostly thanks to Alex's cigarette addiction. Pres had pulled his sweater off. He was down to a sleeveless tee and jeans. Marley had sensibly worn shorts and a t-shirt – he always got overheated – and Cassie was wearing a pair of cut-off shorts and a t-shirt she'd tied into a knot on her abdomen, exposing a sliver of her stomach.

And yeah, he kept looking at it. The woman was toned all over. According to his mom, who had obviously talked to her more than he had, she'd trained to be a dancer. She'd been with a dance company in New York when she'd been involved in a bad accident that meant she couldn't dance professionally anymore.

He'd wanted to ask her about it during one of Alex's many smoke breaks but he didn't know how. God knew he hated answering questions about himself.

So they'd just shoot the breeze, and he'd try not to look too much at the pretty woman who taught his daughter dance class.

How's that working out for you?

They finished the last song. This was one of his. During the band's hiatus, he'd written a lot of music. It had been his outlet after Delilah went to bed and the house felt too quiet and too empty.

He'd fill it with the sound of his guitar chords and voice.

This one was poignant, though. He'd written it back in the days when Delilah would wake up calling for her mom. When she'd asked him all the questions he didn't have answers to. And the ones he did, but he didn't want to answer.

Cassie's sweet voice wove around his gritty vocals, lifting them, making them feel prettier. Less emotional. Her eyes met his across the studio, and he could see understanding there. Sympathy, even.

But he didn't want it. Hated it more than he hated anything else.

Nobody should feel sympathy for him.

He looked away, down at the chords his fingers were forming, finishing the final chorus off before they played the outro, a bead of sweat running down his face before he strummed the last note.

"Fuck, that was good," Marley said. "Anybody ready for a drink?"

"Hell yeah." Alex pulled his guitar strap over his head. "I'm just popping out for five minutes and then it's all about the beer."

"I'm gonna head home," Cassie said softly.

"You sure?" Marley asked. "We're just gonna take some drinks out into the yard. Shoot the breeze."

"There's no fucking breeze," Alex muttered. "That's the problem."

She smiled at his joke. "It's fine. Thank you anyway, but I have an early class tomorrow."

Pres looked over at Cassie. She was tidying up the keyboard. He kept meaning to ask her if she was okay with the studio one, or if she'd prefer to bring her own.

But then she'd usually disappear after rehearsal and he hadn't picked Delilah up from dance class after that one evening when he was late.

Probably best to let Marley do the talking, anyway. He was better at it, and he didn't make her frown every time he spoke.

"Good night," Cassie called out, pulling her bag strap over her shoulder. She was wearing her thick hair up in a bun. A few dark tendrils had escaped, and the heat had stuck them to her neck.

"Night." He nodded at her. She flashed him a hint of a smile before turning and walking out.

No, gliding. She didn't walk, she fucking floated. How was it possible to walk like that, anyway?

"You could be nicer to her, you know," Marley said, as Alex ran out with a cigarette already between his lips.

"I am nice to her," Pres said, frowning. "When am I not nice?"

"You could've asked her to stay and have a drink."

"She didn't want to. She said so." He put his guitar on the rest and blew out a mouthful of air. "She has work tomorrow."

"And so do we," Marley pointed out.

"And?" Pres lifted a brow at his brother.

"And we're having a drink. She leaves because she thinks

you don't like her." Marley was walking around the drum set toward him. "If you fucking smiled occasionally…"

"I smile."

"When?" Marley looked skeptical.

"I smiled at Delilah when she left." Pres wrinkled his nose at him.

Marley shook his head, looking somewhere between annoyed and amused. Funny how often Pres had that effect on him.

"It's okay to be attracted to somebody else," Marley said softly.

Pres blinked, not sure he'd heard right for a second. But he had, he knew that. "Where the hell did that come from?"

"I'm just saying what I see." Marley shrugged. "And there's no need to look so fucking guilty."

"I'm not looking guilty." Pres looked away anyway. "And I'm not attracted to her. I just don't gush over people like you do. Or flirt like Alex. I'm a professional."

"You're an idiot. And I know you like her."

"Jesus, are we back in school again?" Pres asked, shaking his head. "Since when did I need you to organize my love life?"

"Since you didn't have one?" Marley asked. "And if it helps I can tell she's into you too."

No, it didn't help, actually. Not one bit.

"Can we change the subject? Talk about the weather or something?"

Marley lifted a brow. "I see a lot from behind the drums. You don't realize I'm watching but I am. I see the way you look at her. The way she keeps looking at you."

"We're singing together. I'm making sure we're in sync."

"Sure you are." A ghost of a smile passed his brother's lips. Marley could be a cynical asshole when he wanted to be.

"Why are you so adamant for me to admit something

that's not true?" Pres asked. "We both know what happened to the band the last time there was a relationship."

Marley shrugged. "Because I watched you crumble after Jade died. And you stayed crumbled for a long time. It killed me not being able to help. You not *accepting* any help. Did you know the reason Mom calls you every day is to make sure you haven't done something stupid? We worry ourselves sick about you because you've built this wall up and you can't seem to tell us how you feel."

Pres' chest contracted. "I know you worry. But you don't need to. Delilah and I… we're doing fine."

"Fine." Marley shook his head. "That's the worst fucking word in the English language. Is that what you want for your life? Is that what you dream of Delilah being? Just fine? What happened to amazing? What happened to happy? What happened to living life again?"

"I am living life," Pres said, his voice low. He felt cornered, like an animal.

Marley ran his hands through his hair, looking agitated. "No, you're not. Or you haven't been. Did you know the most alive I've seen you since losing Jade is when you're singing with her? For a few minutes it feels like my brother is back. Like you're letting him out of his cage to play."

Pres' mouth felt dry. He knew Marley cared. More than cared. They were twins, there was this invisible chord that bound them. If Marley hurt, he hurt.

And the other way around.

"I'm sorry," Pres said, his voice gritty. "I know it's been hard for everybody."

"We love you, man. We want you to be happy. You and Delilah."

"That's what I want, too," Presley told him. "And I'm trying. For her. I really am."

Marley opened his mouth to reply, but the door opened

and Alex breezed in. "What's going on?" he asked. "Are we getting some beers or what?"

Pres looked over at Marley who shrugged. Conversation over.

And yeah, he was good with that. Talking about emotions had never been his forte.

Singing about them, however. Yeah, he could do that.

CHAPTER
Eight

DELILAH WAS ALL OUT SOBBING, her red face stained with tears. "Where is she?" Her breath hitched. "I need her."

"I don't know," Pres said softly, trying to soothe his daughter. He brushed her hair from her face. "Try to go to sleep. We'll find her in the morning."

"I can't sleep without Lola," she wailed. "What if she's hurt? What if she's in pain? She needs me."

That fucking giraffe. He'd wring that stuffed toy's stupidly long neck when he found her.

"Try to think again," he murmured. "When was the last time you saw her?"

"I don't know." She clutched at the covers like they were a lifeline. She'd only noticed Lola was missing when she'd come up to bed. It had been one of those overwhelming evenings – he'd had a customer demand to meet him at six, so he'd been late picking Delilah up from his mom's. And of course she'd wanted nuggets for dinner and he had none in the house.

So they'd had another battle about that before she finally

took a shower and pulled her pajamas on, pouting all the way.

And now here they were, one giraffe missing, one little girl in tears. Damn, he needed a drink. Or about a hundred night's sleep.

"I had her at dance class," she whispered.

"Okay…" Well that was something. "And did you take her to Grammy's?"

"I think so."

Relief washed through him. "Don't move. I'll call her now and see if she's there."

Five minutes later the relief was gone.

"She didn't have her when I picked her up," her mom said. "I just assumed she'd left her at home."

And yeah, sometimes she did. Delilah was attached to Lola, but not as much as she used to be. After Jade died, she'd been practically glued to the stuffie. Everywhere she went, Lola went too. Her school principal had given her permission to take the giraffe with her to class when she needed the extra emotional support.

But he thought it was getting better. Maybe it was.

Until now.

"Shit." What a mess this was.

"I told you to buy a second one," his mom said, her voice light.

Yeah, but he'd known that Delilah would never be convinced by a brand spanking new giraffe, even if he'd been able to track one down.

"She's probably at the dance school," he said. "I'll call them tomorrow."

"Well, good luck, sweetheart."

He smiled grimly. "I'm going to need it."

It was another twenty minutes later before he couldn't stand it anymore. Not because Delilah was openly wailing

THAT ONE TOUCH 67

but because she was trying so hard to get to sleep but she couldn't stop the sobs from coming. It hurt him to the core.

She was such a good kid. She didn't ask for much. Just one damn giraffe to sleep with when she got a little scared or upset.

Fuck it.

"I'll be back in a minute," he whispered to her. She nodded, her face turned to the side.

Grabbing his phone from his pocket, he walked into the hallway and dialed the one number he never touched. But there was nobody else that could help, he knew that. Not until morning when the school was open.

And it was a long damn time until morning.

"Hello?"

He swallowed hard as he heard Cassie's soft voice. The band had all exchanged numbers a few weeks ago. At the time, he'd thought it was a bit much, but he was glad now.

"It's Presley Hartson."

"I know. I have this magic screen where your name appears when you call." Her voice was light. Teasing. Any other time she might have made him smile.

"I need your help." There it was. Another admission that he couldn't do this thing alone. He knew people said it took a village to raise a child, well it took a whole small town to help with his kid.

"What's up?" she asked, her tone changing. He had the feeling that she was good at helping. She certainly didn't sound surprised.

"Delilah's giraffe is missing. Do you know if she had her in class today?"

There was a pause, like she was thinking. "Yeah, I'm pretty sure she did."

Well that was one mystery solved at least. "Okay. Thanks. I'll let her know. She's kind of missing her."

"I could check if you'd like?" she offered. "I have a set of keys and it's not far away. I know how attached she is to Lola."

Weird how his chest tightened at the fact that his kid's dance teacher knew her giraffe's name. If Marley was listening in he'd laugh right now.

"It's okay, we take up enough of your time." There was no way he could ask this of her.

"Honestly, it's fine. I was feeling bored anyway. I'll let you know if I find her, okay?"

He swallowed down his pride for his daughter's sake. "I really appreciate that."

"It's not a problem. I'll speak to you soon." He heard the jingle of keys. Damn, the woman was fast. "Tell Delilah to hang in there."

"Thanks. I will."

———

It felt strange walking through the dance school's corridors at night. The whole place was silent and it sent a shiver up Cassie's spine. During the day it was full of life – music spilling out of rooms, children running to classes or to meet their parents.

But now it was just Cassie and her thoughts as she pushed open the door to her studio and flipped one of the light switches.

The overhead light flickered for a moment, the pitch black room looking like some kind of horror movie. Then it came to life, and she laughed at the way her heart was hammering against her chest.

Damn, her imagination was way too good.

Turning around on her feet, she scoured the room for Lola. There was no sign of her on the floor where Delilah had sat waiting for her grandmother to pick her up, or by the hooks where they hung their coats.

But as she turned to look by the dance mats, she saw a flash of orange underneath the piano. A little leg was sticking out. She walked over and hunched down to pull her out.

It took a little tugging. It was like somebody had deliberately pushed the toy under there. Cassie frowned. Had one of the other kids done it to play a trick on Delilah?

"Come on," she muttered, taking care because there was no way she wanted to rip the giraffe's fur. With a little twisting and turning the toy was finally free.

Elation rushed through her. She felt like she'd just delivered a baby, not freed an inanimate object.

When she stood she pulled her phone from her pocket and navigated to the last call, clicking the phone button.

Pres answered within seconds.

"I've got her," she said, a smile pulling at her lips.

"You're a fucking miracle worker," he said. "Ah shit. Sorry for swearing."

It was impossible not to laugh. It was stupid how giddy she was feeling. "Give me your address and I'll drop her off on my way home."

"You don't need to do that." His voice was low. She wondered if he was in the room with Delilah but then she remembered the swearing. He may have a dirty mouth, but she was pretty sure he wouldn't swear in front of his daughter.

"It's not a big deal," she told him. "Honestly."

He took a long breath. "I'll owe you big time if you do."

"It's just a giraffe, Presley."

He chuckled.

"What?" she asked, that smile still pulling at her lips.

"The only person who calls me Presley is my mother."

"Do you prefer Pres?" she asked him.

"No, I like it when you say my name."

Oh. Her heart did a weird flutter thing. "Then Presley it is. So are you going to give me your address or will I have to hunt you down? Because Lola is looking mighty angry right now. She needs her owner."

There was that laugh again. She wished she was there to see it. But somehow it was easier to talk with him over the phone than face to face.

She got too discombobulated when she could see him. That was the problem. Men like him shouldn't be so attractive.

"I'm the next street up from my parents' place," he said, reeling off the address. "Take the left before their house. We're about halfway along the road. You'll see my truck in the driveway."

"The Beast," she said. She'd heard Delilah calling it that.

"Yeah, that's right."

"Okay then. I'll see you in a few minutes." She disconnected and took a deep breath. She shouldn't feel this excited from just talking to him.

But that didn't stop her from smiling as she locked up the dance school and headed back toward her car.

———

"Is that her? Is she here?" Delilah ran over to the living room window, pulling open the curtains and pressing her nose against the glass. When he'd told her that Cassie had found Lola, his daughter had insisted on coming down to wait for them. Pres walked behind her, looking over her head at the headlamps sweeping over the driveway.

Yeah, it was her. He ran his tongue along his dry bottom lip.

Cassie climbed out of the car. She was wearing a pair of black yoga pants and a cropped hoodie, her hair loosely tied back from her face. She looked like she'd been dressed comfortably to hang out and watch tv at home, not perform a rescue mission for a stuffed animal.

She still looked good though. He had a feeling she'd look good in anything.

Or nothing.

He blinked that thought right out of his head.

"I'll open the door," Delilah shouted, running into the hallway.

"Wait!" Damn, he needed to teach her about stranger danger. "Don't open it until I'm there."

But she was already opening it and shouting out Cassie's name. The poor woman was only halfway up the driveway by the time Delilah was jumping up and down in the doorway.

"Hey. Look who's been missing you." She wiggled the giraffe in her hand.

"Lola!" Delilah looked over her shoulder at him. "Daddy look, Cassie brought her home."

"What do you say?" he prompted, because they hadn't quite gotten the politeness thing right yet.

"Thank you!" Delilah took the proffered toy and hugged her. Then hugged Cassie.

"No problem." Cassie stroked her hair then looked up at Pres. She smiled softly at him.

And yeah, he smiled back. No big deal. "Hi," he said.

"Hi."

Delilah released her death grip on Cassie and stepped back.

"And bye, I guess." Cassie ruffled Delilah's hair. "It's past your bedtime, right?"

Delilah frowned. "Daddy, can Cassie read me a story? Please?"

Cassie looked at Pres and back at Delilah. He lifted a brow, and she shrugged.

He was okay with it if she was. It felt churlish to send her away after she saved his ass, anyway.

And she didn't seem to baulk at the idea either. She looked kind of pleased.

"Just one story. That's it," Presley warned Delilah, because he knew what she was like.

"Yes!" Delilah did a fist bump and stepped aside so Cassie could walk in. Pres leaned around her to pull the door closed, his arm brushing her chest.

"Sorry. Old habits."

"It's okay. No harm done." She sounded almost breathless. Weird how he felt the same.

He pressed himself back against the wall as she stepped inside and looked around the hallway, as though taking it in.

It was painted white with warm wooden floors, photos of Delilah and his family – along with a few of Jade – fixed to the wall. Mostly taken by his mom.

"You have a big family," she said, her gaze washing over them.

"Yeah. They're a lot. Family get-togethers are a blast."

She smiled softly.

"Come to my room," Delilah urged, tugging at Cassie's hand. "It's a princess room." She was grinning from ear to ear. "It's pink. To make the boys wink."

Pres rolled his eyes. "Did Gramps teach you that?"

"He might have," Delilah said. "It rhymes. Like a poem."

Cassie laughed, and he grinned too. "Come on then," he said. "Let's get you into bed and ready for a story."

"Not you. Just Cassie," Delilah said.

And fuck if that didn't feel like the softest of knives to the heart.

"You okay if I go up with her?" Cassie's eyes met his.

He nodded. "Have at it." Delilah blew him a kiss, and that softened the blow a little, as she led Cassie up the stairs while he stood at the bottom.

Not looking at Cassie's ass at all.

Nope.

When they'd disappeared from view he sat on the bottom step. When was the last time a woman he wasn't related to was in this house? He frowned, trying to think. His mom came over all the time, of course. Occasionally bringing along one of his aunts.

And his girl cousins would come over to spend time with him and Delilah, too. Grace was his oldest female cousin, but there was Sabrina, his younger, wilder cousin, too. He had the worrying feeling that Delilah took after her.

Or she would. When she was grown up.

"See, it's pink," he heard Delilah saying to Cassie.

"It's beautiful."

"And I have a heart cushion. And I can pull the curtains closed around the bed if I want. But I don't because it scares Lola. She likes to see what's going on."

"Why don't you climb into bed?" Cassie said. "I bet Lola's exhausted after all her adventures today."

"Where did you find her?"

"In the studio. I get the feeling she crawled away to play hide and seek but forgot to find you after class."

"Cassie?" Delilah piped up.

"Yes?"

"You know Lola isn't real, right? She can't actually crawl anywhere."

Presley smothered a laugh. Damn, his kid had sass.

"You and I know that," Cassie mock whispered. "But Lola doesn't."

Pres stood and walked into the kitchen, so aware of the two of them upstairs. He put the last of the dishes into the dishwasher and wiped up the counters. He'd let them have some girl time. It was what Delilah wanted.

And he was a damn sucker for his kid. Always.

It took him ten minutes to get the kitchen clean. He ran his hands under the faucet, washing them with some dish soap before he dried them on the towel.

It was silent when he walked into the hallway at the base of the stairs. He tipped his head, his brows knitting, before he climbed up them to make sure everything was okay.

Delilah's door was ajar. He looked through the gap, to Delilah's bed. It was just as she'd described to Cassie. A princess bed, with four posters and a roof, voile curtains hanging down and tied to each bedpost.

He'd made it himself. It had been an easy design for somebody who knew what they were doing with a jigsaw. The hardest part had been hiding it from Delilah as he worked. In the end, he'd made up a story about the garage being dangerous and that she couldn't go in there without asking.

He'd spent nights sanding, priming, and then painting. More getting the curtains right. And then she'd spent the weekend with his mom while he and Marley had built it in her room for a surprise.

He smiled at the memory. It had been good spending time like that with his brother. The same way it was good spending time with him at rehearsal.

Delilah was asleep, her eyes closed, her rosebud lips slightly opened as she inhaled rhythmically. Her head was resting on Cassie's lap and her hands were clutching Lola against her chest.

His breath caught in his throat, because damn, they looked like they were supposed to be laying like this. Like Delilah was supposed to have somebody soft and feminine to take care of her.

He knew she missed her mom. Or at least the idea of her.

Of having something all the other kids at school had.

Sure, some of them didn't have dads. But that was normal, if there was any such thing. But no mom. That was tough.

Cassie looked up, and a soft smile pulled at her lips. "She went out like a light," she whispered. "I'm scared to move in case she wakes up."

"She's a pretty deep sleeper." He kept his voice low, walking into the room. "Let me help you."

Cassie nodded, and he slid his hands beneath Delilah's head, his knuckles pressing into Cassie's thighs. Their faces were close as he held his daughter while her dance teacher wiggled off the bed.

Once Cassie was out from under Delilah, he gently lowered Delilah's head to her pillow. She muttered something he couldn't quite hear and rolled onto her side, her giraffe still tight in her arms.

Cassie was waiting for him outside Delilah's bedroom when he softly made his way out of her room, closing the door behind him.

"Thanks," he told her. "I owe you."

"You don't owe me anything. I was glad to help."

She was close enough for him to smell the citrus on her skin. Was it her shower gel? Perfume?

He inclined his head at the stairs and she went down first, him following behind her.

"Can I get you a coffee or something?" he asked her when they reached the bottom.

She stopped walking and turned to look at him. He hadn't expected the sudden slow down, and he was inches from her, looking down.

Right into her eyes.

Her lips parted. And fuck, he wanted to kiss them. A rush of desire went through him. Strong enough to make him blink.

When was the last time he'd been this close to a woman?

He wasn't sure. But his body liked it, he knew that much.

It was like a drug he'd taken so long ago that he'd forgotten the effect it had on him. His muscles tightened, his teeth clenched.

And his dick, yeah, that was paying attention, too. Way too much.

Step back, he thought. He wasn't sure whether he was talking to himself or her. One of them needed to, though. And he wasn't sure he had the willpower to do it.

She tilted her head, and he could see the sweet tenderness of her neck. He wanted to scrape his teeth over her skin until she gasped. Wanted to bury his face in the curve where her neck met her shoulder.

Cassie's breath hitched. And yeah, he knew she was feeling it too.

Whatever it was.

A little bit of fucked up magic in a world where he'd been lost for too long.

"You have fuzz on your cheek," she whispered. And before he could stop her, she reached out to brush it away.

With that one touch, he was gone.

His hand covered hers until her palm was flat against his rough jaw. Her gaze flew to his. She looked surprised, but something else, too.

Something darker. The same thing he felt.

"Pres…"

"Come here." His voice sounded like a strangers. Rough and needy.

She didn't hesitate, and he loved that. One graceful step forward and her chest was brushing against his. Her head tipped further, her cheeks pink.

Everything about her was so soft, and it made him ache for her.

Without thinking, he traced the line of her cheek with his rough fingertip. She let out a sigh, and he traced her pink lips, too.

But it wasn't enough. He needed more. So much more. His hand slid down her jaw, angling it until her lips were a breath away from his.

And yeah, he had to dip down to close that gap because she was short and he was tall, but damn it only took a second before his mouth was against hers. She was as sweet as he knew she would be. Her lips tender, as his mouth stole what it needed. His tongue swept along her seam and she parted her lips. Her own tongue grazing his.

Hot blood rushed straight from his brain to his dick as he moved his hands down her sides, pushing at her hoodie until he felt her warm skin.

Cassie's arms looped around him and he slid his palms further still, over her hips, beneath her behind, lifting her up and turning so her back was against the wall.

Her breath was hot and short against his mouth as he pressed his hardness against her. Her fingertips were tugging at his hair, her lips stealing his kisses. And as his tongue caressed hers again, he imagined the sweetness of her mouth around his cock.

Jesus. It had been too long. Way too long.

Cassie rolled her hips against his and he was mentally calculating how quickly he could get her naked when a bolt of sense rushed into his brain.

This is happening in your hallway. In your home. Where your daughter is, motherfucker.

And this is her teacher. Your band mate. And if you fuck this up your brother will be pissed.

He never knew thoughts could be like cold water, but he felt icy as he pulled back, gently releasing his hold on her until Cassie's feet met the ground.

Oh.

Shit.

What the hell had he just done?

His skin was still electric. His body still pulsing. Like an addict looking for its next fix. He stepped back, putting distance between them, all too aware of the thick swell of his dick still pressing against the seam of his jeans.

"I should go," she whispered.

He nodded, because that's what he wanted, wasn't it? For

her to leave and forget that this ever happened. No coffee required.

"Thank you for bringing Lola home," he said roughly.

She ran her tongue along her bottom lip. It fucking hypnotized him. "No problem."

Tugging at the hem of her hoodie, she covered the sliver of flesh he'd revealed with his touch. "I guess I'll see you at rehearsal." There was a flash of a smile and then it was gone.

He walked over to the door, pulling it open, then stepping aside so she didn't touch him as she passed.

Say something, motherfucker.

But what could he say that wouldn't make everything worse?

She was on the porch now, her keys in her hand. She pressed the button on them and her car lit up. Then she turned and walked down the steps to his driveway.

"Cassie?"

She turned back to look at him. "Yes?"

"Drive carefully."

"I will."

He stood in the doorway until she'd gotten safely in her car and started the engine, the headlamps illuminating his beast of a truck.

And then she reversed out, and he closed the door, frowning as he realized his dick was still semi hard.

Jesus Christ, he needed to get a life. Or touch himself until he stopped thinking about the way her ass felt in his palms.

Why was it everything he touched turned to shit? His band, his marriage, his kid's dance teacher?

The only good thing he'd done was keeping that little girl upstairs happy.

And that's the most important thing, he reminded himself.

Nothing else mattered. Just Delilah. And that's why he wouldn't kiss her dance teacher again.

CHAPTER
Nine

"HEY, aren't you supposed to be going to rehearsal?" Gemma asked, looking up from the laptop on the counter as Cassie organized some messy fliers on the desk.

"Um, yeah." Cassie looked out of the window. The sky was overcast, but there was no rain in the forecast. At least not until overnight, when she'd be safe in bed. "I guess."

But she didn't want to. Not after that kiss. It had been two days since she'd practically thrown herself at Presley Hartson, only for him to march her out of his house.

How embarrassing. She still hadn't gotten over it. Hence why she was procrastinating when she should be driving to the studio.

"Is there something wrong?" Gemma asked, frowning.

"Why?" Cassie's eyes met hers. Damn her friend and her perceptive ways.

"Because you've been quiet for a couple of days. I was wondering if your mom had called or something."

Gemma knew that Cassie and her mom didn't get along, and when they did talk, it always put her in a funk. Not that they spoke often, especially now that her mom didn't get to bathe in the light of Cassie's dancing on stage.

"I haven't heard from her," she admitted.

"I'm sorry. Is that what's upsetting you?" Gemma's voice was soft.

And damn it, maybe she needed to talk to somebody. "I kissed Presley Hartson," she blurted out.

For a moment, Gemma said nothing. And then she started laughing. "What?"

"I said I kissed Presley. Delilah's dad. You know him?"

"Yeah, that's what I thought you said." Gemma was grinning from ear to ear. "And of course I know him." She closed her laptop, as though she wanted to give Cassie her full attention. "So…?"

"So what?"

"So when did you two kiss?"

"The other night. Remember when I told you I had to come back and find Lola? I dropped her off and…"

"Ohhhhh." Gemma's eyes sparkled. "I'm losing my touch. I should have known. I can't believe you've been keeping this from me. So you two kissed and then…"

"And then?"

"Then what happened?" Gemma asked. "Don't keep me hanging here."

"Then he pulled back, looked white as a sheet, and I went home." And she was still mortified at the memory.

"And that was it?" Her friend looked disappointed. "No touching. No hanky panky?"

Cassie shook her head. "No." She frowned. "Well, he thanked me for finding Delilah's toy. And then he told me to drive safely."

"See! He cares." Gemma lifted a brow. "He's worried about your safety."

"No. He's being a dad. Telling people to drive safely is what dads do."

Gemma looked like she was enjoying this way too much.

Maybe Cassie shouldn't have said anything. But who else could she talk to?

"Tell me this. Did you force him to kiss you?" Gemma asked.

Cassie frowned. "No. I wouldn't do that. You know that."

"So he did it of his own free will." Gemma nodded.

"Yeah. I guess…"

"And did he enjoy it?" her friend continued.

"Um, I don't know. I think so…"

Gemma cleared her throat, still smiling. "Do I need to tell you the facts of life? You can usually tell if a guy is enjoying a hot kiss…"

"He enjoyed it, okay?" Her cheeks were flaming with embarrassment. "Is that what you wanted to hear?"

"Pretty much," Gemma admitted. "So how big is he? I've always wondered. I mean he's a built guy…"

"Stop it." Cassie grimaced.

"I can't. Do you know how long it's been since I had a first kiss with somebody? I need all the details. I'm starving for romance here."

"There was no romance," Cassie told her. "Just a kiss." She took a breath. "Do you think I should say something to him?"

"Like what? Nice kiss, want to do it again?"

"No! I mean should I apologize?"

"For kissing him? No. There were two of you there. Last time I looked he's got muscles growing on muscles, if he didn't want you to kiss him he wouldn't have let you. And anyway…"

"What?"

"I don't know. Your version sounds a little one sided. He's almost a foot taller than you, what were you doing, jumping like a kangaroo until your lips hit his?"

Cassie laughed, despite herself. "No. He leaned down."

"Of his own free will…"

"Yes." She let out a long breath, because Gemma was

right. She hadn't kissed him. They'd kissed each other. And she'd spent the entire night beating herself up over it. "But that still doesn't help me with what to do next."

"What do you want to do?" Gemma asked her.

Kiss him again. She blinked that thought out of her head, because no. Once kissed twice shy.

She would not embarrass herself again. "I'm going to be a grownup about it, I guess." She sighed. "Do my best to avoid him."

Gemma smiled. "Good luck with that."

"I think I'm going to need it." Because every time she closed her eyes all she could think about was that kiss. How good his lips felt against hers.

How he'd pressed her against the wall and taken everything she wanted to give. How it had felt like sex as he'd rolled his hips against hers. *If only they'd been naked.*

And it was weird, because as a dancer she'd been used to being lifted. But during rehearsals her partners would huff and puff and accuse her of putting on weight because she felt heavier than last time.

When Presley had lifted her, it was different. It felt like pure brute strength. The kind she didn't think she'd like, but it had sent a shot of excitement through her that had lit her up from the inside.

She'd felt safe in his arms. Not like she was on the edge of falling, the way she always feared as a dancer. She felt womanly. Desired.

It had been a long time since she felt like anything but a failure.

But she'd see him soon. And she needed to be cool and collected then. Because as much as she enjoyed kissing him, making the band work was important. Not only because she'd finally started finding some friends, but because she sensed it was important to him, too.

"I just don't know what to say to him," she admitted to her friend.

"Do you need to say something? Can't you pretend it didn't happen?" Gemma asked her.

Cassie blinked. "I mean I could. But we have to sing together. And it's going to be embarrassing."

"Ah, just channel your inner Stevie. Pretend you're singing to Lindsay tonight right after he bad mouthed you around town. You're a big girl, you'll be fine." Gemma's voice softened. "You've dealt with worse than this."

Their eyes met and Cassie nodded. "You're right. I'm building this into something it doesn't need to be."

"Exactly." Gemma nodded. "Now go sing your heart out. Don't let a little kiss ruin a good thing."

———

The crack of thunder was loud enough to make the whole studio shake. They were packing up – thank God, and Marley looked over at Pres, his eyebrow raised.

"Already secured the site," he told his brother, knowing exactly what he was thinking. He'd checked the forecast before he'd left the house and had seen that there was going to be rain over night. He'd covered everything up and made sure the part of the roof they were working on was watertight.

Sure, the rain had started earlier than predicted, but all was good.

Marley nodded, looking relieved.

"I hate it when you do that," Alex muttered. He was putting his guitar into its case. An unlit cigarette already between his lips.

"Do what?" Marley frowned.

Alex looked up. "Have those conversations in your heads. It's weird."

"We don't have conversations in our heads. I just talked out loud to him," Pres pointed out.

"Yeah, but he didn't say anything to you."

There was another loud clash of thunder, and from the corner of his eye he saw Cassie jump. She wasn't looking at him. She hadn't looked at him all night, apart from when he'd asked her a direct question.

He couldn't blame her. He'd been a douche the other night. And he hadn't apologized to her, even though he should.

Another mess he'd gotten himself into. And one he'd need to sort out if he didn't want to ruin the band and let his brother down.

"Damn, I love a storm. Dad used to tell us it was God playing the drums," Marley said, hitting his stick on the skin of the snare. From the corner of his eye, Pres saw Cassie flinch again.

"Come on, let's get out of here. I need a smoke." Alex lifted his guitar case. Cassie was looking at her phone. She'd been quiet all night, apart from when they were singing. Their voices were working perfectly together now. They'd learned each other's tempos and breathing, when to go high and when to go low.

They left the studio and Pres flicked the lights off, locking the door behind him. When they reached the lobby, the rain was pelting the glass door, running down in rivulets to the ground.

"Shit," Cassie said under her breath.

"I'm gonna make a run for it," Marley said. "Meeting somebody at the bar." He winked at Cassie and lifted a hand at Alex and Pres before he pushed through the door and ran into the rain.

"You think your dad would be okay if I left my guitar here?" Alex asked, pulling his lighter out of his pocket.

"Sure. I'll lock it up in the studio." Pres took the case off him, and carried it back, unlocking the door and placing the guitar gently on the floor. He'd tell his dad it was Alex's before he went home.

When he got back to the lobby, Alex had already left, though the air still held the stale smell of cigarettes. But Cassie was still there. Still looking at her phone.

"Everything okay?" he asked her.

She looked up, surprised. "Um, yeah. I just…" She pulled her bottom lip between her teeth. "I think I'm going to wait here until the rain eases. It wasn't supposed to start until later."

He walked over to the glass doors, looking out at the metal gray sky. "It looks like it's here to stay," he said. "The weather gets like this sometimes. Mostly warm, but when it rains, it pours."

She nodded. "I can wait."

He lifted a brow. "I need to lock up." And he didn't want to leave her here alone. It felt weird. And wrong. "And I need to get home to Delilah."

Cassie blinked. "Oh yes. Of course. Sorry. I'll wait in the car."

He didn't get it. "Wait for what?"

Her eyes caught his.

"It doesn't matter." She shook her head. "Good night, Presley."

There it was again. His full name. He still liked the way she said it, too much.

"Wait. I'll walk you to your car."

She swallowed and said nothing, but she nodded at least. He grabbed a spare umbrella from the stand. "Here," he said, handing it to her. "It's not gonna work great with the wind, but at least it'll keep you from getting too wet."

As soon as they stepped outside, the noise of the storm hit them. Wind whipped the rain against his face, and he automatically put his arm around her shoulder as she tried to keep the umbrella steady.

It was a long walk through the wet grass to the front of his parents' house. There was a light shining from the basement windows – he figured his dad was watching TV in the den – but his mom's car was gone, no doubt she'd left a little early to take Delilah home, before the storm hit.

And he was grateful for that. At least he knew his daughter was safe and warm.

Cassie's car was parked next to his truck. He walked her to it, and she pulled out her key, opening the lock.

"Thank you." She pulled the umbrella closed, handing it to him. It had done little to shelter her in the wind. Her hair was damp, her skin was, too. And her tank was sticking to her chest in a way that he really shouldn't be looking at.

"No problem."

He waited for her to climb into the car before he walked to his truck. He was as wet as she was, and once he was inside the dry cab he shook his hair and switched on the heater. Christ, what a night.

While he waited for her to leave first, he pressed the buttons on his radio, finding a rock station he liked. Then he pulled his seatbelt on and glanced over at her car.

She hadn't moved.

Her seatbelt wasn't on, either. She was staring right ahead, through the windshield, at the rain lashing against the glass. He frowned. There was no way he was leaving until she had.

While he waited, he tapped out a message to his mom.

On my way home in a few. Should be there in twenty. Everything okay? – Pres

. . .

Drive safely, honey. All good here. Delilah's just getting into bed. – Mom

Okay then, that was one thing he didn't have to worry about. The woman not moving in the car next to his though. That was something else altogether.

He sighed and opened his door, walking over to her car as the rain pelted him. She hadn't noticed him approach because she was still sitting there, her hair dripping, her face unmoving.

Pres had to tap on her window with his knuckles to get her attention. And damn if she didn't jump again. He felt like an ass, but he mimicked winding her window down, until she pressed on the button and the glass between them lowered.

"Is everything okay?" he asked her, wiping the rain from his face.

"What?" She blinked.

He leaned in, mostly because he was getting so wet it wasn't funny. He could smell the rain on her. Mixed with something sweeter. Sexier.

"How long are you planning on sitting here?" he asked.

"I was just waiting for the rain to ease."

"It's not gonna happen. Not for an hour at least." He ran his hands through his wet hair.

There was something strange about the way she was holding herself. She wouldn't look at him. Wouldn't move at all. "Cassie?"

"Yes?"

"What's wrong?"

"Nothing," she said, her voice thin. "I'm fine. You can leave. I'll be okay."

He resisted the urge to roll his eyes. "I'm not leaving you here."

Finally she turned her head to look at him. But he didn't expect to see the fear in her eyes. Jesus, she looked terrified.

"Please go," she whispered.

Dammit. He pushed himself off the window and walked around her car, wrenching open the passenger door so he could sit down inside.

Silently, she wound the window up and looked at him.

"You want to talk about it?" he asked her.

"About what?" Her voice was thin.

"Why you won't drive in the rain."

She ran the tip of her tongue over her dry lip. "Not really."

"Okay." He pulled out his phone and tapped another message to his mom.

Been held up sorting something out. You okay to stay for another half hour? Sorry. – Pres

No problem. I was going to stay until the rain eased, anyway. Take your time. – Mom x

He put his phone back in his pocket and turned to look at her profile. Her nose was straight, slightly upturned at the end. Her lips were as soft as he remembered. Slightly parted so she could breathe.

"Cassie," he said. "Are you scared of the rain?"

She swallowed hard. "I thought we weren't going to talk about this."

Okay then. "What should we talk about?"

"How you're going to get out of my car and drive home so I don't feel bad about detaining you?"

"I'm not leaving until you do."

For a moment she said nothing, before letting out a sigh. "Then I guess you'll be here for a while."

A smile was pulling at his lips. Damn this woman was stubborn. He kind of appreciated it though. Because he was stubborn, too.

"Let me drive you home."

She inhaled sharply. "I'm not leaving my car here."

"Okay. Then I'll drive your car."

"I need it for work tomorrow. It's fine. Thank you, but I've got this."

She so didn't have it.

He ran the pad of his thumb along his jaw. He needed a shave. "Have you always been scared of it?"

"We're not talking about this, remember?"

"You haven't given me another subject to talk about."

She let out a long breath and turned to look at him. "You missed a couple of notes on that last song."

The abruptness of her subject change made him laugh. "So did you."

"I was reacting to you," she said.

"We sing pretty well together though, huh?" he asked her. Weird how he was enjoying sitting here with her, the drumbeat of the rain overhead punctuating their conversation.

"Yeah, we do." She nodded. "Marley said we might have our first gig soon."

"You feeling ready for it?" he asked her.

"Is anybody ever ready for it?" She tipped her head to the side. She really was pretty. "But yeah, I think it'll be fine."

"We need to be more than fine," he said. "We need to be good. Great, even."

Her eyes met his. "Then I think we'll be great."

"Yeah. I think we will." He knew it. He'd never sounded so good as when he sang with her. The sweetness of her voice brought out the roughness in his. Their harmonies were already out of this world.

"Delilah will be worried about you," Cassie said. "You should go."

"She's fine. My mom's fine. Everybody's fine... except you."

"But I'm not your problem. Delilah is."

"You're my problem when you're shaking with what looks like fear in my parents' driveway," he pointed out. "And you did a nice thing for me the other night. I'm not going to leave you now."

"The kiss?" She looked surprised. And yeah, that made him smile again.

"Finding Delilah's giraffe," he corrected her, his lips still curled. "But yeah, the kiss was nice too."

"I'm sorry about it," she whispered. Her apology made him frown.

"Are you?"

"Aren't you?" She looked up at him again.

He pushed his hair out of his face again. "Yes and no."

"What does that mean?" she asked him, her brows knitted.

"It means yes, I'm sorry because I shouldn't have kissed you like that. It was inappropriate, and I took advantage." His voice was thick.

"You didn't take advantage. I did."

"I was the one grinding against you," he pointed out.

Cassie blinked. "I was the one who wanted you to."

And fuck if that didn't make him want to do it all over again.

Pres let out a long breath. This conversation wasn't going the way he'd meant for it to. It was supposed to divert her, but he was the one getting diverted. Wanting things he shouldn't.

"It won't happen again," he promised her. "I wouldn't do anything to jeopardize the band. It's too important." To Marley, and therefore to him.

She looked over at him. "I just don't want this to be awkward."

"It's only awkward if we let it be." He offered her a smile and miracle of miracles, she smiled back at him. If he was being truly honest, part of him hated that she took his rebuff so easily.

But they were grownups, and this was how being an adult was supposed to be. You talked things out; you worked through them.

"Then we won't let it be."

"Good." He tipped his head to the side. "So, will you let me drive you home now? I'll get your car back to your house and drop the keys through the door before the night is over."

She was wavering again. He could tell that from the doubt clouding her eyes. She was somebody who hated being helped, that much was clear. Yeah, well, he hated it too.

But he'd learned to accept it.

"You'll be doing me a favor," he told her. "Because I'd like to get to bed this side of Christmas."

That made her smile again, and it felt like he'd just won a damn Grammy. "Okay. But I'll owe you."

"No you won't. I owe you for the giraffe. This is us getting even."

She looked mollified at that. "Are you sure?"

"Yes I'm sure. Now I'm going to get out of this car and run around to your side. You scoot across to the passenger seat so you don't have to go out in the rain."

"Okay. Thank you." And for once – thank the Lord – she did as she was told.

CHAPTER
Ten

THE SUN HAD BEEN SHINING for a week straight. All vestiges of the storm had long since been dried up by the heat, save for Cassie's memory of Presley driving her home that night.

She was still mortified that he'd discovered her fear. That she was scared of some stupid raindrops. What kind of person froze up at a little precipitation falling on their car?

Apparently, she did.

True to his word, her car had been waiting for her in the morning. She'd sent Presley a thank you text, and he'd responded, but that had been it. They were back to being bandmates again. Talking at rehearsal and nowhere else. But to keep her mind off the fact that they were only bandmates, she focused on her dance classes. Drilling in the names of the last few students she had yet to memorize, and experimenting with a few different dance styles to see which ones the kids enjoyed.

"Okay, so we put our baked goods here," Gemma said, pointing at a table that was already overladen with cakes and muffins, cookies and granola bars.

Cassie did as she was directed, setting down the only

cookies she knew how to bake – snickerdoodles. They'd been her staple since she was in grade school and they had a bake sale what seemed like every other week for one good cause or another.

She'd never eaten them, though. Her mom wouldn't let her. She could remember getting lectures about dancers needing to be strong.

"And now we put our chairs down where we want, then come for some lemonade."

"That's it?" Cassie clarified. She wasn't sure if coming here was a good thing.

"Yep. What were you expecting?"

Cassie smiled. "I don't know. Maybe I didn't think it would be so literal. Like I know it's called Chairs because you bring your own chairs, but I just…" She trailed off, because she was going nowhere with this.

A woman called out Gemma's name, and she waved at her. "That's Aunt Gina," Gemma told her. "She's like the Hartson family matriarch."

Cassie looked over at Aunt Gina, who waved at her, too. Cassie smiled back.

"She looks sweet," Cassie said.

"She is," Gemma agreed. "She adores all her family. And they adore her right back. Speaking of which, there's the younger Hartson clan." Gemma pointed at a group of chairs gathered together on the grass. "Let's go over and say hi. I'll introduce you to them all."

They started walking across the grass. There was a warm wind that carried the promise of a beautiful sunset.

When they got to Gemma's friends, they put their chairs out as somebody poured them some lemonade.

Once they had their glasses in their hands, Gemma introduced Cassie like she'd promised. "Everybody, this is Cassie. She's the new dance teacher at the school. Cassie, you remember Grace? You met her at the diner. She works at the distillery right outside of town. And Sabrina, her cousin. She's usually at college. You're just down for the weekend, right?"

Sabrina nodded. "That's right." She had that kind of wild beauty that made you feel electric whenever you looked at her. Grace, her cousin, was equally pretty. Just more... graceful.

Cassie bit down a smile.

"You're in our cousin's band, right?" Sabrina asked. "Altered Reality?"

Cassie nodded. "That's right."

"Marley said you might play a gig soon," Sabrina said, looking pleased. "If you do, I'll be there."

"Well, that's one person in the crowd at least." Cassie smiled at her. She really loved her energy.

"It's nice to see Pres singing again," Grace said softly. She was in the chair next to Cassie's. "For a while there we were worried he never would."

"Yeah, well losing Jade tore him up," Sabrina said.

Cassie took a sip of her lemonade. It wasn't the first time she'd wondered what Jade was like. There were so many photographs on the walls at Presley's house she wasn't sure who was who. And there was no way she was going to ask.

And though Delilah had a photograph of her mom by her bed, it had been dark the night she read to her and she hadn't wanted to upset the little girl by drawing attention to it.

It was none of her business, anyway. And Presley was clearly too closed up to want to talk about her.

Cassie knew all about needing to keep some things buried.

"Speak of the devil and he will appear," Grace murmured.

And of course she had to look. It was like she had no choice. She swallowed hard as Presley and Marley walked over from the parking lot, the two of them laughing together at something. Delilah was skipping ahead of them, her long hair curling around her shoulders.

"Over here," Grace shouted out, waving at them.

Delilah was the first to spot Cassie and her cousins. Her face lit up as she ran over. She looked from Sabrina to Grace to Cassie, her smile so big it looked like it could split her face.

"You're all here," she said.

Grace shot Cassie an amused glance. "Yes we are. You got a hug for me?"

"I sure do." Delilah hugged Grace first, followed by Sabrina, then she looked at Cassie shyly.

"I like your dress," Cassie told her.

Delilah was wearing a fairy outfit, complete with wings. "I'm an angel," she whispered. "A pretty one."

"You sure are."

"Daddy!" Delilah called out. "Look who's here."

Pres' eyes immediately met hers. And yeah, she felt heat rise through her body. The corner of his lip quirked. "Hey."

"Hi," she breathed back.

Marley walked over, grinning. "I was gonna call you later. There's a bar over in Shawlands that's offered us a gig next week. Need to know if you're free."

"Are we ready for it?" she asked him.

"Yeah, I really think we are." He glanced over at Pres. "Funny, he asked the same thing. If we need to we can have a couple of extra rehearsals next week."

"When's the gig again?" she asked him.

"Next Friday."

It would be the first time she'd set foot on the stage since before… *then*. She took a deep breath. This was good for her, she knew that. She also knew that Presley wouldn't let her fail. His voice knew hers enough by now to compensate if she faltered.

Not that she was planning on faltering.

"Okay. That sounds good."

Marley's smile was huge. "Excellent. I'll call them and confirm. Any night next week that you can't make rehearsal?"

"I work a little late on Wednesdays. But I'm finished by seven so I could always head straight there."

"I'll send out a schedule." Marley ran his hands through his hair. He had a mole on his cheek where Presley didn't.

"Can I come to the gig?" Delilah asked, looking excited.

"No." That was Presley. She looked up at him and his eyes were trained on her face. The intensity of his stare made her jolt.

"Why not?" Delilah frowned.

"Because it's in a bar and you're about fifteen years to young to go inside. Plus Granny already said you can stay over at hers that night."

"I can?" Delilah clapped her hands together. "Can we have pizza?"

"That's up to Granny."

"That's a yes then," Sabrina said, and they all laughed.

"Daddy, can I have a muffin?" Delilah asked.

"Yeah. Go for it."

"Will you come with me?" She turned to look at Cassie, who couldn't say no to her adorable expression.

"Sure." She stood. "I was getting kind of hungry myself."

Her gaze hit Presley's again, but he was just so impossible to read. She'd thought she was closed off, but it was nothing compared to him.

Moody, sexy, tattooed. And probably the best kisser she'd ever met.

No wonder every time she looked at him her body clenched.

"Come on then," Delilah said. "Before all the good ones are gone."

————

It was getting late. Somebody had lit the fire, and all the younger generation had gathered around it. Pres' mom had taken Delilah home despite his protests, telling him he needed to stay and spend some time with people his own age.

He didn't bother pointing out that Marley was almost exactly his own age, and he spent a hell of a lot of time with him. Because he knew his mom well. She was sweet to everybody, but inside there was steel and she wasn't afraid to show it.

If she'd decided on something, you did it. No questions.

Cassie was talking to Marley, the two of them laughing. They'd built up this easy going relationship which he liked. Envied, even. Because whatever was going on between him and her, it was definitely not easy-going.

It was sharp. And dark. And needy as fuck. Their eyes kept meeting all night and all he could think about was the way she'd opened herself up to him after finding Delilah's giraffe.

The way he'd wanted to bury himself inside of her until she forgot her own name.

And that was why he wouldn't. Why he'd keep the space between them. Relationships and him didn't mix. He'd learned that from his marriage. And Cassie was way too sweet to be ruined by him.

Even if every muscle in his body *wanted* to ruin her.

He'd never met anybody who knew their body as well as she did. It was a weird thing to notice, but it was so clear in everything she did. In her smile, her movements, the way she talked. Hell, even in the way she sang.

It was entrancing. And he needed to snap the hell out of it.

"Pres?" Marley called out. "Come over here."

He didn't need asking twice. Because as much as he knew he couldn't touch her, it didn't stop him from wanting to be close. He walked over and his gaze washed over her.

"Hi."

"Hi."

"We were talking about the opening song. I really think we should go for 'Beautiful Liar'."

"'Beautiful Liar' is slow." They always opened on a fast number. Got the audience going. Or at least they used to. It had been a while.

"I know. But it's the second best song we have. The way you two sing it…" Marley trailed off. "It could work. I know it could."

"What do you think?" He looked at Cassie.

"I think you should decide." She shrugged. "You and Marley. It's your band."

"Why don't you decide?" he asked her.

She bit down a smile. "Because I've never sung at a gig before."

Well there was that. "Okay, but how does a ballet begin? Do you start on a fast note or a slow note?"

"It varies."

Of course it did. And now he was picturing her dancing in a tight outfit and fuck if he didn't wish he could see it. "I just think starting on something faster works. We can do 'Beautiful Liar' as our second song. If we started with 'Slammed' we could segue into it nicely."

"Break up and make up," Marley said, because "Slammed" was definitely angry. The two of them had written it years ago, when Marley had walked in on his then girlfriend cheating.

"More like break up and then have great break up sex," Cassie said.

Marley laughed. "Yeah, that's a good description. And you two do delightful break up sex."

She lifted a brow at him. He smiled because what else could he do?

"By the way, how's your car?" Marley asked her.

Pres' hackles immediately rose.

"My car?" Cassie repeated.

"Yeah. I meant to ask you the other night but I forgot. Pres said you've been having trouble with it. That's why he drove it to yours and got me to pick him up the other night."

Her lips parted as she let out a breath. Now she knew he'd lied to his brother for her. Because he clearly got the impression she didn't want people to know about her not driving in the rain.

"It's fine now. And thank you for helping." She glanced at Pres. "Both of you."

"I know a good mechanic if you need one," Marley said.

"It's sorted," Presley replied.

Marley tipped his head to the side, his gaze on his brother. "Okay…" Somebody called out his name, and he lifted a hand. "Gotta go. A few of us are heading over to the Moonlight." He looked at Cassie. "Want to join us?"

She shook her head. "Thank you, but it's been a long day. I'm going home to crash."

Presley liked the fact that she wasn't going. Too much.

"Okay then. I'll give you a shout tomorrow. Talk about rehearsals and the set list."

"Sounds good." She nodded.

As soon as he was gone, she moved closer to Pres. "You lied about my car."

"I figured you wouldn't want your business being broadcasted around town. But I needed his help to get home." He shrugged, it wasn't a big deal.

"You didn't need to cover for me."

"You want me telling everybody?" he asked her.

"Not really." A ghost of a smile passed her lips.

"That's what I figured."

She nodded.

"You worried about the gig?" he asked her. "I saw you frown when Marley mentioned it earlier."

"Not worried. Just… I don't want to let any of you down."
Her words sounded true. Genuine.

"You won't let us down. We wouldn't be playing without
you. And it's only a small venue."

"On a Friday night."

"Most places aren't open except on the weekends around
here. And you're ready. You know you are."

"Do I?" she asked softly.

"Yeah, you do." The corner of his lip quirked. "You're a
hard worker. You know the songs, you know the emotions.
You hit them every time."

"And if I don't, you'll be there to catch me."

"Something like that." His voice was thick.

"Then I'm not afraid." Her gaze was sure as it caught
with his.

And damn if he didn't like that. A little too much. "Glad
to hear it."

CHAPTER
Eleven

PRES HAD BEEN RIGHT, she realized the next week when they were on the small stage in the corner of the bar. Starting their set with a fast song had been the right thing to do. The floor was full of people – locals and fans who'd traveled to watch Altered Reality's comeback gig. And they were all on the dance floor, their bodies swaying, their voices moving as they sang in time.

Cassie's heartbeat was thumping to the sound of Marley's drums.

There was a sense of expectation as the song came to an end, and she started to wonder if they should have segued into another fast hit. They had enough of them. And Presley always took the lead with the fast songs, while she could kind of hide behind the keyboard and sing the harmonies when needed.

But not the next song. No, this one required her to step into the light. And she should want that, right?

She'd yearned for it as a dancer. And sure, half of that yearning came from a desire to please her mom. But still, it was what she was trained for. So she squared her shoulders and grabbed the wireless mic stand, carrying it over to the front as Presley smiled at the audience.

"We're gonna take it down a notch," he told them in a low voice. "This is a new one. Hope you like it."

He looked down at his guitar, his lashes sweeping as he moved his fingers to form the first chord. A sudden memory of how rough they'd felt against her soft skin washed over her.

Then he strummed and glanced at her, his eyes heavy lidded and she felt it.

The electricity. The need.

The pulse between her legs.

"You walked toward me, your body full of grace,
   The wind in your hair, the sun on your face,
   Your lips full of promises you never meant to keep
   Your eyes empty of the tears you would later weep,"

She loved how gritty his voice was. How he stared at her like she was that woman. The one he couldn't stop loving. The one who betrayed him but he'd take back anyway.

"I danced to your tune, in your delicate embrace
   You were lost in the moment, in your time and space
   Your words always felt like petals, fragile and sweet
   Yet in the silence, it felt like my final defeat…"

They'd got to the bridge. Marley's drum's kicked in, a thud of a heartbeat that added to the pain of the music. Pres was strumming louder now. Alex was, too. She felt the rush of blood thumping through her veins as they reached the crescendo.

"You told me that you loved me,
Your lips knew it was a lie,
You said you'd never leave me,
Then every touch was a goodbye,
You ripped my heart and crushed it,
And you laughed at all my pain,
So don't come around here asking for more
Because I won't let you in again…"

Their voices meshed so perfectly it was like a shiver down her spine. This was what she loved about singing with him. It wasn't just about their voices, or the lyrics. It was about feeling it, living it. Right now, they were lovers who tore each other apart again and again.

And damn, they'd have good make up sex. So good it made her skin heat up.

Pres walked out from behind his mic, toward her, his fingers still strumming. He was so close she could feel the heat of his skin, smell the heady mix of his cologne and sweat, as he leaned in to sing with her into her mic.

Calling her baby. Telling her she was the only one who knew how to cut his heart out with her bare hands. And his eyes were still on her. She couldn't look away.

She sang that he'd broken her. Left her lying on the floor. That she was a dead woman without his love.

And then the music slowed again. Into his final vocals. She stepped back to give him space, but he nodded at the mic, the smallest of smiles playing at his lips.

He wanted her to sing the last lines, too. Which wasn't what they'd rehearsed. But the audience was captured by them, swaying, singing along even though they didn't know the words. She moistened her lip with her tongue and gave him a slight nod before they moved in together, their voices meshing, dancing.

Making the kind of music that made her heart throb.

This was better than dancing. It might even be better than sex, though she wasn't sure. All she knew was that singing with Presley Hartson felt like she was riding a permanent wave. One that made her muscles clench and desire rush through her body.

And she wasn't sure she'd survive the rest of the set.

———

Pres leaned into the mic, his heart slamming against his chest. "We're gonna take a twenty minute break. Go buy some beer, kiss your girl, do whatever you can do in twenty minutes. Then come back, because we have more songs for you."

He flicked off his microphone and pulled his guitar over his head. Sweat was dripping off him and he had to grab a towel to dry his face.

"Fucking A," Alex said. "We've got them in the palm of our hands." His eyes were bright. Maybe too bright. Alex had been known in the past for using drugs to get him going. Pres hoped to God he wasn't now.

That's not what he wanted the band to be known for. He had a kid to think of.

Marley grinned at him as he climbed down from the drum set. "You were amazing."

"Cassie was the one that carried us," he murmured, looking over at the keyboard. But she wasn't there.

He frowned.

"We need to record 'Beautiful Liar'," Alex said. "Put it up on YouTube or something. It was fucking electric. Did you see the crowd?"

"It's a second song," Pres murmured, and Marley laughed.

"But what a fucking second song."

He looked over at the keyboard again. Then across the stage. There was no sign of her. "Where did Cassie go?"

Marley followed the line of his gaze. "I don't know. She okay?"

Pres wasn't sure, that was the truth of it. Something happened while they were singing. He wasn't sure what it was. And he wasn't sure he could put it into words even if he knew. But it was there and it was in him.

Like electricity, you couldn't see it or taste it. But damn, it was powerful.

"I think she went outside," Alex said. "Through the back." He inclined his head at the emergency exit to the right of the stage. "Want me to go get her?"

"No." Pres said it a little too fast. Alex blinked. "I'll get her. Maybe she messed up a vocal or something. I can talk her through it."

"She didn't mess anything up," Marley said.

And no, she didn't. But he needed an excuse and that was it. "I'll be back in a minute. Can you grab me a soda or something?"

"They have non alcoholic beer," Marley told him.

"Then that'll work."

He put his guitar against the stand and walked to the edge of the stage, jumping down onto the floor. It took him a couple of minutes to make it outside, mostly thanks to fans and friends wanting to tell him how good they'd sounded, and how much they'd missed the band.

When he pushed the emergency door open a little alarm sounded, but he ignored it, stepping out into the sultry night. There'd been no rain since the last storm they'd had, and the ground beneath him was dusty and dry. He looked around, taking in the few smokers and the late arrivals, before stalking around the corner to the back of the bar.

And there she was.

Leaning against the brick wall of the building, her head lifted as she stared up at the moon. The light of it caught her face, illuminating her profile so that she looked almost otherworldly.

She was wearing a pair of cut off shorts and a black Fleetwood Mac tank, that she'd knotted at the front. Her hair was long and wavy, tumbling down over her shoulders.

He wanted her like he'd never wanted anything else.

And yeah, he knew it was the effects of the performance. It was a drug like no other – he'd forgotten how potent it was.

But his body didn't care. It needed what it needed.

His jaw was tight as he walked into her view.

Her lips parted as she saw him. Her gaze was as foggy as his. Yeah, she had the high, too.

It was intoxicating.

"You okay?" he asked gruffly.

She nodded. "I…" Her breasts rose as she took a deep breath. "That was something, huh?"

"You were something, yeah."

The corner of her lip tilted. "So were you."

He stepped closer, like he didn't have a choice. Her eyes darkened, her chest still rising and falling with her breath. She reached out, her fingers touching his arm, and it took him a moment to realize she was tracing one of his tattoos.

He knew which one. The heart with the barbed wire around it.

"If you keep touching me…"

"What?" she asked breathily, her eyes flicking to his.

"Then I'll touch you back."

Her lips curled more, like it was the kind of threat she wanted. "No you won't."

"Won't I?" he asked. Her fingertip was tracing circles

along his skin now. It felt maddeningly good. But not enough. Not anywhere near.

"No. Because you're like this tattoo. Closed in. You can't escape."

He leaned closer. He could see the individual colors of her hair strands, lifting in the breeze. "I'm not the one caged in right now."

"Maybe I want to be caged in. Maybe I want you to break me out."

He dropped his brow to hers. "You don't want that."

"Why not?"

"Because you're light and I'm dark. I'll ruin you."

Her fingers feathered up his arm, his neck, until her hand was cupping his jaw. This close to her he could feel the difference in their heights. In their weights.

Their power.

He was stronger. Bigger. Could hurt her without trying.

And damn, he didn't want to hurt her.

"It's just the music, you know?" he whispered. "We're just playing the roles the lyrics tell us to."

Her fingertips brushed the back of his neck and it made him shiver. And he couldn't stop himself anymore. He'd tried, damn it. But she was so soft and sweet and everything his body wanted.

His mouth crashed against hers.

Blood pumped through his body as she kissed him back, her fingernails scraping against his neck, her body arched into his. He was hard, throbbing, aching for her. He slid his hand down her neck to her breasts, cupping them, feeling the peak of her nipple pressing against his palm.

She was hungry for him. He could tell that much. The same way he was starving for her. They'd sung to each other for the last forty-five minutes. They'd loved each other, they'd hated each other, they'd yearned, and they'd pretty much made love on the stage.

But this, the touching, the kissing, the feeling…

It was like liquid adrenaline straight to the heart.

She was grinding against his leg, her breath rapid against his lips. He slid his hands down her body and she let out an achy sigh.

And when he cupped her between her legs, his palm pressing where she felt like she needed it, blood rushed to his groin.

God, she was warm. Hot. She let out a sigh against his mouth. He moved his hand, using the heel of his palm against her, his mouth moving against hers with the same, needy rhythm.

Her thighs tightened around his hand. Her breath coming in short bursts. Like little punches. She was clinging onto him like he was the rock *and* the storm.

And all he could think about was making her come. He was so hard it hurt, but he didn't press himself against her. He needed this to be about her.

Needed her pleasure.

Needed the release of it so he could fucking think straight again.

Her back arched against the brick wall, her fingers digging into his shoulders as he took her to the edge. She let out a soft cry, his mouth swallowing it as he kissed her, her whole body stiffening with pleasure as he took her to the peak.

She was shaking, her thighs so tight he could barely move his hand, her head slumping against his shoulder as she orgasmed against his palm.

"Oh my God. Presley…"

Her eyes were shining, her cheeks pink. Her lips looked like they'd been stung. He'd never seen anything more beautiful.

Or felt so wrong.

What was up with him? Why did he keep doing this? It was like the worst kind of addiction.

He opened his mouth to say sorry, but it would have been a lie. He wasn't anywhere near sorry. He would have done it again.

Would have done anything to feel her come against him.

"Pres?"

The two of them jumped at Alex's voice. Cassie looked at him, her eyes wide.

"You okay?" he asked her. Because they had about five seconds before Alex walked around the corner. She touched her hair, as though checking that it wasn't a complete mess.

"I'm fine." She didn't sound it.

He took a step back, taking a deep breath. "We're here," he called out.

Alex rounded the corner, his brow lifting when he saw them. "Your drinks are on the stage. We got you a beer, Cassie."

"Thank you," she said, but her eyes were still on Presley's. Like she wasn't sure what had just happened, but she liked it.

And fuck if he hadn't liked it too.

———

They hadn't been alone again. And maybe that was a good thing because she had no damn idea what just happened.

You came on Presley Hartson's hand.

Her cheeks flamed. Because that was the truth. The man barely had to touch and kiss her before she'd imploded with pleasure. Yes, some of it was the adrenaline from the gig, but most of it was him.

The man knew how to touch her to bring her pleasure. Understood that she'd needed pressure, movement.

Him.

Oh God, she needed to stop thinking about this and concentrate on singing.

Despite her turmoil, the second half of the gig went just

as well as the first. The applause and stomping of feet had gone on until they'd come on for one final song, then the crowd had slowly drifted away as they packed up their instruments and the guys had started carrying them to the van.

She'd tried to help but they'd all waved her off. So she'd watched as they easily hefted the heavy cases. Okay, she'd mostly watched Presley.

The man was born to perform, that much was clear. His grouchy persona just worked, along with his thick, rough voice and the slight air of menace that accompanied him wherever he went.

And then you let him make you come.

And her whole body was still on fire because of it.

"Okay then," Marley said, pulling up outside of her house. He was driving and Presley was up front with him, leaving her and Alex in the back. Thankfully, Alex was mostly snoozing, leaving her to her thoughts. "Here you go, Cassie."

She pulled the door open. Their instruments were all in the back, but Marley and Pres would unload them back at the studio. "Thanks for a good evening," she said, looking back at them.

Pres caught her eye but said nothing. Like he knew she was talking about more than the gig.

"You were amazing," Marley said. "We'll talk tomorrow. Discuss next steps. But I think we can all say tonight was a success."

"Wha?" Alex blinked his eyes open. "Oh, we're here."

"Want me to walk you to your door?" Presley asked, ignoring him.

"No, it's fine." Truth was, she couldn't stand to be close to him and not touch him. And something about his demeanor told her there wouldn't be a repeat of that kiss. Not tonight.

She grabbed her jacket and her bag and jumped down from the cab, walking up the driveway to her little house.

When she got to the door she slid the key in and waved to them.

Alex and Marley waved back. Presley just nodded.

As soon as she stepped inside she let out a long breath. Tonight was… interesting. And electrifying. She wasn't sure she'd be able to sleep, which wasn't great because tomorrow was Saturday and she had classes most of the day.

She dropped her bag on the floor and hung up her jacket before heading straight upstairs. The heat of the bar still clung to her, so she shucked the rest of her clothes off and walked into the bathroom, turning on the shower.

The warm spray on her body felt like heaven. She tipped her head back, feeling the spray dousing her face. Her eyes were closed and all she could see behind them was Presley.

His intense stare as she'd spasmed against him. The way his voice hit those low, aching notes during the gig. She let out a long breath and moved her hands to her chest, slowly cupping her breasts, remembering how hard his body had felt against hers. How demanding his lips were.

How good his hand felt.

She moved her own hand down, between her thighs, feeling the slickness of her desire. She pressed her finger where she needed it most, her mouth parted as she circled once, then twice, imagining it was his fingers.

His lips.

Her thighs were shaking. All of her was. Behind the curtain of her eyelids she saw him walking into the shower, as naked as she was. Seeing her hand between her legs and lifting a brow.

"Let's get one thing straight. Nobody touches you but me."

She'd seen enough of his body through the drenched t-shirt he'd been wearing tonight to know the thick hardness of his chest muscles, the plane of his abdomen dipping into that low v.

He wouldn't be gentle. She knew that much from the way he'd gotten her off. And maybe she craved that. Craved the roughness of him. The raw need that she'd seen in his eyes.

Her breath caught as she pictured him lifting her the way he had at his house, pressing her against the shower tiles and thrusting in.

He was big. She knew that much too. He'd fill her until she was breathless. Until the pleasure coiled in her stomach, the same way it was coiling now.

With her other hand, she pinched her nipple. Hard and rough, like him. And then she felt it. The tightness. The darkness before the dawn.

"Presley..." His name caught in her throat as she came, her body tightening around her fingers, her legs barely able to keep her upright. She contracted again and again, leaning against the tile so she didn't fall, imagining him kissing her through her orgasm, his face tender.

Loving.

And when it was over she felt her cheeks flush. Dear God, what was wrong with her? Yes, there was some kind of connection there, some kind of raw attraction that she felt to the deepest of her bones. But he'd made it clear that was all it was. From the way he'd apologized for the kiss to the way he'd so easily replied to Alex a few seconds after making her come.

He was complicated, and maybe a little broken. And he didn't want her, apart from in her imagination.

"So stop it," she whispered to herself, grabbing the shampoo because she needed to get clean and go to bed. "It's not going to happen. And it shouldn't."

It was time to wash that man right out of her hair.

CHAPTER
Twelve

"DADDY, can you do my hair like a princess?" Delilah asked, skipping into the kitchen in her fairy outfit. It was almost lunchtime on Saturday.

"Do princesses wear their hair in a ponytail?" he asked, hoping to hell she did. He was feeling tetchy and his third coffee of the day wasn't cutting it. He'd spent the morning shopping for new shoes with Delilah – princess ones, of course, with glittery leather and little straps with sparkling buckles.

Why the hell did everything have to be princess? He'd tried to steer her toward a pair of cute little engineer boots, but she was having none of it. Fuck the patriarchy.

"No she doesn't, silly." Delilah pouted, and for a second she looked so much like Jade it made him blink. Most of the time he didn't see that much of his late wife in her. Delilah was a Hartson through and through. But these occasional glimpses were like a fist to the stomach.

Another reminder that he'd failed to give his kid everything she needed.

"I want my hair to look like Cassie's," Delilah said firmly. "With pretty waves that go down around my shoulders."

Pres blew out a mouthful of air. Of course she wanted to look like Cassie. And damn if that didn't get him thinking about her again. The same way he had last night, remembering the way she'd looked when she'd shattered against his hand.

Christ, he needed a cold shower.

"She told me that I didn't need to call her Miss. We're friends," Delilah said, full of satisfaction. "Can you do my waves now?"

"I can't put your hair in waves. It needs to be set."

"What about a curling wand?"

Where the hell had she learned about hair appliances? The kid was six. "I don't have a curling wand."

"Cassie does."

Of course she did. Cassie had everything. Including his balls every time he looked at her. Or touched her. Or made her come.

Ah fuck. He needed to get over this.

"I'm not calling Cassie to borrow her curling wand. She's working today anyway."

"At the dance school?" Delilah asked.

"Yep." She'd mentioned it last night. Marley had made sure they dropped her off first since the rest of them had the weekend free.

"Can we go see her there?"

"You're going to a party," he said patiently. "That's why we're doing your hair." There was something kind of funny about a six year old's attention. It wandered like a nomad, like her thoughts were always ten feet ahead of reality.

"Oh yeah. Like a princess."

"A princess with a ponytail," he reminded her.

"Can you at least do a braid?"

Fuck. Well, he could try. "If you promise not to cry while I'm doing it."

"Just don't tug too hard. You can wet it like Cassie does."

Twenty minutes later, they were walking out of the door. Delilah's hair was in some kind of braid, though it wasn't his best effort. Not his worst either. But she'd praised him anyway, like he was the kid and she was the parent.

"Well done, Daddy. That was a great try." She'd patted his face.

His lips twitched. Damn, she was growing up too fast. She skipped in her new shoes and fairy dress and hair-that-was-almost-a-braid to his truck, waiting patiently as he locked up and grabbed the gift that his mom had bought for Delilah's friend, Lucy, and walked over to help her into the cab.

The party was at one of those trampoline play areas. As soon as they walked in Delilah saw her friends and they squealed, welcoming her into their group as she showed off her new shoes.

He put the gift on the table next to some others and stuffed his hands in his pockets, looking around for somewhere to sit.

"Pres," a voice said. He turned to see Alice. She'd been one of Jade's friends. They'd been pregnant at the same time and had attended some birthing classes together. He'd known Alice's husband – her ex-husband now – a little. Enough to have someone to talk to when the girls were babies.

"Hey." He gave her a smile. "How's things?"

"Great. Listen, Maisie was asking if Delilah could come back to ours after the party. She could stay over if that works? The two of them haven't seen each other for so long."

They were at different schools now. And shamefully he hadn't kept up the friendship after Jade died.

"I haven't got her pajamas. Or clothes for tomorrow."

"You could go home and pack them up," Alice said hopefully. "I'll be here to keep an eye on the girls."

"Let me ask Delilah."

"Sure." Alice smiled.

Of course she didn't need asking twice. By the time the

words were out of his mouth, she and Maisie were jumping up and down with excitement. So he went home and packed some clothes and her toiletries, being sure to put Lola in there just in case. And then he drove the twenty minutes back to the trampoline play center, handing the bag over to Alice.

Delilah ran over to him. "Did you pack my unicorn pajamas?" she asked breathlessly. The braid he'd worked so painstakingly on was half undone, and her face was red from all the bouncing.

"Yep. And your favorite dress for tomorrow. And Lola's in there in case you need her."

It felt strange saying goodbye to her. But it shouldn't. She had plenty of sleepovers at his parents' after all. But this was different. He trusted his mom implicitly. He knew Alice was a good person but...

It was still hard letting go.

Delilah hugged him. "Bye, Daddy," she said cheerily.

"I can stay until the end of the party," he told her. "There's no rush."

She wrinkled her nose. "Don't do that. You can go."

Well okay then. Apparently only one person here was feeling a little sentimental right now. He hugged her back, told her to be good, and then she was running back to the party.

"If there are any problems, call me," he said to Alice. "I can be there in ten minutes."

"She'll be fine. I promise," Alice told him.

Yeah, she would. He just wasn't so sure about himself.

When he climbed back into the cab of his truck he let out a long breath. What a couple of fucking days it had been.

He'd spent last night tossing and turning, thinking about Cassie. Thinking about kissing her, about touching her.

Making her come.

It had been a hell of a long time since he'd thought about being inside of a woman. Truth be told, he'd been surprised by how much the softness of her skin turned him on. How the way she sang made his chest ache.

How he wanted to lift her against the bar wall and thrust inside of her until she saw stars.

He dropped his brow to the wheel, letting out a groan. He needed to go home. To get her out of his mind.

Good luck with that. You have the whole night to yourself. What else are you going to think about?

Fuck, at this rate he was going to pleasure himself raw.

With a sigh, he started the engine and backed out of the space, turning left out of the parking lot back toward Hartson's Creek.

He would get through this. He would.

———

"Everything okay?" Gemma asked, peeping her head around the door to the dance studio.

Cassie looked up. She'd been sorting through music tracks, getting prepared for next week's lessons. And truth be told, she was also avoiding going home.

Because being alone with her thoughts wasn't the best place to be right now. Not when they were full of him.

"Hey." She smiled at Gemma. "Sorry, didn't notice the time."

"I was about to head out," Gemma told her. "I should be able to see the last twenty minutes of Lucy's softball game."

"Oh, of course." She immediately felt bad for holding Gemma up. "You go on ahead, I can lock up."

"You sure?"

"Of course."

Gemma tipped her head to the side. "Is everything okay? You've been really quiet today. You didn't even tell me how last night went."

And now she felt worse. "I'm sorry." She offered her a

conciliatory smile. "I've been all over the place. Can we do dinner next week?"

"Of course, I'd love that." Gemma grinned. "You sure you're okay to lock up?"

"I'll be fine. I won't be that long behind you."

"Okay then. Have fun. I'll see you on Monday." Gemma blew her a kiss, and Cassie returned it. A minute later, she heard the front door close and she was alone in the studios.

Pulling the music list up again, she slid her finger down until she found it. The song.

The one that would get her out of this funk.

She'd always loved *Flashdance*. What dancer didn't? There were never enough movies about dancers making it.

But Jennifer Beals was something else. Cassie had fallen in love with the character she played in the movie. Alex had fought against all odds to be accepted at the Pittsburgh Conservatory of Dance. More odds than Cassie had to face, being the daughter of a dancer.

And she'd succeeded where Cassie had failed.

She pushed that thought right out of her head where it belonged, and pulled up Irene Cara's song, the music filling the studio as she took a deep breath.

It started slow. A steady, throbbing beat that matched the rhythm of her heart. She felt her muscles react, the memory of learning this dance as a teenager with her friends rushing through her.

They'd loved it so much. At the end of every lesson they'd put this song on and dance until nothing else mattered. Not their arguments with their parents or their grades at school. It was just them and their bodies and the music.

And it was what she needed right now.

She moved slowly at first, her back arching, her leg extending, her body turning in a mixture of ballet and modern dance. And then the beat hit in, and she sped up, spinning and jumping, her breath fast, her heart racing, and damn, it felt so good.

She was only wearing a leotard and tights, her ballet shoes were off and her feet were bare as they hit the wooden floor of the studio before she launched herself again. And yes, she could feel a twinge in her ankle as she landed, but it didn't matter. The pain felt good.

Everything did.

It was just her, her body, the music, and nothing else.

By the time Irene Cara reached the crescendo, Cassie was breathless. Her body was flushed, and her muscles were loose. She had music, she had rhythm, as she arched her back one final time and dropped to the floor.

And that's when she saw Presley.

Standing at the doorway, his eyes dark, his jaw tight. Irene's voice faded away and there was silence in the room, save for the sound of her rapid breaths and the pulse of blood rushing through her ears.

Presley was wearing a pair of jeans and a gray t-shirt, his hair falling over his face in the way it always did. She noticed one of his hands was curled around the door jamb, his knuckles bleached white.

And the way he was staring at her made her body want to throb.

She opened her mouth to say something, but no words came out. Just another breath. One that was full of need.

And as though he could hear it, he let go of the doorway and stalked toward her, his lips saying nothing.

But his eyes said everything.

He held his hand out to her. She took it and he pulled her up. She'd barely gotten to her feet before she was pulled against him, her body flush against his.

She could feel the hardness of his body...

And other parts.

He tipped her chin up until their eyes locked. She ran the tip of her tongue along her bottom lip and his eyes narrowed.

"How long were you watching?" she asked.

"Long enough." His palm pressed against the dip of her spine. She could feel the heat of it through the thin fabric of her leotard.

"I didn't know you were there," she murmured.

"I know. You dance like a fucking angel. You're beautiful."

Weird how she felt beautiful, too, in his arms. Even if she was a little sweaty and overly worked up. But she could see his reaction to her. Could feel it.

It sent a pulse of need straight between her legs.

"Are you going to kiss me again?" she asked him.

"Do you want me to?"

She swallowed hard. "Yes. It's all I can think about."

He didn't need asking twice. It was like a dam breaking as his lips took hers, the need and the ache and the desperation pouring into that single kiss. His hands were all over her, tracing the curve of her sides, her hips, her ass. He pressed his fingers into her soft flesh, their tongues clashing, and she moaned against his mouth.

His hand moved between her thighs, and memories of last night flooded her thoughts as his fingers touched her there. God, this man knew how to make her feel good. And then she was in his arms and he was walking over to the piano, his mouth never releasing hers. And when he sat on the stool, he brought her with him, until she was straddling his body.

Feeling the thick ridge of him between her thighs.

"I want you," she told him.

"I want you too," he whispered against her mouth. "So damn much."

His hands were touching her face, her chest, her breasts. Her nipples peaked obscenely through the fabric. He leaned down to capture one in his mouth, dampening the cloth of her leotard, making her arch her back.

The only reason she didn't fall was because he had a hold on her. Still steadying her back, keeping her safe. He sucked and scraped and she ran her fingers through his hair.

"We need to stop," he murmured. "Before I take you here and now."

"There's nobody here."

He let out a groan and pushed the neck of her leotard down, exposing her breast to the air, the coolness of it making it harder still. This time when he licked her sensitive skin she let out a long, low moan.

Every part of her was on fire. And they were both still fully clothed.

He kissed her jaw, her cheek, her lips again, pushing the leotard down her arms, exposing all of her chest to him. His eyes roamed over her, taking her in.

"So fucking beautiful."

And she felt it. Because he meant it.

She leaned forward to press her lips to his neck. Where the curl of a black tattoo was emerging from his t-shirt. Her breath was fast, her heartbeat faster, as she moved her hands down his t-shirt, feeling the hard planes of his chest. Her fingers stole beneath the fabric, until she was touching his stomach and he groaned out loud.

He groaned even louder when her fingertips grazed his nipple. "Cassie…"

"What?" she asked breathlessly.

"You okay with this?"

She wanted to laugh. Couldn't he feel how okay she was? Couldn't he tell from the way she was flushed and breathless? Her senses were full of him. She could feel the tautness of his thigh muscles beneath her. Smell the warm pine of his soap on his neck.

And yeah, the thickness of him was obvious. She was doing everything that she could not to squirm against him.

But she was fighting a losing battle.

"It's more than okay."

His hands cupped her waist, and he tipped her back, until she was arching again, her breasts exposed to his heated stare. He lowered his head until she could feel the warmth of his breath against her skin.

Then he captured her nipple with his mouth, sucking her in, making her gasp.

He knew how to hold her so she wouldn't fall. Those large, rough hands of his came in super handy as a backrest. And as he licked and teased and scraped his own teeth against her, she found herself squirming again.

So needy, so turned on.

"Come home with me."

She blinked at his voice. "What?" He was still stroking her breasts, plucking her nipple between his fingertips. Pain and pleasure rushed through her, making her feel heady.

"I'm not having sex in here. This is where my kid learns to dance."

She started to laugh. She couldn't help it. Mostly because he was right. This couldn't happen, not here, not now. It was one thing to get a little handsy with him, another to go full blown porn star.

"You're right," she said, her eyes meeting his. "You can't."

"So come home with me," he said again.

"What about Delilah?"

"She's at a sleepover."

Oh. That flush was showing no signs of disappearing from her face or her skin. "All night?"

"Yeah, all night."

She took a long breath. "Okay then. But you can come to my house."

He tipped his head, as though scrutinizing her. "You prefer your place to mine?"

She shrugged. "It'll be easier to kick you out in the morning."

"I'll follow you home." He pulled her leotard up, until her breasts were covered again. Then he wrapped his arms around her, pulling her into a kiss that made her toes curl.

He'd done the right thing in stopping. They were grown ups, not little kids.

But when they got back to her place, it was on.

CHAPTER
Thirteen

"I WAS THINKING on the way home," Cassie said as he followed her through her front door. She had the world's smallest house, and he had to stoop to walk through the front door.

"That's a dangerous thing to do," Pres replied.

She turned and grinned at him. "We should lay down some ground rules. In case things get messed up."

He blinked. He wasn't expecting that. "What kind of ground rules?" And what kind of messed up? He'd been hard as he drove. The memory of her dance played over and over in his mind.

He'd never met anybody this flexible. This at one with their body. It was pretty much the hottest thing he'd ever seen.

"This thing," she said, pulling her sweater off, revealing her leotard and tights beneath. "Whatever it is between us. I don't want it to cause any problems for you or me."

"How would it cause problems?" He couldn't take his eyes off her ass as she leaned down to pull of her sneakers.

Cassie looked up, lifting a brow. "You've already gotten

weird on me twice. And that was just from kissing and touching me."

"You think I'm gonna get weird if we have sex?"

She bit down a smile. "I'd say it's pretty much guaranteed. And that would be fine if you and I never saw each other again. But we play in the same band. I teach your daughter. We can't walk through town without bumping into each other. So I need you to promise me it won't get weird."

"That *I* won't get weird," he corrected. There was a half smile on his lips because she wasn't wrong. He knew he'd been an ass to her after they'd touched before. Mostly because he didn't want to feel this way.

Pulled to her. Entranced by her. Every time he pictured her his dick got hard.

His shower had never seen so much damn activity.

She pulled her leotard down and his whole body went on high alert.

"What are you doing?" he asked.

"I need to take a shower. I've been working all day." She rolled it down her thighs, followed by her tights.

She was naked. And he was staring at her, open mouthed.

Like he'd thought. Completely at one with her body.

Jesus.

"Have we finished with the ground rules?" he asked.

She turned and started walking up the stairs on her tiptoes, the movement making the cheeks of her ass jiggle. "Are you planning on being weird?"

"No."

"And you won't treat me any differently when we're singing together?"

He frowned. "You want me to treat you like you're just a friend?" He needed to clarify what she was asking. But his mind was hazy. And a little bit distracted by the sight of her climbing the stairs naked.

He kicked his own shoes off and followed her.

"I want you to treat me like you would anybody else." She'd reached the top. "And maybe this will help. The UST is stupidly distracting, right?"

"The UST?" he murmured. She was pulling her hair into a bun.

"Sexual tension. Maybe we both need to get it out of our bodies." She reached for the door, pressing the handle down then stepped inside.

The bathroom. Of course.

"Sometimes that can cause problems," he murmured. "Sometimes the sexual tension is what makes the band work."

Her eyes widened. "You're right. You can leave now."

"What?"

Cassie started to laugh. "I'm kidding. You just looked so serious again. If we're doing this, can you at least crack a smile?"

"I can smile."

"I know you can. But will you?"

He lifted the corner of his lips.

"Oh god, not like that." She screwed up her nose. "I'll tell you what. If you smile, I'll get on my knees in the shower for you."

He opened his mouth to answer, but she was already reaching in and turning on the spray. The shower was small, barely big enough to fit them both.

It'd be cozy though. Very. Damn. Cozy.

"Are you coming in?" she asked, stepping into the steaming spray.

"Yes I'm fucking coming in."

"Then get undressed."

His eyes caught hers. It was weird how much he liked her teasing. It made things easier. Made him not think so much.

Made him want to show her who was the damn boss around here.

He pulled his t-shirt off and it was his turn to smile because she was staring at his chest, her throat undulating as she swallowed.

Then he flicked the button of his jeans, pulling the zipper down, climbing out of them until they were a pile of blue on the floor. His socks were next, and then his shorts.

His dick slapped against his stomach. She ran the tip of her tongue over her bottom lip, her gaze dipping, her eyes widening.

"You could hurt somebody with that," she told him.

"That's the plan." It wasn't. But it got a smile out of her.

And he liked that too much.

Her eyes flashed. "Come here and prove it."

He lifted a brow and walked toward the shower, stepping around the glass barrier to where she was standing, naked and wet.

He pulled her to him until their bodies touched. And fuck, she felt perfect. His dick twitched in approval as his lips lazily captured hers, their tongues sliding, their fingers caressing.

Learning each other's bodies. Each other's tells.

He kissed the skin beneath her ear and she gasped. Moved his lips lower to where her neck met her shoulder and she shivered.

This was fun. Why had he been fighting this? He was finding it hard to remember.

When he kissed her breasts she let out a long, deep groan, her head tipping back until it was against the tiles. He took his time sucking and scraping them, teasing them until they were hard and swollen, before he kissed his way down to her stomach.

Then dropped to his knees and pushed her thighs open.

"I thought I was going to get on my knees," she said

breathlessly, as he pressed his thumb against the soft skin between her thighs.

"Ladies first," he leaned forward to kiss where his thumbs had been. Then moved his lips up.

Water was pouring down her, but she was wet already, he could tell from the slickness between her legs. He leaned forward, his tongue touching her right where she needed him.

She let out another loud sigh, her fingertips scraping against his scalp.

God, she tasted like heaven. He licked her again and again, his cock throbbing with every cry she made, until she was unsteady on her feet, and he had to hold her thighs tightly.

"I need you inside of me."

And that's when he remembered. "I don't have anything."

Shit. Fuck. That's what happened when you're out of practice. If his friends found out about this, they'd laugh their asses off.

Not that they'd find out. This wasn't something he planned to share.

"I'm on birth control," she told him. "And I'm clean."

He looked up. Her eyes were on his. And fuck if she didn't look so trusting it made his heart twinge.

"Me too."

They should still use a condom. He knew that. But he had nothing, and he wanted her.

Too much.

"I'll pull out," he promised. Himself as much as her. He stood, cupping her face. "Are you sure about this?"

He needed her to say it. To be clear.

"Did me almost coming on your mouth not tell you how sure I am?" she asked him.

"Say yes," he whispered, pressing the thick length of his cock against her.

Her lips curled up. "Yes. Fuck me, Presley."

He slid his hands beneath her, lifting her until the angle meant he could grind against her most sensitive part. He thrust into her, their mouths clashing, her body sandwiched between him and the tiles, his body taking over, taking what it needed.

Giving her what she needed.

Another thrust and he was in to the fucking hilt. A wave of dizzy euphoria washed over him. So fucking tight, so fucking warm.

He was being rough, but she was begging him for more. So he gave it to her, still kissing her, still whispering her name, still telling her how beautiful she was.

As he defiled her beautiful body.

Her arms tightened around his neck at the same time her pussy tightened around his dick, her breath coming in pants against his lips.

"Presley…"

"I know," he soothed. "I've got you."

And then she was coming around him. Not just her pussy but her whole body. Convulsing and arching like she'd never come before. He stopped thrusting, pinning her against the tiles, letting her orgasm wash over her. Holding her tight because there was no way he was letting her go.

"Keep fucking me," she whispered against his ear.

And so he did. Moving his hips, moving inside of her. Until he could feel the peak too, uncurling in his spine, making his balls tighten.

"Fuck…" He pulled out, coming hard, and his lips captured hers. His heart slammed against his ribcage, the pleasure wracking his body the same way it wracked hers.

And when he finally stopped surging, he gently set her down on the floor.

"That's the first shower I've taken where I've ended up dirtier than I started," he told her.

She lifted a brow, her face lighting up with the most beautiful smile. "Somehow I sincerely doubt that."

———

Cassie's eyes fluttered open, adjusting to the dim light in the bedroom. It took a moment for her to realize there was somebody else in her bed.

No, not somebody. *Presley.* Her breath caught as she looked at him, remembering last night.

They had sex twice more before she'd finally drifted off to sleep, her muscles aching in a delicious way. One time on the floor once they'd finally dried off – this time he'd insisted on getting her off with his mouth first – and then on the bed, which they'd laughed all the way through because he'd discovered she was ticklish on the sides of her body and had taken advantage.

So she'd returned the favor.

Sundays were Cassie's only real day off. And she usually spent it by being lazy in bed for as long as possible before attacking her laundry pile and doing what she could to clean her house.

But this morning, she was apparently spending it staring at Presley Hartson.

He was laying on his front with his head facing her, one arm flung above his head, his eyelids flickering as he dreamed about whatever hot single dads dreamed about. But it was his tattoos that drew her eye. He had a big one of wings on his back, so intricately drawn that they almost looked like real feathers.

She reached out to touch it. No, it was definitely skin.

Warm, hard, masculine skin.

"I got that one for Delilah," he muttered against the pillow.

Her lips twitched. "Did I wake you?"

"Nope. Still asleep."

This time she grinned. "What time do you have to pick Delilah up?"

That made his eyes open. His little girl was definitely his achilles heel. "What time is it?" His voice was croaky. It reminded her of all those dirty words he whispered in her ear the second time they had sex.

Her cheeks flushed.

"Almost eight."

He groaned into the pillow. "Why are you awake so early? Didn't I wear you out?"

"Obviously not. But I'm younger than you so…"

Presley turned his head, his eyes open now. Narrow, though. "You're not *that* much younger. What? Five years?"

"Something like that." It was six, actually, but he didn't need to know that right now. But the truth was he felt older. Not just because he was a dad but because he was actually a considerate love maker.

He'd made sure she came before he did. Three times that last time, when tickling and touching all mixed in together until she was riding a wave she couldn't get off.

You definitely got off, honey.

She was pretty sure she wasn't the most experienced lover he'd had. But hopefully what she lacked in skill she made up for in energy. Like a puppy.

No, scratch that. A kitten. Yeah. Like a delighted kitten, all over him.

"What are you smiling about?" he asked, his arms stretching.

"Just thinking about how soon I can throw you out of my bed."

His brows knitted. "You want me to go?"

"I'm kidding," she promised. "I was actually thinking that you have so much more experience than me."

He blinked but said nothing.

"Did I say the wrong thing?" she asked him.

"No. I was just..." He shook his head. "You say things I don't expect you to. And then I have to figure out how to respond."

"Why would you have to figure out how to respond?" she asked him, confused.

"Because I've been known to piss you off. Hell, I've been known to piss a lot of people off." He shrugged. "I find it's best to think first and speak second."

"That sounds exhausting," she told him.

"Yeah, it can be."

No wonder he was so brooding. His head must be a mess of thoughts. Sure, they were grown ups, they'd all had to learn to censor their thoughts somewhat. Her mom always said that what happened in your head didn't need to come straight out of your mouth.

But still, this was different.

"Were you like that with Jade?" she asked him. It was weird saying his wife's name. Not least because they were naked in bed together. But also because he'd never mentioned her. He'd certainly never told her his dead wife's name.

She'd heard it though. From Marley and Alex. And probably his mom, too.

He opened his mouth and closed it again, and this time she knew what was happening. Whatever he was going to say was censored.

"I hate the way you won't say what you think."

"I think I should go home, shower, and pick my kid up."

Okay, so she'd taken the wrong tack. Noted. He didn't like talking about his dead wife, and why should he?

Especially with another woman.

"Sure," she said smoothly.

He ran the tip of his tongue along his bottom lip to moisten it. "Are you still okay?" he asked, his voice thick. "About this?"

"I will be after we go tell everybody about us."

"About us?" he repeated, looking confused.

"We had sex, so we'll be a couple now, right? Isn't Sunday the day you go to your parents' house? What time should I get there?"

His mouth fell open. His eyes were so wide she could almost see his thoughts clouding inside them.

"I'm kidding," she told him, rolling her own eyes. "Of course I'm alright. The sex was good, you're funny when you remember to speak before you think. And now I'm also going to take a shower and start my day."

"Okay…"

"And you're still not going to make this weird, right?" she asked him.

"No?" It sounded like a question. He was clearly having a hard time with this.

She sat up, pulling the sheet up to her chest. "Say it with conviction."

His lips twitched. "No."

"No you won't say it with conviction, or was that a lame attempt to actually say it like you meant it?"

"No," he said again. "To both."

She opened her mouth to tell him to try again, but he curled his palm around her neck and pulled her to him, his lips brushing hers in a way that was intended to shut her up.

And it worked.

His mouth was warm, demanding. He climbed over her, kissing her again, caging her in with his arms.

"How long do we have?" she murmured.

"Gotta be out of here by nine-thirty." His lips trailed down her jaw, her neck, as he slowly pushed the sheet down to reveal her breasts.

"Plenty of time then." She gasped as he captured her nipple between his lips.

"My thoughts exactly." He kissed lower and lower until her eyes rolled into the back of her head.

The man knew how to make her feel good. And she planned on taking advantage of it for as long as she could.

CHAPTER
Fourteen

"YOU'RE BEING WEIRD," Cassie murmured to Presley the following weekend as they unpacked their instruments at the bar. "You promised…"

"I'm not being weird." He frowned at her. "How am I being weird?"

"You insisted on carrying my bag in," she pointed out. "Even Marley thought that was weird."

"I'm a fucking gentleman," he said, looking annoyed.

"I know." She lifted a brow. "With an emphasis on fucking."

Okay, now he was pissed. He was pretty damn sure that if he'd ignored her as they drove to the bar for their next gig she'd have been annoyed at that, too.

He wasn't sure how he was supposed to behave. Especially when she was wearing jeans that looked like they were painted on her ass and a top that barely covered the parts of her he loved the most.

All he could think about was how she'd felt when he slid inside of her. How her skin flushed whenever he'd touched her.

And yeah, it had been a week and he'd been busy as hell,

but they'd managed to talk a couple of times on the phone once Delilah was in bed.

He'd seen her at rehearsals, too. Then followed her home afterward so they could make out in his car for twenty minutes before he headed home to take over from his mom.

But his life was complicated. Between his work and his daughter he didn't have a whole lot of time. Even less now that they had the band. But he wanted to see her.

Wanted to see her tonight.

Wanted to make her breath tight and short the way he had when his head was buried between her thighs.

"What are you thinking about?" Cassie whispered.

Busted. "About how much of a pain in my ass you are."

A smile pulled at her lips. "I'm not the weird one."

"Don't you have a keyboard to set up?" he muttered.

"Just going over there now." She smiled at him over her shoulder and left him standing there. Staring at her sweet ass.

There was a bigger crowd here tonight. They were playing the Rainbow Bar. It was a roadhouse kind of joint, right outside of Hartson's Creek, and they'd attracted a big local crowd.

"Everything okay?" Marley asked him, as Presley walked over to help him set up the drum kit.

"Everything's fine. Why?"

"I saw you and Cassie having a heated conversation. Don't tell me you've pissed her off right before the show."

Okay, now this was too much. Even his brother had it in for him. "What the hell do you mean by that?"

It came out more vehemently than he'd intended. And Marley actually flinched. "Whoa," he said. "Where did that come from?"

He ran his hands through his hair. "I don't know. Sorry. It's just all a bit intense in here. A lot of old faces, you know?"

"It's nice that they've all come to watch us," Marley said. "We've been gone for so long."

And yeah, that was his fault. "Not anymore."

"Nope." Marley grinned. "So everything's okay then? I don't have to worry about you and Cassie screaming at each other on stage?"

"No."

"Good."

From the corner of his eye, Presley saw his two girl cousins arrive. Sabrina was the youngest, currently in college. And technically she wasn't old enough to be in a bar. But he'd squared it with the owner. If she sat with a chaperone and drank sodas all night she'd be good.

So his other cousin, Grace, had agreed to be the chaperone. And right now Grace was hugging Cassie.

Cassie had been right. This was a small town.

Too fucking small.

And that's when he saw Sadie. Jade's sister. Standing with a group of friends at the bar down from Cassie and his cousins. She caught him looking at her and smiled.

He nodded back.

Fuck. Guilt at staring at Cassie immediately washed over him. Had Sadie seen them talking? He hoped to hell not. Sadie was a few years younger than Jade. He'd gotten along with her fine, but she was still a kid when he and his wife had started dating.

"Come on, let's go say hi to Sabrina and Grace," Marley said, punching his arm lightly. "You can give Sabrina the riot act again."

"I'm not her dad," he muttered.

Still, they walked over and hugged their cousins. Sabrina ranting about something her dad had said about her clothes. He tuned it out, all too aware that he'd have said the same fucking thing if Delilah had tried to walk out of the house half-dressed.

Shit, he was so not looking forward to her being a teenager.

"Presley," Sadie called out. Marley lifted a brow.

"Did you invite her?" he asked.

"Nope. But it's a free world." And it was kind of sweet that Jade's sister was here. He walked over to hug her.

"Hey. Thanks for coming."

Sadie smiled at him. "You should have told me you were playing. I had to find out from a flier at work."

Sadie ran a shop a couple of towns over. She lived above it. She was busy, he knew that, but she still made time for Delilah. She and her parents saw her every month.

"Who's that?" she asked, looking over his shoulder.

He turned to look. And of course it was Cassie, back on stage. Staring at him with her brows pulled tight.

"Our new keyboardist."

"What happened to the last one?"

"Alex."

Sadie wrinkled her nose. "I remember Jade telling me about him."

Yeah, Alex had a reputation. "I gotta go. Have a good time tonight," he told her.

"And you break a leg."

"I'll try not to." He winked. That would finish Marley off completely. "Don't drink and drive, okay."

Her eyes met his and he could see understanding there. "Of course I won't," she said softly. "I promise."

———

"You're definitely being weird," Cassie hiss-whispered after the first song. He'd barely looked at her the whole time they'd been on stage. What was it with his mood swings? She felt like she was watching a damn tennis match. "Can you at least look at me when you sing?"

"I *was* looking at you."

Alex wandered over. "You two ready for the next song?"

She nodded and walked back to the keyboard. They'd already chosen to go with the previous playlist. Starting off with a fast song, segueing into the slower one.

And at least she could hide the fact that Presley was completely ignoring her with the fast one. But "Beautiful Liar" needed him to be singing to her.

This is your fault for telling him not to carry your bag.

He'd swung the other way. Was completely ignoring her. And truth be told, she didn't like it.

She watched, her breath catching in her throat as Presley tipped his head down, his fingers forming the first chord. She could see the tip of his tattoo as it snaked up his neck, and the beads of perspiration that were breaking out on his skin.

And then he leaned forward. The room was so quiet she could hear the sharp inhalation of his breath before he strummed the first note and sang into the microphone.

"You walked toward me, your body full of grace…"

His voice was thick. True. It sent a shiver down her spine. She'd never met a man who put more emotion into his songs than Presley Hartson.

His eyes slid to hers as he hit the second line.

"The wind in your hair, the sun on your face."

She parted her lips. His eyes narrowed but didn't move from her at all. She felt the rush of blood through her veins as his lips formed the lyrics. A shiver snaked down her spine.

"Your lips were full of promises you never meant to keep."

The corner of his own mouth quirked up at that line. She half smiled back, because she knew he was singing about himself here. The promise that it wouldn't be weird.

But maybe she'd been wrong. Of course it would be weird. They'd had mind blowing sex and she was expecting him to act normally.

She was the weird one for making those kinds of demands.

It was hard to breathe as he continued to stare at her, the

atmosphere between them thick and electric. She could vaguely hear a woman in the crowd scream out Presley's name, but it just made her smile.

Because right now he felt like he belonged to her.

Her heart started hammering against her chest as he made it to the bridge. She had to pull her microphone toward her, take a breath to steady her heartbeat. And then she sang like her life depended on it.

"You told me that you loved me,
Your lips knew it was a lie,
You said you'd never leave me,
Then every touch was a goodbye."

His brows knitted as he sung. Like he was trying to work her out. Work himself out, maybe. She'd noticed before that he wasn't great with words when they weren't lyrics. He was a man who didn't talk when it wasn't needed. He guarded his emotions like they were bars of gold.

But right now it felt like he was cutting himself open. Revealing himself to her. She wanted to do the same for him.

She wanted to do everything for him. That was the problem. This man was addictive in the worst kind of way.

The way that broke up bands and shattered hearts. He made you want to dig deep to find out all his secrets.

Only to find out they could cut you like a knife.

It was her verse now. She sang of hurt, of being rejected. Of never trusting love again. And he watched her, his eyes hooded, his fingers slowly strumming his chords.

She was so hot her cheeks were flaming. She shook her hair to get rid of the perspiration, and he gave her another one of those half smiles.

The ones that she liked to fantasize were only for her.

When they got to the chorus this time, he walked toward her, still playing the guitar, leaning into her microphone like he did the first time they sang this song.

But he was closer. Hotter. She felt his arm brush hers every time he strummed the guitar. And as they reached the crescendo she didn't know if they were working together or fighting each other.

He sounded almost angry. Lost. So rough against the sweet notes she was hitting. It was magical and heartbreaking.

She never wanted it to end.

But then they were on the last note and he leaned in so close she could feel the roughness of his jaw touching hers. His lips were a turn of the head away, his cheek warm against hers.

Her muscles tightened at his nearness. Like it wanted more.

Wanted everything.

He sang the final word, his voice fading into nothing and the crowd exploded with applause. Marley was grinning, Alex was staring out into the audience, lapping it up.

"I'm so turned on right now," Pres whispered in her ear, his voice so low she had to concentrate to make it out. "It's taking everything I've got not to carry you off this stage."

She looked at him, breathless and shocked.

"Thank you, everybody," Marley shouted into his own mic, clearly bored of waiting for Presley to move things on. "Now let's get this bar rocking. Our next song is 'Rising From The Flames'."

———

"What are you doing?" Cassie asked Alex later, when the four of them were sitting at a table, along with Presley's cousins. Pres was busy talking to Grace about something, the two of them looking serious. And Marley was messaging somebody, she assumed either a woman or one of his friends from the fire station.

"I got somebody to record us playing 'Beautiful Liar'," Alex said. "I'm uploading it to our TikTok."

"We have a TikTok?" she asked, surprised.

Alex blew out a mouthful of air. "Kind of. Pres and Marley are shit at social media. I always took the lead. First on Facebook, then Insta. We even had a Snap for a while. But then TikTok came along so I made an account last year and added some old stuff, but this is the first new video I've posted." He held his phone up. "Look how good you look."

She watched as she was singing into the mic, Presley staring at her like he hated and loved her at the same time.

"You two are fucking gold together."

"Our voices work well," she murmured, almost certain that Alex finding out about the other night would be the last thing Pres would want.

"I used to sing sometimes," Alex told her, changing the subject. "Maybe we should try a song together."

She tipped her head, surprised. "Is that a euphemism?"

He laughed and shook his head. "No, but should it be?" He shrugged. "If you ever need somebody to sing a song with, I'm your guy."

"I've heard a little about you and keyboardists," she said, batting off his suggestion. Presley or no Presley, she'd never go there.

"So you've been talking about me?" he said, looking pleased at that.

The man was virtually impossible to dislike. Sure he was a bad flirt, but he didn't mean anything by it.

"I've been warned off," she told him, trying not to grin. "And it was effective."

He took a sip of beer and gave her a lopsided smile. "You'll change your mind."

"You have a big opinion of yourself," she said lightly.

"I figure if I don't have it, nobody else will. You've got to be your own biggest supporter in this game. It's dog eat dog."

He looked down at his phone. "Hell yeah, we have our first like."

"Does that make us famous?" she asked dryly.

"No, but we will be." This time he wasn't smiling. He was deadly serious. And she hated to burst his bubble and point out that they were just a little band in a small town that got the locals excited.

Let him ride the wave of the euphoria for a little longer.

"Sure." She smiled at him, lifting her glass.

Over his shoulder she noticed Presley had stopped talking. His eyes were on hers.

He looked annoyed about something.

"I'll tell you what, let's make a bet," Alex said. "If we get famous, you owe me a date."

"It's not going to happen." She was certain of that.

"Then there's no reason to refuse the bet."

She frowned. "That's the first logical thing I've heard you say all night. It's kind of scary."

"Is that a yes?"

"You're not getting a kiss."

"Okay." He shrugged. "But you're getting famous."

A chill went down her spine despite the heat of the room. She looked up again. Presley was back talking to his cousin, shaking his head at something she'd said.

Truth was, she didn't want to be famous. She liked things the way they were. Easy. Fun. In control.

Especially the control part. Because her life had been out of her control for so long, it felt like she was finally getting back on an even keel.

CHAPTER
Fifteen

"I'LL TAKE CASSIE HOME," Pres said once they'd finished loading Marley's van. He'd driven here separately from the rest of them, thanks to having to drop off Delilah at his mom's.

"It's fine, I got it." Marley shrugged, clearly not getting the message. "Her house is on the way."

Pres gritted his teeth. "Seriously. I want to talk to her about a song."

"What song?" Marley asked him.

This was the problem with brothers. They knew you too well to let anything slide. "Just something I want us to work on."

"Then we all need to work on it," Marley said slowly. From the corner of his eye he could see Alex talking to Cassie again. She laughed at something he said, tucking her hair behind her ear.

And that pissed him off even more.

"I'm. Taking. Her. Home." *There*. Could it be any fucking clearer?

Marley blinked at the edge in Pres' voice. For a moment he said nothing. Just stared at his twin, as though trying to work him out.

"Okay?" Pres prompted.

Marley turned his head to look at Cassie before turning back to look at Pres. "What's going on?"

Well great. Now he'd laid it on too much. Cassie was right, he was a damn weirdo.

He couldn't get it right if he tried.

He let out a long breath. "There's nothing going on."

"There's definitely something going on," Marley said. "But I get it, you don't want to talk about it." He looked over at Cassie. "Just promise me something."

"What?" Pres kicked at a stone with the tip of his sneaker. He had a feeling whatever his brother wanted, he wasn't going to like it.

"Just don't hurt her. Or yourself." Marley looked him in the eye. "Definitely not yourself. You've been through a lot."

"I'm fine."

"Sure you are. That's why you're sneaking around behind your twin brother's back with a girl."

"That's your move, not mine," Pres pointed out.

"Only because the girls always preferred you."

"That's when we were younger. Not true anymore, my friend. I've seen your Instagram likes."

"You're not even on Instagram, you idiot." Marley laughed, and the atmosphere between them lightened. Pres felt his muscles relax. This was how they were meant to be.

Easy. Fun. Brothers who loved each other fiercely.

He wasn't planning to let Cassie come between them. Just the opposite.

In a weird way she was bringing them all together.

"Take her home," Marley said, shaking his head, a wry smile pulling at his lips. "I'll deal with Alex."

"What are you gonna tell him?" Pres asked.

"Leave it to me." Marley pulled the keys from his pocket.

"Alex, get your butt over here and help me finish loading the truck. We've got some things to do."

———

Pres was silent as she climbed into the Beast. He closed the door softly behind her before walking around to the driver's side of the cab. She buckled herself in, wondering what he and Marley had been talking about.

By the way they kept looking over, it was either her or Alex, and she was pretty sure neither of them were that interested in the bassist.

The parking lot was dark, almost empty of cars and trucks now. The lights to the bar had been switched off, only the owner and a couple of staff members were inside the locked building, cleaning up after tonight's full house.

Her phone buzzed. She pulled it out and saw Alex's name on the screen.

Is he kidnapping you? – Alex

"What's got you smiling?" Presley asked as he pulled the driver's door shut. He started the engine up.

Pink Floyd blasted out of the speakers.

"Alex thinks you're kidnapping me," she said, tapping out a reply.

Yes. He's asking for a reward of one bass guitar and two Big Macs. Leave them by the trash can in the town square. – Cassie

. . .

"You messaging him now?" Presley asked. He didn't sound too pleased about it.

"Yes. Are you jealous?" she replied. Part of her hoped he'd say yes.

"Nope."

"That's good. Because we have a little wager. If we get famous I've promised to go on a date with him."

Presley frowned. "Why the hell would you do that?"

To get a rise out of you.

"Because I can't resist a gamble. And because he's going to lose." She smiled. "But don't worry, my lips won't be going anywhere near his."

"Glad to hear it," he muttered. "You deserve better than Alex."

Well this was going somewhere unexpected. "Do I?"

His lips twitched at the teasing tone of her voice. "Yes."

"Who would be better," she said, touching her fingertip to her mouth. "Hmm, let's see. There's one guy in the band who's completely hot and every time I look at him I blush at the things he could do to me."

Presley pulled onto the road, shaking his head.

"Don't you want to know his name?" she asked.

"Surprise me."

"Marley." She grinned. "The guy is hot as hell."

"He's my identical fucking twin."

She started to laugh because teasing Presley was way more enjoyable than she'd ever expected. He actually looked grumpy as he took a left and headed back to Hartson's Creek.

"But can you play the drums like him?" she asked.

"Actually, I can. We both learned, much to my mom's distress."

"You did? Why didn't I know that?" It gave her a weird thrill that he'd volunteered something to her. He wasn't always this talkative.

"There's a lot about me you don't know." They'd reached

a stoplight. The red reflected through the windshield, onto his face.

"Like what?" She shifted in her seat to look at him. His eyes were still on the light, his hands tight on the wheel.

"Like I love the way you growl my name when you come."

She took in a sharp breath. Well that was unexpected. "I don't growl."

"Yeah, you do."

"Prove it." She was grinning now.

"That's the plan."

She liked Dirty Presley so much more than Angry Presley. The light turned green and he started to accelerate, and she put her hand on his denim clad thigh, her fingers dangerously close to her favorite part of him.

"So you're driving me home to fuck me?" she asked.

"I'm driving you home because I want to make sure you get there safely. The rest is up to you. Obviously, I'd like to come in."

"In more ways than one." She moved her hand up further. Cupping the thick ridge of him. Damn, he was hard. "If it makes you feel any better, I'd like you inside of me, too."

His neck undulated as he swallowed. "Keep touching me like this and I'll be pulling over long before we get you home."

"Keep making promises like that and I'm never going to stop touching you," she teased. But she released him anyway, sliding her hand back down to his thigh. Keeping one hand on the wheel, he placed the other over hers, sliding their fingers together in a clasp.

She tried not to smile too hard.

Presley Hartson was holding her hand and it made her giddy. Damn, she was an idiot for this man.

———

"Oh my God," she whispered, her cheeks pink as he moved her up and down on him. "Presley…"

She was going to come. He could tell by the way she'd tightened around him. The way her nipples were taut and she couldn't keep a rhythm so he was having to help.

Christ, she was beautiful. Her hair was down and a little damp with perspiration, her makeup smeared, but he'd never seen her looking better than she did right now, riding his cock like it was her favorite sport.

"Do it…" he rasped. He wasn't going to be far behind her at this rate. Not with the way she felt so tight and so good. He pulled her down for a kiss, their mouths moving together as he rolled his hips underneath her.

And then he reached for her nipple, pinching it until she called his name out again.

"That was a growl."

She started to laugh against his mouth. But it turned into another groan as her orgasm overtook her, her pussy fluttering around his cock, her fingers pawing at his hair.

And then he was following her into the sweetest damn oblivion he'd ever experienced. Surging inside of her as she collapsed onto him, her body still in the throes of her own delight.

He was breathing so fast he wasn't sure his heart could take it. Could feel the thud of his pulse against his ears. He pushed the damp hair away from Cassie's face and smiled at her.

"You're fucking beautiful."

"Am I also beautiful when I'm not fucking?" she managed to rasp out.

"You know you are."

She was laying on his chest, her body splayed out over his. They'd have to move soon. But right now he couldn't shift a damn muscle even if you paid him to. He was spent and he liked it here too much.

Holding her tight.

"It's funny," she said. "But I grew up thinking about everything that was wrong with me. I wasn't thin enough. I wasn't pretty enough. I couldn't do the right kind of bun with my hair."

"You thought that?" He frowned. "Why?"

"Mostly because that's what my mom told me." She traced the tattoo on his bicep. He liked the way her fingers felt on his skin.

Like an anchor. Keeping him right where he needed to be.

"Your mom told you that? Seriously?"

"She said it was for my own good. That I needed to be realistic about who I was. And realistic about the things I put into my mouth, if I wanted to be a dancer."

"That's messed up."

"I know." She lifted a brow. "Years of therapy taught me that."

"You've had therapy?" he asked.

"Yes. Have you?"

"I took Delilah to therapy after her mom…" He trailed off. He didn't want to talk about another woman when Cassie was lying naked on top of him. "Kind of. Not really."

"I'd highly recommend it. It helped me love who I am."

He kissed her bare shoulder. "I'm glad. And your mom was wrong, by the way."

"Thank you," she said softly.

"What's wrong with some parents?" he asked. "I can't ever imagine saying something like that to my kid. I want her to be confident. To be happy."

"That's because you're a good dad."

"What happened to yours?"

"He left my mom when I was a baby. For another dancer."

"Ouch." He wrinkled his nose.

"Yeah. I suspect her wanting me to be perfect came from

that. She wanted to show him that she could bring me up without him."

"He wasn't around?"

"Not much. I hear from him at Christmas and that's about it."

"And your mom?" he asked.

"She travels a lot. She used to come see me if I was in a show, but there haven't been any of those for some time."

He swallowed. "She sounds like a bit of a bitch."

Cassie laughed again. Damn he liked the way it sounded. "Yeah, well lucky for you, you won the parent lottery."

"Yeah, they're pretty good parents."

"And Delilah won too."

His heart clenched at that. But he wasn't going to follow the thought that kept poking at his mind.

Wasn't going to think about his past at all.

"Can I ask you something?" he said.

"Sure."

"You said I was being weird because I was carrying your bag. Do you not want me to do that?"

She lifted her head, their gazes connecting. "I'm sorry. I shouldn't have said that."

"But you meant it, so I'm wondering what the non-weird thing to do is."

"To treat me like you treat anybody else, I guess. But I do like the little gestures. Most girls do, I think. It's nice that you have this kind of protective thing about you."

"I have a protective thing?"

"I think so." She nodded, looking thoughtful. "How have you been with other women after…"

"After sex?" he asked.

"Yeah."

"I don't know," he said, honestly. "You're the first woman I've slept with since…" Since Jade died. He still couldn't bring himself to say it.

From the shock in her eyes, Cassie understood it anyway.

"But it's been what... three years?"

"Yeah," he replied gruffly.

"And you haven't had sex with anybody at all?"

"I've had a lot of sex with myself."

Her mouth twitched. "I'd like to see that sometime." Her cheeks flushed, like she was imagining it.

"I'd like to see you touch yourself, too," he told her. "But maybe we should shower first. I'm still sweaty from the gig, and then from you."

She grinned at him. "That sounds good to me."

"It does, doesn't it?"

CHAPTER
Sixteen

"HE HASN'T HAD sex in three years?" Gemma gaped at her. "Seriously?"

"That's what he said." They were sitting in the diner drinking coffee. Gemma's kids were with Riley's mom, so they'd decided to come in for a late breakfast, although since it was almost twelve it was probably more like an early lunch.

Cassie had pretty much devoured her stack of blueberry pancakes, thanks to last night's exertions.

Presley had left early in the morning. He'd had to pick Delilah up and take her to church. She got the impression he really didn't want to go, but he'd promised Delilah and if there was one thing this man did, it was keep his promises. Especially those made to his daughter.

He'd asked her if she wanted to go to, but she'd shaken her head.

"I think I'd spontaneously combust if I walk into church after the things you did to me last night," she'd murmured.

"In that case, I'll be a pile of ashes on the fucking steps." He'd kissed her softly. "If you change your mind let me know."

She hadn't though. After last night's gig and then Presley

coming back to her house, she'd felt like she needed some space to think. Because yes, she loved being with him, and she loved having sex with him, too.

"The man must have the bluest balls this side of a pool table," Gemma muttered, pulling Cassie out of her thoughts. "Or at least he did. Until you did a public service and emptied them for him."

"Eww." Cassie screwed her nose up. "You make it sound so romantic."

Gemma started to laugh. "Seriously, though. Three years. Riley gets grumpy if we don't do it for three days."

"I guess it's hard being a single dad."

"Obviously." Gemma wiggled her brows.

Cassie opened her mouth to reply, but right then the door to the diner jingled open and Delilah walked in. She was wearing a green flowery dress, her hair up in bunches, one of them a little higher than the other. Her face lit up when she saw Cassie sitting with Gemma.

"Hi Cassie!" She ran over. "Guess what?"

"What?" Cassie leaned forward, all ears.

"I've been picked for the choir. To sing. I get to make my de-boot next month."

Cassie grinned at her pronunciation of debut. "That's wonderful. Congratulations."

"But I want my hair in a fishtail braid," Delilah said. "Can you do it for me? Daddy can't."

From the corner of her eye she saw Presley walk in, with his parents and brothers. She'd only seen Hendrix once, but apart from his blonde hair, he was a carbon copy of his two older brothers.

All three of them were wearing suits. They looked devastating. Heads turned to watch them walk.

Presley's eyes caught hers and he smiled. She smiled back.

"Hey." He put his hand on Delilah's shoulder. "Is she disturbing you?"

"Not at all." She shook her head, feeling ridiculously pleased to see him. "How was church?"

"Tolerable."

Gemma kicked her under the table, and she kicked her back.

"Daddy, can we sit with Cassie?" Delilah asked.

"There's not enough seats," Presley said. "And anyway, she's with a friend."

"That's not a friend. That's Gemma." Delilah rolled her eyes at him. "She says hi every time I go into class."

"Sorry," Pres said to Gemma, who was openly staring at him. "She's a little overexcited."

"I mean, she isn't wrong," Gemma said, smiling at him. "I am just Gemma."

"Hi Cass," Marley said, coming to join them. He'd already loosened the knot on his tie and unbuttoned the collar of his shirt. He looked about as comfortable in a suit as Presley did.

But they were both hot. In every single way.

"Hi." She smiled at him. "You look fancy."

"Mom insists on dressing up for church. Usually I'm at the station but Pres called and told me that if he had to go to church, I did too." He shrugged. "Anyway, did this animal get you home okay last night?" he asked, bumping his shoulder against Presley's.

"Yeah. It was all good." She gave him a smile.

And then the rest of the family walked over. She got an official introduction to Hendrix, and Presley's mom and Gemma started talking about the annual dance show they put on every Christmas.

"You want your check?" their server asked Cassie and Gemma, because the diner was filling up.

"Hey, Rina," Maddie said.

"Hey, Maddie." Their server grinned. "I didn't see you there." She looked around. "Want to take the big corner booth?"

"Yeah, that would be great." Maddie smiled.

"But I want to sit with Cassie," Delilah said.

"We have to go," Cassie told her. "Maybe another time?"

"Daddy, can Cassie come over for dinner instead?" Delilah asked.

Gemma kicked Cassie again. She wrinkled her nose at her friend. Did she need to make it so obvious?

"We're going to Grandma's for dinner." He ruffled his daughter's hair. "But we can have Cassie over another time."

"Tomorrow?" Delilah questioned.

Cassie met Presley's eyes. They were crinkled at the side, like he was amused.

"I'll talk to Cassie and we'll arrange it, but not tomorrow, okay?"

Delilah gave a loud sigh. "Okay."

The server gave them the check. Cassie picked it up. "I'll get this," she told Gemma.

"You sure?"

"Yep. My turn." She hopped up and walked over to the counter, but not before she whispered quickly in Presley's ear. "You should wear a suit more often."

He harrumphed and she smiled again. She'd never get sick of teasing him. By the time she reached the counter to pay, there was a line there. As she stood waiting, her phone vibrated. She took it out and smiled when she saw the message from Presley.

You look pretty hot yourself. – Presley

Glancing over her shoulder, she saw him next to Delilah, who was talking to Gemma. Thankfully her friend was so used to little girls she was joining in the conversation with animation.

Marley wandered over to the corner table to join his

parents and Hendrix. She could see Pres urging Delilah to take a breath and say goodbye.

Wear that suit the next time I see you. I want you in my mouth just like that. – Cassie.

Was it too much? She wasn't sure. It was true though. They hadn't had a lot of time for foreplay. Not when they were both so desperate for him to be inside of her every time they were alone together.

But she did want to taste him. To please him.

The thought of it made a blush steal up her chest.

When she turned to look at him this time, he was smirking. He glanced over and gave her the dirtiest look.

"You ready to pay?" the cashier asked. She blinked the thought of Presley's body out of her mind, trying to concentrate on the poor woman in front of her.

"Yes, thanks." She handed the check over, and passed over some cash. This was about the only place in town that didn't take card. But she kind of liked it. Liked that it stayed old fashioned and untouched.

Even if she did have to remember to go to an ATM every time she came here.

"Okay," she said, walking back to the table. "We're good to go."

"I'll see you at class," Delilah called out. "And when you come over to dinner."

"You will."

"And you can do my hair," Delilah said, as though she was offering Cassie a treat.

"Sure." Cassie laughed.

She looked at Pres, who had an exasperated expression on his face. "I'll see you around," she said, her voice soft.

"Yeah, you will."

She wasn't sure if that sounded like a promise or a threat, but either way it worked. Gemma grabbed her bag and slid out of the booth to join her, saying goodbye to Delilah and Presley before they reached the door.

As soon as they stepped outside she felt the warmth of the sun blasting down. Cassie didn't bother putting her jacket on, letting the balmy air caress her skin. The door closed behind them and Gemma put her arm through Cassie's.

"So, what did he text you?"

"Sorry?" Cassie blinked.

"I saw him on his phone. He was messaging you, right?"

Her cheeks pinked. "Um, yeah."

Gemma's grin was huge. "That man has the hots for you like nothing else. You should have seen him looking at your ass as you walked to the counter."

"He was looking at me?" She felt a little breathless.

"All the damn time. Like he wants to do all the dirty things to you." Gemma sighed. "I remember those days. The heat, the excitement. Don't get me wrong, married life is good, but… that early passion. Man, there's nothing like it."

"I told him I want to blow him in his suit," Cassie said.

Gemma almost choked. "Give a girl a little warning before you start with the dirty talk, will you?"

It was hard not to smile. "You asked what he texted. I thought I'd give you the short version."

"That suit though," Gemma said, fanning her face with her hand. "It really did look amazing on him. He's great in jeans and engineer boots but…"

"But there's something about a suit."

"Damn right there is. I might have to ask Riley to put his on later."

"For what?"

"For a blow job." Gemma rolled her eyes. "Of course."

Cassie laughed. Damn, she was laughing a lot these days.

Life was good and she appreciated that. Between her teaching, the band, and friends like Gemma she felt truly blessed.

And maybe add a hot grumpy single dad in there, and it was almost perfect.

How did she get this lucky?

———

It was Sunday evening and they'd cleaned up the dishes from dinner, and Presley, his dad, and his brothers were sitting in the den, having been thrown out of the kitchen by Delilah and his mom who insisted they wanted to watch the live action *Beauty and the Beast* in there.

Not that being in the den was a hardship. When their parents had this house built a year before his mom had gotten pregnant with twins, they'd future proofed it for a family. When they were kids this had been their playroom. Full of plastic toys and coloring books and tiny little instruments that they learned to play on.

And then when they'd all moved out, his dad had it remodeled into his man cave. It had a pool table and a fussball set, along with a bar that stretched the length of one wall. On the wall opposite was the biggest damn television you'd ever seen. And the four of them were sitting on the sunken leather sectional sofa, watching the ball game.

"Your mom was happy you came to church today," his dad told Pres, as on the game went to commercial.

Pres shrugged. "Delilah wanted me to be there. It's no big deal."

"Of course it's a big deal," Marley said. "You made us all go."

Pres met his brother's eyes. "If I have to suffer, you do too."

"I know that," Marley said grinning. "The story of my damn life."

Truth was, going to church hadn't been as bad as he'd thought it would be. And it made his kid happy, and wasn't that what it was all about?

"Whatever the reason, thank you," his dad said. "Your mom keeps saying how different you've been recently."

Pres had no idea what to say to that. One thing for sure – he wasn't going to tell them that one of the reasons for his difference had been screaming his name beneath him last night.

Thankfully, Hendrix's phone started vibrating, taking the attention off Pres. Marley looked over at the screen and smirked. "Who's Mollie?" he asked.

"Shut the hell up." Hendrix accepted the call and jumped up from the sofa. "Hey, give me a sec. I'm with my asshole brothers."

"Less of the asshole," Pres said, lifting a brow.

"Sorry, I'm with my big brothers. Who are pains in my ass." He wrinkled his nose at Pres and walked through the door to the stairway.

"He's in love again," their dad said, shaking his head. "He's always moody when there's a girl around."

"Who isn't?" Marley asked. "You've seen Pres around Cassie, right? He's moody as hell."

Their dad turned to look at Pres. "You and she a thing now?"

Thanks Marley.

He swallowed hard. "It's complicated." Not that he wanted to explain it to his father, anyway.

"So what, you were just at her place last night to do her plumbing or something?" Marley asked, grinning.

"How do you know I was at her place last night. You tracking me now?"

"Nope." Marley shrugged. "I drove past early this morning. Had to pick something up from the station. Your car was still there."

Well shit. That's what he got for letting his horndog ways override his common sense. He could have at least parked down the road. If Marley noticed, that meant half the town had.

"She seems like a nice girl," his dad said.

"Too nice for Pres," Marley teased.

"At least I'm not yearning after somebody I can't have," Pres said, finally getting annoyed with the focus being on him.

Their dad blinked and turned his attention to Marley. "Who are you yearning for?" he asked, and then he shook his head. "Actually, scrap that, it's probably better that I don't know. Your mom will squeeze it out of me and then she'll hunt you down for all the juicy details."

"There are no juicy details because I'm not yearning for anybody," Marley replied, shooting Pres a dirty look.

Yeah, sure. And that's why he hadn't been on a date for a year. But that wasn't Pres' problem. If his brother wanted to break his own heart by wanting somebody he couldn't have, that was Marley's problem.

As for Pres, well he didn't have any problems. Yeah, it was awkward seeing Sadie at the gig knowing he'd finally slept with somebody for the first time since Jade died.

But she'd been kind. Sent him a message saying she'd enjoyed the show and would hopefully catch another.

But it was one thing feeling more relaxed about finally seeing somebody. Another thing having his entire family knowing. And his dad was right. Once you told one member of the family, you told them all.

And he had a damn big family. Sometimes it felt like he was related to half of Hartson's Creek.

"Anybody want a beer?" their dad asked, just as Hendrix walked back in, looking a little flushed.

"I'll take one," Hendrix said. Marley nodded.

"I'm driving. I'll take a non–alcoholic, please," Pres said.

His dad gave him a pleased nod and grabbed four bottles, carrying them over to the sofas.

"So," he said, handing out the bottles. "What about the Pirates this year? You think they stand a chance?"

"Not if they keep playing like this," Marley muttered.

Pres smiled, because they all appreciate their dad's change of subject. Even Hendrix, who was typing on his phone, only half his attention on his family.

"Hey, did you know your band's song has gone viral?" Hendrix asked.

Pres blinked at yet another change in conversation. "No. How?"

"On TikTok. Mollie saw it. Apparently you've got a million views."

"What does that mean?" their dad asked. "What's TikTok? They paying you?"

Pres bit down a smile. Their dad's fame came at a time when social media wasn't a big thing. He didn't get why any bands would expose themselves to that kind of scrutiny. Especially without being paid directly.

"I don't think so," he told him. "It's just some free publicity. Alex likes doing it, so we let him."

"It's still cool though," Hendrix said. "When are you playing next?"

"A couple of weeks," Marley told him. "Why, does your girlfriend want to come watch how real men do it?"

"She's not my girlfriend," Hendrix said, his eyes narrow. "And you're not a real man."

"Sure about that?" In the blink of an eye Marley reached for Hendrix, wrapping his arm around their little brother's neck and pulling him into a noogie. He rubbed his knuckles on Hendrix's head as their younger brother tried to squirm out of his grasp, fruitlessly hitting his hands against Marley's rock hard chest.

"Get the hell off me," Hendrix protested.

"Just showing you how a real man deals with annoying little brothers." Marley let him go, smirking.

Until Hendrix launched himself at Marley, pinning him down in an attempt to noogie him back.

Pres' eyes met his dad's. How many times had they all fought as kids? Way too many times to remember. His mom used to hate it, even though their dad admitted he'd done the same with his own brothers.

It was how they solved problems. How they communicated.

Sometimes, it was even how they showed each other they loved them. And yeah, he knew that was messed up. And they'd mostly grown out of it.

"Touch me again and your head is going down the toilet," Marley said, extricating himself from Hendrix's grasp.

Okay, *he'd* grown out of it. And he thanked God daily that Delilah hadn't picked up the habit of punching out her feelings.

She talked them out and he liked that. Even if sometimes she talked just a little too much.

"Is somebody fighting down there?" their mom's voice echoed down the stairs. Hendrix and Marley immediately separated and Presley bit down a smile.

Sure, their dad let them fight it out, but their mom never did. And truth be told, all three of them were more scared of her than they were of each other.

"Not anymore," their dad shouted back. "You can get back to your movie."

"I'm on it," she called. "And I'm telling you, the Beast is way better behaved than any of my damn children."

CHAPTER
Seventeen

"DO YOU LIKE PASTA?" Delilah asked as she opened the front door to Cassie later that week. She was wearing a tiny apron with a unicorn on the front of it. "Because I love pasta.

"I do like pasta," Cassie told her, her expression serious. "Is that what you're cooking?"

"Yes. And I'm making a salad and garlic bread. But you can't eat too much of it because then your breath gets smelly. Or at least my dad's does. He pretends he's a dragon and breathes on me and I have to run away."

It was impossible not to smile at this little girl. Especially when she was giving away all of Pres' secrets. "I'll remember that after dinner. Do you have a good hiding spot?" Cassie asked.

"Um…" Delilah frowned. "We could call Granny and go over there?"

"Are you going to invite Cassie in?" Pres appeared behind her. He was wearing a pair of jeans and a Henley, unbuttoned enough that she could see the ink on his chest. "Hey." He smiled softly at her.

She smiled back. "Hi. I brought chocolate and flowers." She held them out to him.

"Ooh," Delilah said. "Those are pretty."

Pres took them and glanced at her. "I don't think I've ever been given flowers before."

"There's a first time for everything I guess."

"I like it." His voice was thick.

"We're making pasta fredo," Delilah announced.

"Alfredo," Pres gently corrected her.

"That's what I said, silly." Delilah walked back to the kitchen counter and clambered onto a stool, kneeling so she could reach the bowl. "Do you like tomatoes?" she asked Cassie.

"Yeah," Cassie nodded.

"I hate them. But they look pretty in a salad, don't they?" Delilah continued.

"They sure do." She looked over at Pres. "Is there anything I can do to help?"

"I got it covered. But thank you. Would you like a drink?"

"A soda would be great."

He pointed at the stool next to Delilah's and she took it.

"How was work?" she asked him.

"Tiring. Our current customer is pretty demanding. We've had to retile the bathroom twice."

She wrinkled her nose. "Ugh."

"Right? How was your day?"

"It was good. We started a new dance today."

"Do I get to do a new dance?" Delilah asked. "I've got class tomorrow."

"Yeah, you will." Cassie nodded. "I think you'll like it."

"Can you show me it *now*?" The little girl was oozing excitement.

Her eyes met Presley's. He looked like he was biting down a smile. And yeah, she knew how much he liked watching her dance.

He'd told her so last night when he'd called to invite her

for dinner and they'd spent an hour on the phone, including him listening to her getting ready for bed.

And into bed.

And then him asking how often she touched herself in bed.

Was it getting hot in here? She tried to push away the memory of his low, dirty talk as he persuaded her to touch herself as he told her what he wanted to do to her.

In every way possible. With his lips, his teeth, his fingers. And of course the hardest part of him.

Inside of her. In her mouth. And it reminded her that she still hadn't gotten to make good on her promise. It was difficult to find alone time when you were sleeping with a single dad.

But they'd gotten to talk a lot on the phone this week and she'd liked that. He made her laugh, and sometimes she made him laugh too, and when she heard his throaty chuckle it felt like she'd won something big.

Something nobody else got to see.

"Cassie!" Delilah said, getting impatient.

"Sorry, did you say something?"

"Please dance for me. She should dance, shouldn't she, Daddy?"

His mouth curled into a half smile. "Yeah, I could live with that."

Of course he could.

"How about Daddy dances for us," Cassie suggested. "I've never seen him dance before."

"You've seen me on stage," Pres pointed out.

"You play guitar and sing. You don't move your hips."

He smiled as he grabbed some onions to chop up.

"What do you think?" she asked Delilah.

Delilah's brow wrinkled as she thought through her answer. It was kind of sweet how long it took her to decide. It reminded her of Pres, the way he always got trapped in his head before he could actually say what he thought.

Speak of the devil, Presley's gaze flickered to hers. She could see the heat there.

She felt it too. And she needed not to because this dinner was supposed to be strictly PG rated. She'd eat, probably help clean up, and then go home. She was here as Delilah's teacher, not as Presley Hartson's booty call.

Damn, she liked being his booty call though.

"I think…" Delilah finally said, looking from Cassie to her dad. "That you should both dance."

She could see Presley's shoulders shake as he burst into laughter.

"Okay," she said to Delilah. "That works for me. But you have to dance, too." Mostly because she couldn't let herself get that close to him. Not here. Not in front of his daughter.

"Sure. We can all do it. You show us and we copy, right?"

"Right." Cassie nodded. "Where's your biggest space?"

"I'm not doing it," Pres told her.

"Yes you are," Delilah said. "You promised."

"Did I?" He frowned. "I don't remember doing that."

"Daddy, please…"

It was funny how his expression changed at Delilah's pleading. Like he really wanted to say no, but he couldn't.

She got the feeling he could be strict when he wanted to be. He probably had to be, as a single dad. But it didn't stop his daughter from having him wrapped around her little finger.

"Dinner will be ready soon," he said.

"It'll only take ten minutes," Cassie promised, trying not to smile at his horrified expression.

"Okay, ten minutes. But you…" he pointed at Delilah, "have to promise to go to bed on time tonight. No arguments."

"I promise," his little girl said excitedly. "Now let's go dance."

———

If the guys at the construction site ever found out about this, he would never live it down. They'd spent the first five minutes with Cassie patiently teaching Delilah three different moves for the new dance. And yeah, it hadn't been bad watching as the woman he thought about constant-fucking-ly arch her back and lift her leg and spin around until he was dizzy just watching her.

She was so damn patient with his kid, too. That's what he liked most of all. The way she didn't blink when Delilah got frustrated. The way her voice stayed patient and calm.

And yeah, he liked the way his daughter responded to her. She clearly idolized Cassie.

He knew the feeling.

He'd spent the last few days alternately worrying that he shouldn't be getting involved with his kid's ballet teacher – and his band mate – and not being able to think about her without needing a cold shower because his body wanted her more than ever.

Truth was, it wasn't only his body. He liked talking to her. He liked the way she'd tease him until he laughed. Like she'd found the little chink in his armor that nobody else knew about.

Their little secret.

Take last night. He'd called her to invite her to dinner because Delilah hadn't stopped talking about it. It had been late by the time he'd called her because he wanted Delilah in bed first, or she would have begged to talk with Cassie.

And Cassie had admitted she'd just gotten out of the shower. And then she'd admitted that she'd touched herself a few times in there, thinking of him.

Fuck if that hadn't made him as hard as steel. He needed to hear her do that again. So he'd sweet talked her into getting into bed naked. And touching herself the way he needed to touch her.

He'd talked her into an orgasm that made her groan his name out loud and damn if he hadn't almost come in his pants even though he hadn't touched himself at all.

"Are you hard?" she'd whispered.

"Painfully so."

"I still owe you that blow job."

He'd closed his eyes, thinking about the velvety warmth of her mouth. The way her eyes were wide and trusting whenever they were together.

And when the call was over, he'd stroked himself into oblivion. But it still wasn't enough.

"You need to concentrate," Delilah said, bringing him back into the here and now. "You're the worst dancer, Daddy."

"No he's not," Cassie said. "He's just a beginner, that's all. You were once, too." She walked over, adjusted his position. Because yeah, he was in the first position, standing in his living room, his shoes off, his socks covering his feet as he tried to copy what his kid and Cassie were doing.

"Let me show you," Cassie murmured, leaning down in front of him to reposition his feet. Her hands were soft, and he looked down to see her hair cascading around her face as she concentrated on him.

And then she looked up. "That's it."

"Show him second position," Delilah said, clapping her hands.

"Ready?" she asked him.

"As I'll ever be," he muttered.

"Okay, here it is." Cassie started in first – the one she'd taught him. Her heels together, her arms out in front of her and curved, like she was holding a large ball against her chest.

Then she stepped out, her feet still wide, her heels apart by about twelve inches. Her arms lifted, as graceful as a swan, until they were out to her sides, and yet still somehow rounded.

He could see the rise of her neck, the strong line of her spine. She was elegance in human form.

And all he could think about was that he needed her to dance for him again. All the fucking time.

"Daddy, your turn."

He tried to copy, but dammit he didn't have the grace.

"Your heels are too far apart," Cassie murmured. She adjusted him again, and he let her, feeling the warmth of her hands on him.

Wanting them everywhere.

And then – thank God, the timer on his phone started to blast.

"Saved by the bell," Cassie said.

"My kind of salvation." He winked. "Gotta go finish up dinner. You two can keep dancing."

"Will you watch us?" Delilah asked.

"Sure will." He walked over and switched the timer off, then grabbed some plates and silverware, putting them on the kitchen counter. He and Delilah usually ate here, at the breakfast bar, and he wasn't planning on doing anything fancy tonight.

Sure, his mom could make a table look like a masterpiece when she set it, but he made it look a mess.

Delilah was trying to twirl, calling for Cassie to watch her. She was clapping her hands, giving Delilah encouragement and for a minute all he could do was be mesmerized by his girls.

No, not his girls. Only one of them was his. His heart tightened.

"Oh no!" Delilah called out, tottering on one foot before she collapsed to the floor. Cassie pretended to collapse next to her, then started tickling her. The two of them were in a fit of giggles and he had to take a moment.

Delilah would never remember moments like these with her mom. She'd never get to show off her dance skills or be tickled or loved by Jade.

And yeah, he and Jade had their differences, but she'd also given him the best gift in the world. The one thing he woke up for every morning.

Their daughter.

"Dinner's ready," he said, pushing the plates toward the stools where they usually sit and ate.

Delilah sat up. "I'm so dizzy," she said.

"Come here." Cassie reached for her, pulling her up to standing. "I used to get dizzy, too. But you can practice not to. Just by keeping your eye on one spot when you spin."

"You can?" Delilah tipped her head to the side. "But isn't getting dizzy part of the fun?"

"Not when you're on stage," Pres said. "Now come on, eat your dinner before it gets cold."

CHAPTER
Eighteen

PRESLEY HAD BEEN quiet all evening. Ever since Delilah had made him dance. Cassie wasn't sure if it was because he was annoyed that she'd made a spectacle of him, or if she'd done something wrong.

Softly closing Delilah's door – because she'd promised to read a bedtime story to her – Cassie tiptoed down the stairs, shaking her head at herself for thinking that way.

Old habits died hard. Especially when you were used to taking the blame as a child. Every time something went wrong in her mom's life, it was Cassie's fault.

If Presley Hartson was in a bad mood, that wasn't her doing. She'd come over, played with Delilah, helped him clean up. Sure, she may have inadvertently done something, but she wasn't going to take the blame for it.

She sighed. Maybe she should just grab her bag and go.

When she walked back into the kitchen he was standing by the open back door, a beer in his hand as he looked out into his yard. The sun had set and the trees were casting shadows over the grass. Delilah's swing set was a dark castle shaped silhouette.

He turned when he heard her footsteps.

"She's asleep," Cassie told him.

He nodded. "Thank you for reading to her."

"She's never a problem. I like spending time with her."

Was that a wince? It looked like one. She shifted her feet. "So I think I'm gonna go home. I have an early start in the morning."

It wasn't as though she was hoping for anything else, anyway. She knew Presley well enough to know that he wasn't going to go for a full on make out session while his daughter was sleeping upstairs.

"You sure you don't want to stay?" he asked her. "I can make you a drink."

"I'm driving."

He held up his beer. "Non-alcoholic."

"It's fine. I'll grab a water when I get home before I crash. It's been a long day, you know?"

His eyes caught hers. "Please stay."

Her breath caught in her throat. There was that little boy lost look again. It seemed so out of place in this man – and he was definitely all man. Strong and silent and protective.

When she was in his arms it felt like the world could collapse around them and he'd still keep her safe.

"Do you want me to?" she asked.

"Yes."

"Okay then." She nodded, and he turned and walked over to the refrigerator, pouring her a glass of water from the dispenser. When he handed it to her, their fingers brushed and she jumped from how cool they were.

"Want to sit outside?" he asked her. "It's warm enough."

"That sounds nice." She followed him out through the open doors. He was right, it was warm, even with a breeze in the air that ruffled the leaves in the oak trees and lifted her hair as she walked.

He had an old pair of white painted chairs, set around a table that looked like it barely got any use. "My mom's old set," he told her. "I was supposed to replace it a couple of years ago. Haven't gotten around to it yet."

"Do you not sit out here much?" she asked, pulling out a chair and sitting down. The moon was low in the sky, looking like an overripe fruit. Pres pulled out the seat next to her and sat in it, stretching his long legs out.

"Not really. Between Delilah and work I'm pretty busy. And now there's the band."

"Did you see the group message from Alex?" she asked him. "Another video went viral."

"Yeah, I saw." Presley shook his head. "I swear he's addicted to that app."

"A few of the moms at the dance school have seen it. They wanted to know when our next gig is."

"Did you tell them?"

"Yeah. I think they have the hots for you and Marley. Kept asking if you're both single."

He turned his head to look at her. "What did you tell them?"

Funny how interested he was now. She lifted a brow. "Wouldn't you like to know?"

The ghost of a smile passed his lips. Warmth rushed through her, because it felt like the sun was blasting after days of rain.

"Want me to make you tell me?"

"And how are you planning to do that?" she asked lightly. The final word had barely left her mouth before he was standing and pulling her out of her chair, throwing her over his shoulder like she was as light as a feather. She started to squeal as he walked through the backyard with her, blood rushing to her head, the tips of her hair brushing his legs.

"Hush," he told her.

"I can't hush. The world's turned upside down."

He lowered her down to the grass. They were in the

middle of his yard. And yes, she felt giddy. She had to hold onto his arms to steady herself.

"Why did you carry me here?" she asked him breathlessly. "Did you think I'd get intimidated by a bit of grass?"

He chuckled again. Music to her damn ears. "If I'm going to torture you, it's probably best not to do it under my daughter's bedroom window."

"You're going to torture me?"

"I need answers." He looked amused.

"You'll never get them." She pretended to zip her lips. "Torture me all you want." Then she frowned. "Wait, ignore that *Reservoir Dogs* reference. I'd like to keep both my ears in tact."

"You watch too many movies," he said.

"I was alone a lot as a kid."

Presley reached his hand out, cupping her face. "What did you tell them when they asked if I was single?"

"I told them you were single as fuck and to have at it." Her own lips curled.

"No you didn't." He shook his head. "You wouldn't give the answer up as easily as that." His fingers feathered across her jaw, tipping it up. Then he closed the gap between them and pressed his lips to hers. "What did you say?" he murmured against her mouth.

This man. This stupidly complex, moody, gorgeous man. He gave her goosebumps every time he touched her. She should have known the torture wouldn't involve pain.

Pleasure worked so much better.

"What if Delilah sees us?" She glanced hesitantly up at the closed curtains of the little girl's room.

"I wasn't planning on stripping you naked and taking you on the grass," he muttered. Then he frowned. "Although…"

"Although?" she prompted, because now she wanted to know what he was thinking.

He gave her the softest of smiles. "If I have to do it to get the truth, it's a sacrifice I'm willing to make."

She started to laugh because she knew he was lying. There was no way he'd risk upsetting Delilah. And nor would she, come to that.

They'd both claw each others' faces off if it meant protecting that little girl.

"You want to fuck the truth out of me?" she whispered.

"I want to fuck you. That's about it. I wanted to since you taught me to do that stupid one position."

"First position," she corrected. "You went quiet after that."

He brushed the hair from her face. "You noticed, huh?"

"Yeah." She ran the tip of her tongue along her bottom lip. "Did I do something wrong?"

He shook his head. "Not at all."

"So what were you thinking?"

Presley blinked. "I'll tell you if you tell me."

"Tell you what?"

"What you told the women about whether I'm single or not."

She laughed again. Why was it he could go from being completely morose to stupidly amusing in the space of a few moments? And why did she like that so much?

Because you're addicted to drama.

Ugh, no she wasn't. Of everything she wanted in life, being drama free was at the top of it.

She nodded. "It's a deal."

And then he was lifting her up again, like a damn football, and carrying her further across the yard.

———

"So, who's going first?" Presley asked. He'd carried her to Delilah's swingset, where he'd deposited her on the wooden platform that led to the yellow slide. He was leaning against it, the two of them looking at the house, which was around fifty yards away. From here he'd be able to see if Delilah came out looking for them.

Not that they were doing anything.

Although somehow her sitting here, swinging her legs next to him, felt more intimate than when he was inside of her.

And that thought made her cheeks flush. She was glad he wasn't looking at her right now.

"I told them that I thought you had your eye on somebody," she admitted. "I didn't tell them about us."

"Why not?" He ran his fingers down the back of her calf. It made her shiver.

"Because I thought we were keeping this a secret."

"It's a pretty bad secret. Marley already suspects. If Alex wasn't so busy trying to go viral, he'd probably suspect as well."

"Yeah, but there's something different between our bandmates knowing and everybody knowing. And you know Delilah would find out, too."

"Not if I told her first."

Cassie blinked. "Do you want to tell her about us?"

"I don't know." He was still facing the house. "I guess it depends on what this is." He turned to look at her. "I went quiet because I started feeling guilty. That the three of us were having such a good time and Delilah's mom wasn't part of it."

"You miss her," Cassie said softly.

"It's complicated. We were friends long before she got pregnant with Delilah. We'd see each other at gigs and have some fun. It was always supposed to be light, and then…"

She held her breath, not wanting to break the spell of Presley Hartson actually talking about his past with her.

"She got pregnant. And we got married because we both wanted to prove that we could be adults about it." He blew out a mouthful of air. "I know it sounds kind of quaint, but I thought that this was my sign. It was time to be a grown up. To stop messing around and settle down."

"And did you?"

"Yeah. But Jade, she…" He shook his head, looking into the distance. "Delilah was a real colicky baby. And Jade was the one at home with her all the time. I was trying to build up the construction business to support us, which meant long hours. I thought I was doing my bit, providing for my family. But I wasn't. I didn't see how much she was struggling."

Cassie swallowed. She could taste the bitterness of his words.

"She tried. And that's what kills me, she really tried to make it work. But I was too much of an idiot to listen to her distress calls. She talked about wanting to be in a band again, wanting to play gigs, and I thought I was placating her by telling her she could do that once Delilah was older."

He turned to look at her. The sadness in his eyes made her whole body feel achy. "Pres…"

"Don't say anything yet. I haven't told you the worst part."

He looked away, shook his head. She could feel the tension radiating off of him.

"She got an offer from a band. One of their backup singers had pulled out right before they were set to tour and they needed a fast replacement. She wanted to go so badly. We argued about it for days. I had no idea how we were going to make it work with her away. I told her that if she left we were over."

His shoulders slumped. "And she screamed at me that I had no idea how hard it was for her, then jumped in the car to go see her sister. But she never made it there."

Oh God. Cassie's heart clenched.

"It was a drunk driver. On their way home from an afternoon bender. The doctor told me it was instant. She wouldn't have known what was happening." He cleared his throat. "Our little girl lost her mom because I wouldn't listen to her needs. Wouldn't meet her half way."

"You didn't know…"

This time when their eyes met she could see the misery inside his. Is this what he'd been living with for three years? The pain, the agony. The constant guilt?

She exhaled softly, putting her hand on his shoulder.

"I'm sorry."

"Not as sorry as I am. And today, watching you with Delilah, it brought back everything I took from her."

"You didn't want her to crash. You weren't the one driving drunk…"

"But I'm the reason she went out in that car to see her sister."

"Do you think she'd want you to keep beating yourself up about it?" Cassie asked him? "What if it had been you who'd left? What if you'd been the one who died instantly? Would you have wanted her to put her life on hold?"

"No." His voice was rough. "But logic doesn't always help."

"I know," she said softly. She gently lowered herself down from the swing set, her bare feet touching the grass. He stared at her wordlessly as she took his hand in hers, and pulled him down, until they were both on their knees. She turned and crawled into the cavity beneath the swing set, laying down on her back. "Are you going to join me?"

He lifted a brow, then crawled in after her, laying down next to her, both their legs extending onto the grass.

"I broke my leg in four places in a crash," she told him. "One minute I was in the New York Ballet Corps, the next minute I was in the hospital, with my leg in pieces and a doctor telling me it was going to take months until I could walk again. They tried to make me as good as new, but I never danced professionally again." She took a long breath, the memories making her feel anxious. It had taken five surgeries and a year of recovery and rehab for her legs to heal.

It was her ankle that had been the biggest problem. The doctors told her she'd never be able to dance en pointe again.

Which meant she'd have to leave the New York Ballet.

He threaded his fingers through hers, squeezing them tight. She wasn't sure why she was telling him this. Maybe because their quid-pro-quo felt so uneven. She'd admitted something stupid about some dance moms and he'd cut himself open and bled out to her.

"I called my mom and begged for her to come be with me. But she was in Australia and didn't want to cut her trip short. She was supposed to come to New York the following month to see me in the show, but when she heard I wouldn't be recovered for it, she canceled her visit."

"Jesus." Presley's voice was full of compassion.

"And I know losing your dream is nothing like losing your wife or your mom. I know that." She squeezed his fingers. "And even worse, I realized it was never my dream. My dream was to have a mom who loved me. Who was proud of me. And dancing did that. Made her proud. Until it didn't…"

"I'm sorry." He ran the pad of his thumb over her palm. "Nobody should ever treat their kid like that."

"I know. And that's the thing. I look at you and the way that you are with Delilah and I know that if I was Jade I'd be happy. Because you make your daughter happy. She's everything you think about. If she loses her stuffie, you don't stop until you find it. You didn't rejoin the band for three years because you couldn't bear to be apart from her." She lifted her brow. "You even went to church for her. You're a good dad, Presley."

"I stole her mom away."

"No you didn't. You just made some mistakes. Some very human ones. If she'd left a minute later, maybe you'd still be together, maybe you'd be divorced. Who knows? But it was one stupid twist of fate, not something of your own design."

He rolled onto his side to look at her. She rolled too, until they were facing each other.

He leaned forward, cupping her jaw with his strong hand, brushing his lips against hers. "Next time somebody asks, tell them I'm taken."

Her lips curled against his. "Oh yeah, by who?"

"This sweet little ballerina who knows that every time she dances for me, it makes me hard as fucking nails."

"SO, it's your birthdays next week," Maddie said to Marley and Presley. The two of them had finished work early and when Marley heard Pres was heading straight to their parents' place to pick Delilah up, he'd tagged along, looking inordinately pleased at the prospect of a free dinner.

"The anniversary of you shitting the both of us out," Marley said, grinning. "Congratulations, Mom."

She rolled her eyes. "I did not... do that." It was funny how she couldn't bring herself to swear. When they were kids, Pres and Marley used to have bets over who could make her curse first. "And anyway, I was about to offer something nice. How about we have a cookout? The weather is good and Dad has a new grill he wants to try."

"So you're inviting us over and Dad will do all the work?" Marley said. "Sure."

"Dad doesn't do all the work," his mom said, shaking her head. "We all know that the women do all the work for the cookout and the men get all the glory. We marinade the meat, we prep the salads and the veggies, we put out the plates and the silverware and the cups and the drinks. The guys just slap some steaks on the grill and then somehow they're Michelin starred chefs."

Pres' lips twitched. His mom wasn't wrong. He'd seen how hard she cooked for them all. "Why don't we do it at my place?" he suggested. "I can do the work."

"On our birthday?" Marley frowned.

"Mom did all the work on our actual day of birth. Why make her do it again?"

"I always did like you better." Their mom winked and patted his cheek. Marley started to laugh because she'd never played favorites. Between Pres, Marley, and Hendrix there had always been more than enough love to go around.

Cassie was right. They'd lucked out in the parent department.

"Honestly, I'd love to do it here. And you boys can always come over early and help set up," she told them.

"It's a deal." Pres nodded.

"So we just need to decide who to invite. Family, of course. And some of the guys from the fire station?" She looked at Marley who shrugged.

"Sure."

"And the band?"

"If you invite Alex to the cookout you'd better buy extra steaks," Pres said. "The guy is little but he can put it away like nobody else."

"That's because he can't cook for shit," Marley pointed out. "Remember that time he tried to make a lasagna to impress a girlfriend?"

"I do." Presley nodded. Marley had been on call that day. When the fire department had been called out and raced to Alex's apartment his day had been made.

He'd never let their bassist live it down.

"And Cassie, of course," their mom said smoothly, glancing at Pres from the corner of her eye.

"Of course." Marley bit down a grin. "Mom, never apply to the secret service. You'd make a terrible spy."

"What?" Her mouth opened in the perfect image of innocence. "She's a band mate, too. That's all I meant." She turned to look at Presley. "Unless she isn't just a band mate?"

"She's also Delilah's teacher," Pres said, his voice full of amusement. "So I guess she isn't *just* a band mate."

Marley started to laugh, as their mom sighed, looking exasperated.

"I'll ask her," Pres promised.

"And will she come as your band mate or…" she trailed off.

Pres glanced at her fondly. Their mom had never been the best at being surreptitious. "She's a good friend. That's how she'll come."

Marley snorted.

"To the fucking cookout," Presley added.

"I didn't say anything." Marley held up his hands.

"But you thought it," Presley pointed out. Because his twin was still smirking.

"Hey, you're the one who's sneaking around thinking you're all clever when in fact half of the town sees your car outside her house every time Mom and Dad have Delilah over for a sleepover." Marley smirked, crossing his arms over his thick chest.

Their mom blinked and looked over at Pres. "You stay over?"

"Come on, Mom, you know he does. You told me that Ria told you." Marley blew out a mouthful of air. "Can we all just talk the truth for once?"

"Jesus." Pres raked his hands through his hair. "Is everybody talking about this?"

"You're not exactly discreet," Marley pointed out. "Even at rehearsal you two eye fuck each other until Alex and I turn green. And the gig the other night…"

The one where he and Cassie had snuck out during the interval and made out until neither of them could breathe. Pres' cheeks heated up at the memory of it.

"What gig?" their mom asked, looking from Marley to Pres. "The one at the Moonlight Bar?"

"No, the one after that," Marley said. "Even Pres isn't stupid enough to kiss a girl in the middle of the town square."

"You and Cassie are kissing?" his mom asked.

Pres let out a long breath. He'd had enough of this. "Yes, we're kissing." He waited for the feeling of regret to come over him. Maybe the need to shut down again. But it didn't. It had been a couple of weeks since Cassie had come over for pasta and the two of them had talked through his feelings about Jade.

Two fucking amazing weeks of talking and kissing and doing more whenever they were alone. Which was nowhere near as often as he liked.

Or his body needed.

A huge smile crept across his mom's face. "Oh my God, that's wonderful."

He put his hand up. "But it's still early. And Delilah doesn't know. And I'd like to keep it that way for now."

"Why?"

"Because I'm not going to confuse her by introducing Cassie as my girlfriend."

"So you'll let her be confused when somebody else tells her?" Marley asked. "I know she's only little, but she goes to school. Kids talk. All one of them has to do is repeat some gossip and soon it'll be around Hartson Elementary."

Pres winced, mostly because Marley was right. You couldn't get away with anything around here without some-body finding out. Look at his cousin, Grace. Her parents had just found out she'd been seeing her much-older step cousin and their families had imploded.

Last Sunday he'd stuck close to her side when she'd been in church with them all to watch Delilah's first choir appearance, mostly because Michael, the man she's in love with, had turned up to try to win her back.

Pres had been amazed they'd managed to keep their relationship quiet for as long as they had. Even he hadn't known, which was a good thing.

First rule of hiding something? Never tell a member of your family about it.

"Yeah, well school's out soon," Pres pointed out.

"And then she'll be at day camp." Marley grinned. "So good luck with keeping things on the down low."

———

The rain had started an hour ago. One of those freak storms that come over the mountains on a hot summer's day, the thick gray clouds engulfing the sky for a few hours.

Unfortunately, Cassie had just started her final class of the day when it began. She'd taken them through the new dance they were learning, to the accompaniment of the rain lashing down against the windows. When the parents came to pick up their children, they'd looked like drowned rats, their too-light summer jackets dripping on the wooden floor, as they waited for Cassie to dismiss them all.

And now they were gone and it was time to go home and she was looking hopefully out of the window for a chink of light between the clouds. But there wasn't one, not yet. The app on her phone told her there were a few more hours until the storm was due to abate.

The thought of getting in her car and driving home made her chest seize up.

It was stupid, she knew that. But her therapist had told her that trauma was a strange beast. It wasn't really driving in the rain that she was afraid of. But what it represented. And they'd worked hard to try to stop her from feeling this over-whelming sense of dread at the thought of getting behind the wheel while the streets were flooded with water.

But she couldn't. She just couldn't.

"Hey." Gemma walked in, a smile on her face. "I'm heading home. Thinking that I should buy a boat instead of a car. You ready for me to lock up?"

Cassie forced a smile onto her lips. "I've just got a couple of things to do before I'm ready to head out. I can lock up tonight."

"You sure?" Gemma asked.

"Yep." She kept her voice as light as possible. She hated lying to her friend, but she just couldn't admit to this weak-ness. And that's what it was. The kind of weakness her mom would hate.

She pushed that thought out of her mind. 'Be kind to yourself,' her therapist had told her when she'd expressed her frustration. 'You got back behind the wheel. That was a huge first step.'

Yes, it was. And it had been hard at first, even driving in the sunshine. Because all she could think of was that damn truck and the shrill screech of brakes before she lost control of her car. She'd avoided the truck, but she'd ended up in a ditch, pain radiating from her broken leg while she waited for rescue.

"You sure you're okay?" Gemma asked.

"Yes, honestly."

"That's good." Her friend gave her a genuine smile. "Oh, by the way, I saw the latest TikTok from last week's gig. You guys are sensational. And I need to find a better babysitter. I can't believe I missed seeing you on stage again."

Cassie smiled. "Thank you." It had been a good one. Espe-cially the part in between, when she and Presley had… *yeah*.

Her cheeks pinked at the memory.

"Let me know when the next one is. I promise to be there."

"I know you have the kids to look after. The TikTok views count." Cassie winked. She just wanted Gemma to leave now. Before she got an inkling about the rain and put two and two together. "Go on, head home before it gets any worse."

"Well don't stay too long," Gemma told her.

"I won't." Just until the rain stops. Whenever that might be. "I'll see you tomorrow."

Gemma blew her a kiss and left, the door to the studio swinging closed behind her. Cassie slowly walked over to the piano and sat down on the stool. She felt like an idiot. A failure.

What kind of person was afraid of a little rain?

Ugh. She stood up again, deciding to make herself a coffee and see if there was any chocolate in the snack stash Gemma kept in the staff room, striding across the studio and pushing the door open.

And walked straight into a hard, wet torso blocking her way.

"Oof." The breath escaped from her lips. She looked up to see Presley standing there, soaked to the bone. He was wearing a pair of sodden jeans and a thin black t-shirt that stuck to his skin. "I didn't see you."

He gave her a half smile. "Clearly."

"What are you doing here? Delilah doesn't dance today."

He was still smiling at her. She felt her body clenched at his warm eyes. "I came to give you a ride home."

"My car's outside."

"I know," he said softly. "And I also know it's raining so you won't be using it. I saw Gemma on my way in. She said you were planning on staying for a while."

Cassie swallowed. "Did you tell her why?"

"No." He shook his head. "It isn't my place. I just didn't understand why you didn't."

"I don't like showing weakness."

He reached for her, his damp fingers curling around her

face. "It's not weakness. It's fear. An understandable one. You've been through a lot."

She blew out a mouthful of air. "You don't need to give me a ride home. I can wait it out."

"I know I don't need to, but I want to. I want to know you're home and safe. I'll call Marley and we'll get your car home for you."

"You'll have to tell him why. Once is understandable. Twice is…" she trailed off.

"Can I tell you something?" he asked her.

She nodded.

"Marley won't care. Not one damn bit. He won't see you as weak because you're not. He won't see you as stupid, because Marley's seen trauma, too. He's a volunteer fire-fighter, he's seen enough fender benders to know it's wise to stay off the road unless you're confident in the rain."

"Was he on duty when…" she trailed off.

Pres shook his head. "No. And I'm glad for that because I would have hated for him to be the one to break it to me."

"Who told you?"

"A police officer."

She blew out a mouthful of air. "I feel like an idiot. I got hurt. You lost everything and you can drive without blinking."

"I didn't lose everything." His voice was thick. Sure. "Now can I take my girl home?"

"Your girl?" A rush of warmth went through her.

"Yeah." His gaze flickered to hers. "I think that's what you are."

Her breath caught. "I think I am too. If you're my…"

"Don't say boy."

She started to laugh. "You're definitely not that. My man."

He held his hand out to her. She slid her palm into his and they walked down the hallway, Cassie turning off the lights as they went. Gemma had already shut down all the computers and locked away everything that needed to be locked. Cassie grabbed her bag from the staff room and turned off the final lights.

"Have you got a jacket?" he asked her. Rain was still lashing against the front doors.

"No." It had been warm and sunny that morning.

"Then we'll have to make a run for it."

She nodded. "Let me set the alarm and then we can go." She keyed in the code and waited for the countdown to begin, then Presley pushed the front door open, his arms bracing against the force of the wind, and the two of them stepped outside.

"I have to lock up," she shouted. She could already feel the rain hitting her body, even though Presley was trying in vain to shield her.

It was funny how chivalrous the man could be. How in everything he did, he was aware of his size, of his strength.

Of his innate masculinity.

When she heard the bolts click into place she pulled the key from the lock and put it in her pocket. "Okay," she shouted over the torrent of the rain. "I'm ready."

He pulled her in front of him, letting her lead the way while his body stooped over hers, but it was futile. By the time the two of them got into the car, they were both soaked. She felt terrible for dripping water all over the leather seats of the Beast.

He started the engine, switching the heat up to high, despite the fact it wasn't actually cold outside. Just as wet as it could get in the summer in West Virginia.

"Okay, so before I take you home, I have a question," he told her.

"Okay. What is it?"

He caught her eye. "Actually, it's two. One, would you like to come to a cookout next weekend at my folks' place?"

She smiled. "I'd love to."

"And two, what do you think about telling Delilah about us?"

Cassie blinked. She wasn't expecting that. Not at all. And part of her wanted to laugh, because damn, this man always took her by surprise. But she got the feeling that laughing was the most inappropriate thing to do in that moment.

"Um… is that what you want?" she asked him.

Pres swallowed hard. "Marley pointed out that people will start to talk about us soon. Very soon." His eyes met hers. "And that kids talk too. Even if they don't always know what they're saying, they could upset her by talking about us."

She nodded. He was right. This wasn't exactly Manhattan where you could disappear into the night after a steamy liaison. His car parked outside her house had to be a dead giveaway.

"I'm okay with it if you are," she said softly. "You're her dad, this has to be your decision."

Their eyes caught for a long moment. He hadn't said it, but this meant he was in this thing. She knew that. He wouldn't be telling his daughter if he wasn't serious.

And yes, part of her felt a thick pull in her stomach at the thought. Because Presley Hartson came as a package. A delicious package, but all the same it was serious.

"I love Delilah," she told him. "I never want anybody to hurt her."

The way he looked at her told her it was the right thing to say.

"Do you regret parking outside my house?" she asked him, thinking back to his earlier words.

A smile pulled at his lips. "Hell no. I've never regretted anything less."

Warmth rushed through her. Did this man know what he did to her every time he opened up a little more? Being with Presley Hartson was like unwrapping a gift, layer by layer. One that kept giving.

"Maybe we should have driven out to the forest to have hot rampant car sex," she murmured.

His eyes sparkled. "There's no forest near here."

"To the desert then."

He shook his head. "We need to teach you some Hartson Creek geography. There's mostly fields. Farms. Corn. All that jazz."

She tipped her head to the side. "So where did you go to make out when you were a kid?"

He lifted a brow. "Where did you?"

"I didn't make out. I was too busy dancing and singing my way through life."

"Then maybe we need to make up for a lost teenage-hood," he said thickly, pulling her toward him and brushing his lips against hers. "By the way, every time I see you in a leotard all I can think of is ripping it off you."

"Spandex is really hard to rip," she told him. "Seriously, these things are made to withstand a nuclear war."

"That sounds like a challenge." His brows pulled together.

"And you sound like a man."

He grinned. "That's because I am. Now buckle up, let's get you home."

CHAPTER
Twenty

"HAPPY BIRTHDAY, DADDY!"

All the air rushed out of Pres' lungs as his daughter landed squarely on his stomach. She leaned forward to smother him in kisses and he wrinkled his nose, pretending not to enjoy every minute.

"What time is it?"

"I don't know. I can't tell the time." Delilah shrugged.

"The clock in your room is numbers." He was suspicious now. Mostly because he couldn't see much light coming in through the curtains. "What did they say?"

Delilah pulled her lips in, like she was trying to stop herself from speaking.

"Delilah…" His voice was low. "Tell me the number."

"I think I saw an eight," she finally said.

"What was the first number?" he said, grabbing her waist and tickling her. It would be easy for him to roll over and grab his phone to check, but he was enjoying this.

Watching his daughter try – *and fail* – to lie was always funny.

"Five," she admitted.

"So it's five am." He nodded slowly. "You know what that

means?"

"Time for cake and milk?" she said hopefully, lifting her eyebrows. That's what they had for breakfast on all of their birthdays. Sure, the cake was usually a little over dry because he wasn't exactly the best baker. But mix it with a little milk like your mouth was a cement mixer and the result was pretty enjoyable.

"No. Time to go back to bed and let your father sleep."

"But I can't sleep," she said. "It's your birthday. I want you to open your gifts."

"No gifts get opened before seven," he reminded her. "That's the rule."

"Santa is no fun." She pouted.

"What's Santa got to do with it?" he asked, confused.

"That's what you told me last Christmas," she reminded him. "That Santa says nobody can open gifts before seven. Birthdays and Holidays."

He'd said that? Pres blinked. He must have been sleep deprived. Not that it was a terrible idea. In fact, he wanted to high five his former self.

"Santa's the one in charge," he told her. "We just have to do what he says."

She crossed her arms in front of her. "We could have cake while we wait?" she said hopefully.

"We could," he agreed solemnly. "But we won't." For a moment he wondered if it would be bad to tell her the Tooth Fairy forbade it. But yeah, lying to his kid was a bad idea.

Especially since he'd never be able to keep track of all the mistruths.

"Why don't you go back to bed for an hour?" he suggested. "Then we can get up and have some breakfast."

She pressed her lips together again, her eyes moving like she was thinking hard. And he knew she was trying to find another excuse to stay here and not have to go back to sleep.

He sighed, because that extra hour felt really enticing. The storm had caused some delays on the construction site, and they'd been set back by a few days, so they'd worked extra hours once things dried up to try to catch up. His whole body ached and all he wanted to do was sleep, spend some time with his family.

And spend some time with Cassie, too.

He lifted the coverlet. "You can stay here if you promise to sleep."

Delilah's face lit up. Mostly because he tried so hard to keep her in her own bed. Not because he didn't love having her sleep with him. For those first few weeks after Jade died, he'd wanted his daughter with him constantly. Had panicked if he couldn't see her at all times.

But he'd also learned that his kid was a messy sleeper. She tossed and turned and kicked and sometimes talked in her sleep.

For the sake of both their sanities, he'd learned that keeping her sleeping in her own bed was the best course of action.

And truth be told, he probably should have insisted now, because she was wriggling under the covers like a damn snake in an attempt to get comfortable. He lay back, closing his eyes, praying to the god of parental sleep that he could have at least another half hour.

"Daddy?"

Okay, so the god of parental sleep didn't exist.

"Yeah?" He didn't open his eyelids this time. He wasn't sure he could.

"I can't wait for your and Uncle Marley's birthday party."

"It's not a party. Just a cookout. No clowns or party games." Thankfully.

"It is so a party. Grammy said so." There was a pout in Delilah's voice. "I can't wait to see everybody."

"Uhuh."

"And Cassie is coming. I love Cassie."

His lips twitched. "Yeah, I know."

"Do you think she'll do my hair if I ask her?"

He groaned. "Not if you don't sleep."

There was silence for a moment. But then it was cruelly broken again. "What if I *can't* sleep?"

"Huh?"

"If I can't sleep does that mean she won't do it?" Delilah persisted. "It's not fair. I can't help not sleeping."

Oh holy hell. He turned onto his side and opened his eyes, almost jumping out of bed because his daughter's face was in extreme damn close up.

"When did you move?" he asked groggily. She was staring at him like he was some kind of ogre.

"I don't know. But what about my hair?"

"Your hair will be fine. I promise. Now go to sleep."

She huffed and shuffled back across the mattress. *Finally.* He let his eyes close and blew out a mouthful of air.

"Do you love Cassie?" Delilah asked.

For the love of god. He opened his eyes again. "What?" he asked, stalling for time as much as anything else.

"Do you love her? I do."

This wasn't exactly the way he'd hoped to spend his birthday morning. And yeah, he'd talked to Cassie about telling Delilah about them, but he hadn't planned to do it this minute. Next week, maybe. When he and his kid had a quiet minute that didn't involve his parents or her dancing or him trying to get some goddamned sleep.

"Cassie's a good friend," he finally said.

"Uhuh." Delilah clearly wasn't happy with that. And then a sinking feeling came over him. Had somebody said something to her already?

This is a small town. Ugh, his brother was right.

And he obviously wasn't getting any more sleep this morning.

He sat up and rubbed his eyes, telling himself that he

could sleep tonight. And tomorrow.

And maybe the rest of the year.

"Why do boys have hair on their chests and girls don't?" Delilah asked. And he'd have laughed at the change of subject if he wasn't so damn exhausted.

"Go get dressed," he told her. "It's cake and milk time."

————

Happy Birthday! Your official gift will be given to you at the party this afternoon. And your unofficial gift… is me. However you want me. Cassie xx

She pressed send and slicked gloss on her lips, stepping back to check her reflection in the bathroom mirror. She had no idea what to wear for a family cookout. She wasn't sure she'd ever been to one. But it was warm outside so a pair of shorts would work. She'd teamed a gray herringbone pair with a white t-shirt and a statement necklace that she could easily take off if it was too dressy.

But the fact was, she kind of wanted to look dressy. For him.

Because Presley Hartson was constantly on her mind nowadays.

Thank you. I'm very much looking forward to both gifts. Especially the second. And just so you know, I was woken up at five o'clock by my kid. Who wanted to know about us… Presley. x

Oh. She blinked at the message, her mind racing. Had he spoken to Delilah like he'd talked with her about? She knew he wanted to do it just the two of them, but she had no idea he was planning to do it on his birthday.

She zipped her makeup bag up and slid it into the bathroom cabinet, trying to ignore the thoughts running through her brain.

But it was no good. They were as persistent as Delilah was with Presley. She grabbed her phone and unlocked the screen.

EEK! How did that go? C xx

She watched as the 'Presley Hartson is typing' text came across the screen then disappeared again. And yeah, she was getting impatient. She knew this didn't mean that she and Presley were about to walk down the aisle or any other such nonsense. He was just telling his kid that they were a couple.

Dating. Friends. Whatever it took so that if the kids at school – or their parents – mentioned it, Delilah wouldn't feel like he'd lied to her.

She knew that was important to Presley. That he was truthful with his daughter about all the things that mattered. It was another thing that made her heart race whenever she thought about this moody, complicated, glorious man.

He loved his daughter more than anything. And he'd do whatever it took to protect her from getting hurt.

He still hadn't responded, and yeah, she felt a little disappointed, but he was probably busy. It wasn't just his birthday, it was Marley's too. And from what she'd heard from Maddie, the family always celebrated big when it came to birthdays and anniversaries.

She was about to go grab a coffee when her phone started to ring. She smiled when she saw his name flash on the screen.

"Hi," she said breathlessly, accepting the call.

"Hi." His voice was low. "Delilah's changing her clothes for the fourth time. I thought I'd take the opportunity to hear your voice."

"How's your birthday going?" she asked him.

"Apart from the early start? Pretty good." He cleared his throat. "The talk with Delilah was fine."

"It was?" She let out a long breath. She hadn't realized how tight her chest had been. "She's okay with it?"

"Yeah. I put it in kid words. That we're very good friends. That we like each other. All that shit."

She laughed softly. "That shit?"

"The G rated stuff."

"She wasn't worried about me being around?"

"Not at all. She asked if you could still be her friend as well as my special friend, and I said yes. Then she asked if she could have another slice of cake and that was it."

"So I'm your special friend?" she asked, her voice low.

"That's what I called you, yes." It was his turn to sound amused. "Should I have said something else? Girlfriend sounded… weird."

"I like special friend," she teased. "Because I have a few special things planned for you when we're alone."

"Yeah. About that…"

"What?" She was grinning now.

"Mom suggested that Delilah stay at theirs tonight. So the party can go on while the kids sleep. Obviously Delilah said yes."

"That's… convenient." She bit down a smile. "Because I have a skintight leotard that needs your attention."

"I was hoping you'd say that. Because all I want for my birthday is you in a fucking bow and nothing else…" He cleared his throat. "No, sweetheart. I don't think furry boots are gonna work in this weather."

And now her smile was huge, because Delilah was almost

certainly wearing the most inappropriate outfit. "I'll let you go," she told Presley. "And I'll see you later."

"That you will." His voice was full of a promise that sent a shiver down her spine.

This man… He'd be so easy to fall for. It would be the getting up again that would be almost impossible.

———

"Ah, no." Their mom slapped Marley's hand as he attempted to steal a cookie. "Don't touch. Those are for the kids."

"But it's my birthday." Marley pouted. "And I want a clown face cookie."

"Because he's a clown," Hendrix said, grinning. Their younger brother had been away for a week, spending time at the beach with friends. He had a glow to him that could light up half of the town.

"Shut up, golden boy." Marley flicked his ear and Hendrix groaned.

"Don't do that. You know I hate it."

"Then don't be mean to me on my birthday."

"How old are you again?" their mom asked. "Six?"

Marley gave her a big grin. "Not being able to remember your kids' ages is the first sign of losing your brain."

"I lost my brain when I gave birth to you," she muttered. "Now get out of here and help your dad." She looked at Pres. "Not you, I need you."

"Why can't I stay?" Marley asked, grinning at Pres. Pres rolled his eyes at his twin. They'd long since grown out of competing for their parents' love, but it didn't stop Marley from pretending.

"Because I say so. Now shoo." Their mom pointed at the door, and Marley leaned forward to kiss her cheek, before he and Hendrix left the kitchen. The wall of glass doors were open that led to the backyard, and his two brothers walked onto the grass, joshing each other as they made their way over to where their dad was setting up the grill.

"So…" His mom smiled at him. "How's your morning going?"

"Good."

"Delilah seems excited about the party," his mom said, reaching up to push his hair out of his face. "Especially about seeing Cassie again."

Ah. So that's the reason his mom wanted him to stay. Pres bit down a smile because damn, news got around fast.

"Uhuh." Not that he was going to make it easy for her. It was his birthday, he could have a little fun teasing his mom if he wanted to.

"Delilah said you and she had a chat this morning,"

"Did she tell you she woke me up at five?" he asked.

"No. Ouch." His mom grimaced. "I remember when you were like that. One Christmas you got so excited you made yourself sick. We had to wait until four before Santa could fill yours and Marley's stockings. Your dad wasn't pleased."

Pres grinned. "Yeah, well I'm paying the price now."

"She said that Cassie is your…" His mom tipped her head to the side. "Special friend." Damn if she didn't hold her hands up and do the old quote mark gesture with her fingers as she said it.

He wasn't sure whether to laugh or roll his eyes.

"Did she?" he said. And it was his mom's turn to look impatient.

"So?" She leaned forward, her gaze intent. "Are you going to tell me what's going on or are you going to leave me hanging forever?"

He smiled fondly at her. This woman had always been his rock. Even before he'd become a single dad and she'd stepped in to help him.

"So Cassie and I are a thing," he told her, his voice low.

"Oh my God." She grabbed him, hugging him tight, her

head resting in the crook of his neck. "Oh, Pres, I'm so happy. So, so pleased for you. You deserve this. You all do."

He hugged her back. Damn, he'd forgotten how emotional she could be. But he couldn't help but smile. When she pulled away she stared up at him, her eyes full of tears.

"Why are you crying?" he asked her.

"Because I never thought I'd see the day," she was trying hard not to sob. "I prayed for it. I longed for it. I just want you to be happy. And for the longest time it felt like all you were doing was surviving."

He shrugged. There was a truth in her words. "We're just dating, Mom. Not getting married."

"Exclusively?" she asked.

This time he couldn't help but laugh. "Do you see a long line of women standing at my door."

Exasperated, she slapped his arm. "Stop that. I'm serious."

"Yes, Mom. We're exclusive." The thought of anything else made his gut twist. "Now can I go out to help Dad? Or do you need me to do something in here?"

"You can go help him." She hugged him again. "I'm so happy for you both. Cassie is just a lovely woman."

"I know."

"And she's so good with Delilah."

His throat felt tight. "I know that too."

"Of course you do. You wouldn't let just anybody into your daughter's life." His mom's voice was soft. "I'm so proud of you, honey. Not just because you're a great dad. I'm proud because I know how hard it's been to let somebody in." She wiped the tears from her face with a tissue."

"Thank you." He meant it. In so many ways. He leaned forward to kiss her.

She nodded. "Now go before I start crying again. Today is supposed to be a celebration. No more tears allowed."

"I can go for that." He winked at her. "I love you, Mom."

"I love you, too," she told him. "So, so much."

CHAPTER
Twenty-One

AS SOON AS Cassie parked behind all the cars lining Gray and Maddie Hartson's driveway, she found herself accosted by Marley.

"Hey." He was smirking at her.

"Pres told you?" she said, because his smile was only getting bigger. He had to know about her and Pres. Officially. Because unofficially, she had the sneaking suspicion he'd known about them all along.

"Nope." Marley shook his head. "Delilah did. And I just came out to warn you that she's been telling everybody that you're her daddy's special friend." He started to laugh. "I'm sorry, it sounds weird coming out of a six-year-old's mouth. So yeah, you're kind of the talk of the party."

"Is it too late to get back in my car and drive away?" she asked him, only half joking. She had a pile of gifts in her arms, but she was willing to drop them and make a run for it.

"Yep, way too late." He glanced at the wrapped presents. "Pres is a lucky guy. Want me to carry these for you?"

She shook her head. "Actually, the top two are for you. Take those and I've got the rest."

"You bought me a gift?" he asked, looking touched.

"Of course. You're a bandmate."

"And your boyfriend's brother." He lifted a brow. "Right?"

"I guess so." She blew out a mouthful of air. "Okay, let's do this."

He winked at her. "It won't be that bad. The Hartson family loves gossip, but they also have short memories. After today you'll be forgotten."

Her brows knitted. "Thank you. I think?"

"Come on, let's go face the music."

She had such a soft spot for Marley. Not just because he was Pres' brother, or because he'd always been so nice to her. But he had this glow to him. He was easy going, didn't let anything get him down. She had the feeling that if it came down to him and a hurricane, the hurricane would apologize and find another place to blow.

Sure enough, as soon as the two of them stepped into the backyard, it felt like every face turned their way. But she kept a smile on her lips, and it turned into a real one when she saw Pres turn and see her, his eyes crinkling in pleasure at her arrival.

"Cassie!" Delilah ran for her. "Are those gifts for me... I mean my daddy?"

Cassie laughed. "Yes they are. Want to help me with them?"

"Daddy, come open your presents," Delilah shouted. "Look at the pretty colors."

Cassie had wrapped them in sparkly silver paper, with iridescent ribbons that criss crossed the boxes then tied in bows.

"Hey." Presley walked toward them. He lifted a brow at Marley who gave a little snigger.

"Hi. Happy Birthday," she breathed.

"I'm just gonna do this," he told her, "And then it'll be over, okay?"

"Do what?"

Before the words had left her mouth, he was taking the gifts out of her arms and passing them to Marley, who was completely unfazed by the move. And then Pres was pulling her into his arms, his hands spanning her waist as he dipped his head to hers. His mouth was warm and welcoming as he claimed hers.

Blood rushed through her ears. She felt him dip her back, as though they were posing for a 1940s black and white poster, and she wrapped her arms around his neck to bring him closer as he kissed her again.

And suddenly the whole backyard erupted into applause.

She was dizzy when Presley lifted her up to standing. "Sorry." He didn't look it. He looked kind of pleased with himself. "I decided to get it over with."

"Like a wedding," Marley said. "Just kiss the bride so everybody can get their kicks."

"It's not like a wedding." Presley frowned. Then his eyes caught Cassie's. "You okay?"

"Yeah," she said breathlessly. "I was just… yeah." She was trying to straighten her mind. Find her thoughts.

She was pretty sure they were there somewhere. Hidden behind this constant need to be touching Presley Hartson.

And he was right, everybody was looking at them. The whole Hartson clan were there – Pres's uncles and aunts, his cousins. And of course, Aunt Gina, smiling widely at both of them like they'd just made her day.

That was a hell of a way to be introduced to the family. But they all looked happy for them. Especially for Pres.

She knew from his cousins that they'd been worried about him for the longest time.

"You sure you're okay?" Pres looked worried he'd done the wrong thing. But actually, he'd been right.

"I'm certain." She smiled at him. "Now open your gifts."

Marley had set them on a table. As they walked, Delilah grabbed her hand. "My daddy kissed you," she whispered.

"I know. Is that okay?"

Delilah nodded. "Yes. Because you're special friends."

Oh boy, Presley really started something with that phrase. "Yes we are."

"Are we special friends, too?" Delilah asked her, her eyes shining as she looked up at Cassie's face.

"Well, we're friends, and I think you're very special so…" She leaned down and tickled the little girl, who laughed with delight.

"Daddy, can I help you open your presents?" she asked him.

"Sure." Presley's eyes met Cassie's. She nodded. There was nothing a little girl shouldn't see in them. She wasn't that stupid.

Delilah skipped around to where Marley and Presley were standing. Marley had already opened his two gifts. A vintage Nirvana album for the turntable Pres had gotten him, and a black t-shirt with white writing on the front. Marley read it and was laughing.

"What does it say?" Delilah asked him.

"It says, *Drummer: A skilled musician who is often forced to the back to preserve the fragile egos of the other band members.*"

Presley laughed with him.

"What's an ego?" Delilah asked.

Marley's eyes met Cassie's. "Ask your dad," he said. "He knows."

"Daddy, what's an ego?" Delilah asked.

Presley rolled his eyes. "I thought you were helping me open these," he said, gesturing at the pile of gifts.

"Oh yes." She grabbed at the paper of the gift at the top, all thoughts of egos forgotten. "What's this one?" she asked, as Presley helped her unstick the tape and open it. "Oh, it's a book."

Presley read the front and looked up at her, smiling. She'd noticed he had a lot of Stephen King books in his house the first time she visited. It was his latest. "Thank you," he said.

"Look inside," she told him.

He opened it up and a little piece of paper fell out.

"What does it say?" Delilah asked, impatiently.

"It says, this voucher entitles the holder to one child free day." He smiled. "Not sure how that works."

"Delilah and I can have a girl's day," Cassie told him. "And you can read the book."

The smile wavered on his lips. "That's incredibly thoughtful."

Her chest tightened. "I just thought you'd probably enjoy some peace."

"We get to have a girl day?" Delilah asked, fist bumping the air. "Yes!"

"You're the gift that keeps on giving," Pres murmured. "Thank you for my presents." He kissed her cheek.

"You're welcome."

"Daddy, can we open the rest now?" Delilah asked, not waiting for his reply as she grabbed the next one. Within a minute all five of them were opened. Like Marley, Presley got a t-shirt, but his had a print of the Rolling Stones on it, another band she knew he loved. Then there was a box of his favorite chocolates, tickets to a concert that was happening in the summer, and a leather wallet, because she'd noticed his was pretty battered.

Delilah wandered off when she realized there were no more to open. And Presley walked toward her, pulling her against him as he brushed her cheek with his mouth. "Thank you," he told her, sounding strangely emotional. "They're all perfect."

"I have one more for you at home," she reminded him.

He smiled against her skin. "That's already my favorite."

"Oh boy, so what's going on here?"

They turned to see Alex walking toward them. He was wearing a pair of cut off jeans, and a sleeveless tee, a pair of aviators covering his eyes. But you didn't have to see his eyes to know he was hungover.

"What's what?" Presley frowned.

"You and Cassie? You a thing now?"

Cassie smiled at him. "Looks like it."

Alex shrugged. "Cool. And since you're all here, I have some news."

"Another viral TikTok?" Marley asked, looking amused. Because Alex was completely addicted to that app.

"Kind of." Alex frowned at him. "But not really. It's what's happened on the back of the TikTok."

"What?"

Alex looked around the party, as though he was waiting for everybody to listen to him. But unlike when Presley kissed Cassie, nobody looked all that interested.

"So I got an email on Friday."

"Scintillating…" Marley murmured. "I got a text message. Isn't modern technology a wonderful thing?"

Cassie bit down a smile. Presley shook his head.

"But was yours from a motherfucking record company?" Alex asked, looking annoyed.

"There are kids here," Presley murmured. "Keep the language clean, please."

"Like you do," Alex said.

"I am today." Pres lifted a brow.

Alex sighed. "Did you not hear me? I got an email from a record company. A big one. They found us on TikTok. They're interested in our songs."

"Sure they are." Presley nodded. "Did they ask for your credit card so they could start promoting us?"

Cassie elbowed him in the stomach. Sure he was funny, but Alex looked so excited, she hated to dash his good humor.

"I'm being serious, man. Look at this." He pulled his phone from his pocket and slid his finger along the screen until an email appeared on it. Holding it out to Presley, he had a triumphant expression on his face. "Read it and weep."

Presley looked over it, his own expression neutral. "Did you click on the sender and see if it came from some weird email address?"

"Of course I did. I'm not an idiot."

"What does it say?" Cassie asked, leaning over Presley's shoulder. Her eyes skimmed the words, taking in the invitation to come to New York for an audition.

"Nah," she said smiling. "That has to be a hoax."

"Dad?" Marley called over to Gray. He turned, his bottle of beer halfway to his mouth.

"Yeah?"

"Can you take a look at this?" he asked. "Dad will know if this person really works for Story Records."

"What is it?" Their dad walked over. Alex quickly got him up to date and Presley's dad took the phone, reading the email.

"I don't know all the A&R guys at Story Records," Gray told them. "But it looks genuine. I can look into it for you if you'd like." Presley's father still produced for some bands and singers, occasionally.

"That'd be awesome." Alex grinned. "Thank you." He turned to look at Marley, a satisfied look on his face. "See?"

"He didn't exactly say it was genuine," Marley pointed out.

"He said it could be, though." Alex shrugged. "Can you believe this? We're hitting the big time. Seriously." His face lit up like Times Square. "Can you imagine if this works out?"

"Let's worry about that another day," Presley said. "If it's genuine, it can wait." He didn't sound very enthusiastic. "Now let's get on with enjoying the party, shall we?"

———

"Wait," Cassie said, a smile on her face as she broke their kiss in his entry way later that night. "I promised you a birthday gift. How do you want me?"

"Just like this." Pres pulled her against him, leaving her in no doubt how much he needed her right away. He'd been watching her all night. Well okay, during the day too. Seeing her laugh with his family, spend time with his kid, talk to his parents like she was born to…

It made him want her like he'd never wanted anything else.

The only reason he hadn't pulled her into the bushes on the way home was because the whole town would find out and they'd never hear the last of it.

But whatever wafer thin restraint he'd had for during the journey home finally snapped.

"You look so beautiful tonight." He kissed her neck, his fingers tugging at her t-shirt, pulling it over her head until just her pretty lace bra and a thick necklace remained. "This needs to go," he murmured, kissing the swell of her breast through the lace of her bra as he reached his hand around and deftly unfastened it, pulling the straps down her arms and throwing her bra to the side.

Christ, this woman was perfect. He wanted to taste every inch of her. To touch her until she was vibrating with pleasure beneath his touch.

"But it's your birthday," she gasped as he pinched her nipple, her head tipping back until it hit the wall behind her. They'd hardly made it inside with the door closed before he'd pounced on her.

He couldn't stop himself. He needed her. Needed this.

"Damn right it is." He dropped to his knees, unfastening those cute little shorts that had been teasing him all day. He pulled them down then leaned forward, kissing the soft skin on her thighs. "Do you know how much I've been thinking about this?"

She gasped again as he nipped at her skin. "As much as I have?"

"More." He tugged at her panties, helping her step out of them. She'd already slid her shoes off, thank god. And then she was naked, which right now felt like the best fucking present he'd ever had, thank you very much.

Naked apart from that necklace. And it could stay. He liked it.

He slid his hand up the inside of her thigh, the movement making her breath catch in her throat. Her skin was so soft. So warm. Her legs parted as soon as he nudged them, revealing the innermost part of her.

She looked like heaven.

He leaned forward, inhaling her, and her fingers threaded through his hair. "Presley, it's supposed to be your birthday, not mine," she whispered.

"Shut up. I'm hungry." He buried his face between her, surrounded by the sweet slickness of her pleasure. He kissed her pretty clit, then licked it, his fingers sliding inside of her in the way he knew she loved. And then he started to fuck her with them, determined to win her pleasure.

It was his birthday and he could do what he liked.

"Pres…" She was breathless. Giddy.

"Call me Presley when I'm on my knees for you," he grunted.

"Presley." She was breathless. "I need you inside of me."

He looked up, and he could see the intensity in her gaze. She was on the edge. Tight and needy. And fuck, he loved it when she came on his mouth.

But that's not what she needed. She needed him.

And he was a fucking fool for her. If she wanted him, she'd have him.

He stood, pulling his t-shirt off, as she reached for his

jeans, her fingers trembling as she unbuckled him. He was so hard it almost hurt as he tugged his jeans down, followed by his boxers. He grabbed a condom packet from his wallet and looked at her carefully.

"Here?"

She nodded, her eyes glazed. He leaned forward and kissed her softly, and she purred like a kitten against his lips. Ripping the foil, he rolled the condom on. Even that short contact of his fingers on his dick was enough to make his body flex.

His tongue slid against hers as he lifted her legs around his waist, angling them both until the tip of his aching cock pushed against her.

And slid inside the place it loved the most.

So tight, so warm. He took a deep breath to center himself. "You ready?" he whispered.

She smiled, knowing what he meant. He wanted to make her come first because he wasn't sure how long he would last. How gentle he could be when all he'd thought about all day were her long legs wrapped around him like this. His biceps flexed as he held her against the wall, his hips pulling back until she almost released him.

And then he thrust forward again. Hard enough to take her breath away. She fluttered around him, a reminder she was on edge, too, as he took her hard and fast against the wall. The same place they'd first kissed.

He'd never be able to walk down the stairs without blushing again.

"Harder." Her mouth was against his ear. He felt the warmth of her breath tickle his skin.

But he was a fool for this woman. If she told him to jump he'd buy a damn rocket to see how high he could go. So he thrust harder, rougher.

Until she was crying out his name and pulsing around him.

"Don't stop."

"Wasn't gonna." It was a lie. He was so, so close. But he wanted to feel her come on him again. Wanted to feel it forever.

Never wanted this moment to end.

———

"Do you think that email Alex got was a hoax?" Cassie asked him the next morning. They'd taken a shower together and now he was cooking her breakfast. Blueberry pancakes and bacon. It had been his favorite combination as a kid.

And technically, it was still his birthday weekend. Which hadn't gone unnoticed by Cassie, who'd woken him up with that belated birthday blow job she'd wanted to give him. And then she'd offered to make breakfast, but he'd batted her suggestion off, because he liked cooking. The same way he liked giving her pleasure.

He'd forgotten how much he liked making people happy. Maybe that was because he'd been so unhappy himself for the longest time.

"Nah, it wasn't." He flipped the pancake over. "Dad checked it out last night. It's legit."

"It is?" Her eyes widened as she leaned forward. She was wearing one of his old t-shirts, her damp hair twisted into some kind of bun. Even freshly fucked and showered she had the kind of grace that made his body feel weak.

She was his Helen of Troy. Or his Achilles' Heel. He frowned. Damn, he should have paid more attention in school.

"Why didn't you tell Alex last night?" she asked him.

He put the pancake on the stack, then poured in some more batter. "Well firstly because he would have lorded it over Marley and it's his birthday too."

"Good point." She nodded. "Alex isn't exactly diplomatic in victory."

He smiled. "You know him well already."

"And secondly?" she prompted.

"Secondly?" he repeated, frowning.

"You said firstly. Which led me to believe there'd be a second reason." She blinked. "Now you've got me questioning myself."

He laughed, pushing the plate toward where she was sitting at the breakfast bar. "Eat," he said, pointing at the plate of bacon he'd already cooked. "And yeah, there was a second. I just don't want to think about it."

She looked up from where she was lifting pancakes onto her plate. "Why not?"

"Because it almost certainly won't go anywhere. And if it does, it'll have to go somewhere without me."

Cassie frowned. "The band couldn't exist without you. You're the lead singer."

"I'm also Delilah's father. And she lives here." He put the empty pan to the side and grabbed his own plate, loading it with pancakes and bacon before taking the stool next to hers. "It's one thing doing an occasional gig at a local bar while my mom takes care of her, another to have to move somewhere to record music and then tour without her."

"Oh. I didn't think of that." She swallowed a mouthful of pancake. "Damn, this is good. Where'd you learn to make pancakes like this?"

"You've met Delilah. You see how much she talks. The only way I can keep her quiet is by feeding her lots of sugar."

Cassie started laughing. "Surely that makes her worse."

His brows knitted. "Now that you say that, it probably does. Why didn't I think of that?"

He took a sip of coffee. Damn, he loved this. The two of them sitting here, just talking. Nobody wanting something, nobody interrupting.

"We could record music here," Cassie pointed out. "Your dad has the whole studio set up for it."

"Doesn't solve the touring part though," he said, popping a piece of bacon into his mouth. When he swallowed it down, he looked carefully at her. "And that's where the money is in music."

"I guess."

He tipped his head to the side. "Are you actually interested in getting signed?" he asked her. "I thought you liked working with Gemma."

"I do." She shrugged. "It just sounded like fun, that's all. But you're right, it'll probably go nowhere. And I'd never leave Gemma hanging."

And now he felt like an asshole for taking away the shine of it. Sure, he had responsibilities, but Cassie didn't. And she'd already had to step out of the limelight once, thanks to her accident. He ate another mouthful of pancake.

"I guess we could go to the audition and see where it goes," he said carefully. "We're probably not what they're looking for anyway. Some old has been single dad trying to sing with a gorgeous younger woman."

She rolled her eyes. "Has been? Old?" she repeated. "Seriously?"

His lips twitched.

"Anyway, even if what you're saying is right, it's a tried and tested trope. In most bands the guys get older and the women get younger. A sad reflection of life." She lifted a brow.

His phone started to buzz. His mom's name appeared across it. "Hey," he said, accepting the call. "Everything okay?"

"Everything's fine," his mom said warmly. "I just wanted to check that we're meeting you at church this morning rather than here."

"Yeah, that's right. Unless you need me to pick Delilah up now?"

"No. We got it covered. Although I think I might wear my fingers out trying to put her hair into a fishtail braid."

He laughed. "Just tell her a ponytail will do."

"I'm her grandma. What Delilah wants, Delilah gets. I'm the one who spoils her, and you're the one who picks up the pieces."

"Great, thanks." But he was smiling, because he knew his mom didn't mean it. "I'll see you at church."

"Yes you will. Bye, honey. Oh, and say hi to Cassie for me."

He looked over at her and she was grinning. Okay, so his mom wasn't an idiot.

"Yeah," he said gruffly. "I will."

"OF COURSE you have to go to New York," Gemma said. "An audition is amazing. Don't worry about the classes, I'll get in a sub or something."

"Are you sure?" Cassie frowned. "I don't want to leave you in the lurch. This place is important to you. And to me."

"I know," Gemma replied calmly. "But I've got this. Seriously, if you don't go to New York, you're fired."

"You can't fire me," Cassie said.

Gemma grinned back at her. "Seriously though. This is important. You said yourself you've been looking for a sign of what to do next. What if this is it? What if our teachers were right all those years ago about the Trifecta? We didn't go through all those years of painful music lessons for no reason."

"But I've only just gotten here." And she liked it here.

"And you'll be back. I don't know why you're looking so worried. This is a good thing."

Cassie took a deep breath. "I know. But it's all so soon."

The two of them were sitting in the diner on Monday evening. Gemma's mother-in-law had taken the children to the movies, and Riley was working so the two of them had decided to head straight out after locking up the dance school.

Gemma tipped her head to the side, looking carefully at Cassie. "Are you talking about the band or you and Pres Hartson?"

"A bit of both, I guess." Cassie let out a mouthful of air. "I just don't like that things could change. Not when I feel like I'm settled for the first time in a lifetime."

And that was the truth of it. It felt like she was finally home, in a town she'd just discovered. She'd hit her rhythm with her classes, she'd found fun with the band, and now there was Pres and Delilah.

"Maybe this is what you need," Gemma told her. "To go back to New York and see what you've been missing."

Cassie frowned. "What do you mean?"

"What if you're settling here because you're afraid?" Gemma lifted a brow. "You moving here was only supposed to be temporary."

"Are you trying to fire me again?" Cassie's throat felt thick.

"Absolutely not. But you're different than me, you always have been. You have the fire that I never had. I've seen you on stage, it brings you to life. That first time I saw you dance in New York was amazing. Don't you want to feel that again?"

Cassie's chest tightened. "I don't know," she admitted. She wasn't sure what she wanted.

"This could be a good thing," Gemma told her. "And you get to audition with Pres. You don't even have to leave him behind. What's not to like?"

Letting out a mouthful of air, Cassie nodded. Gemma was right, this was a good thing. It was just the fear making her feel awkward. The fear of failure. The fear of losing.

The fear caused by that stupid accident.

"Anyway, who else can I live vicariously through?" Gemma asked. "Did you know while you were getting loved up by the hottest single dad in Hartson's Creek, I was being woken up by my seven-year-old daughter who wanted to know what a lesbian was?"

Cassie's eyes widened. "What did you tell her?"

Taking a sip of her coffee, Gemma shook her head. "I was really patient. I lovingly explained about different types of families and relationships. Told her love is love, and that we need more of it in this world, not less."

"Well that's pretty cool," Cassie said.

"I thought so," Gemma agreed. "Until she looked really confused and asked me how this applied to fishies. It took me another ten minutes of questioning to realize she was asking about amphibians. Stupid David Attenborough and his gorgeous documentaries." She pouted.

"Seriously?" Cassie asked.

"Seriously," Gemma agreed. "I don't think I'm cut out for this parenting thing. I just keep making mistakes. So let's talk about you instead." She leaned forward, her eyes sparkling. "I heard you and Presley made it official."

"You and the rest of Hartson's Creek," Cassie muttered. "I can't tell you how many moms asked me about it when they were picking their kids up from class today."

"Ugh." Gemma wrinkled her nose. "People do love to gossip. But don't worry, tomorrow the subject of the day will be my excellent parenting skills."

Cassie chuckled. "You're a great mom. You don't have to worry about that." She took a sip of her coffee. "Even Presley got some questions about us at the construction site. It was so funny. He sounded disgusted when he told me."

"He called you today?" Gemma asked, her head tipped to the side.

"A few times," Cassie admitted.

"Oh that man has it bad." Gemma clapped her hands together. "And he should. I'm so pleased for you."

"It's still new," Cassie pointed out. Because she was trying not to get giddy herself. "Neither of us wanted to tell people yet. It's only because of Delilah and his fear that somebody else would say something."

Gemma put her hands on her chest. "He's such a good dad. Isn't that hot?"

"It's smoking," Cassie agreed, sighing.

"And he has that grumpiness, too." Gemma grinned. "Except when he's with you."

"Oh, he's grumpy with me," Cassie said.

"How?"

Cassie bit down a smile. Because his grumpiness almost always ended in sex. It was hot. It turned her on. She liked the challenge of making him smile.

And when he did, it felt like waking up on Christmas morning to see that Santa had come.

Except it wasn't Santa who got to come.

"Come on. Give me the details. The last time Riley and I had sex I think Clinton was still president."

"You were an infant when Clinton was president," Cassie pointed out. God, she loved this woman. Especially because she knew Riley and Gemma had a great sex life.

"I know. And it was actually last week, but then Andrew started crying because there was a butterfly in his room and he thought it was a baby bat."

Cassie snorted.

"And you can laugh all you want, but when you move in with Presley you'll have to deal with this too. You think Delilah won't try to walk in on you while you're doing the dirty?" Gemma asked. "She'll make it her mission. You'll never be able to have free and easy sex again."

"You make it sound so enticing," Cassie teased. "And anyway, we're not moving in together."

"But you will."

Cassie shrugged. "We haven't talked about it. And I don't think he'd want to take that step without *a lot* of talking. It's a huge commitment. Bigger than marriage because that's just between two people. This is three."

"Do you feel ready for that kind of commitment?" Gemma asked.

Cassie's chest tightened. "It's a little scary," she said. "Because Delilah is such a lovely little girl. I could never hurt her. So I'd have to be ready. We all would." She took a sip of coffee. "I'd hate for her to ever feel the way I felt whenever my mom ignored my calls or didn't visit."

"That's why you're such a good person," Gemma said, patting Cassie's hand. "Because you think of other people before you think of yourself."

———

"We have less than one week until the audition," Alex said, as the four of them sat around in the studio behind Presley's parents' house. "And we have to get this right. It's make or break, kids."

Presley lifted a brow but said nothing. Cassie glanced at him from the corner of her eye. She knew he still wasn't happy about this whole audition. That he was only doing it for the rest of them.

Or for her, more specifically. And it made her feel warm and sad in equal measure.

"It's just an audition," Presley murmured. "Four songs and we go home."

"They're putting us up in the Carlton," Alex said. "It's right in Midtown, near everything. They wouldn't do that unless they were serious." He shook his head. "Come on, don't you want this to work."

Cassie caught Presley's gaze and smiled softly at him. "He's making it work," she pointed out. "He's been working all the hours he can to get ahead on the construction work. And he's gotten his mom to look after Delilah."

"Yeah, well we've all made sacrifices," Alex said, rolling his eyes. "I was supposed to go on a first date that weekend."

Marley coughed out a laugh. "Your sacrifice is appreciated, man," he said, patting Alex's arm. Then he turned to look at Cassie and Presley. "How long after we sign do we have to wait before we replace this goon?" he asked them. "Bass players are a dime a dozen in New York, right?"

Alex blinked. "You can't replace me."

"Bassists get replaced all the time," Marley told him.

"Yeah, but if we get signed, that's our names on the contract." He looked unsettled. "Right?"

"Sure." Marley nodded, looking amused. "Whatever you say, man."

"Can we get on with this?" Presley asked. He'd been edgy all night. Cassie knew it was because he was exhausted. Trying to run a business, take care of his daughter, and keep everybody else happy was taking its toll on him.

She'd had to nag him to go to bed most nights this week when he called her. Told him that paperwork could wait unless it was invoices he was waiting on being paid.

But she was determined to make this up to him. She knew he was doing it for her. Not just her, but Marley too. She'd learned that Presley loved quietly but hard. He was a brick wall of emotions. They were all there, keeping him steady, but you only got to see them if he let you come close.

"Okay, let's go with our first song," Marley said, standing up and walking over to the drum set. He settled himself behind it while Presley lifted his guitar strap over his head, and Alex did the same.

Cassie stood behind the keyboard, her eyes still on the only man she wanted to look at. He glanced over at her and smiled when he realized she was watching him.

When they got to New York this man was getting all the blow jobs. And apart from the audition, she wasn't going to let him lift a damn finger. If he was working his ass off to make the rest of them happy, then she was going to show him how much he was appreciated.

With her hands. Her lips. Her body. And yeah, she'd probably let him occasionally come out into the sunlight and breathe in some fume-filled Manhattan air.

Marley beat them in, and Presley started to strum, his soft, thick voice filling the room.

And as the rest of them joined in, she felt a little shiver down her spine, because they were playing well. Really well.

Somewhere along the line this had gone from a little bit of fun to something serious. Possibly permanent. And yeah, she was talking about the band, but she knew it was more than that.

He was more than that.

She was in love with Presley Hartson. With the lead singer of the band she was playing in. It was so damn predictable she should have seen it coming from the start. But all she knew was she didn't want it to end.

She'd do anything for this man. Even give up her dreams.

Again.

———

"You okay?" Pres asked Cassie as they sat outside her house in his car after rehearsals. She'd been quiet all evening. Like she was lost in her thoughts.

"Yeah, I'm fine." She smiled at him. "Sorry, I know you have to get home. We're wasting time here."

"We're not wasting anything."

"Don't you want to make out?" she asked him. Because that's what they did most nights when he followed her home after rehearsals. He'd park behind her car in the driveway and they'd kiss – and touch – until they were hot and needy.

One time he'd gone inside with her, but that had been

even worse, because once they were in her house he wanted to stay all night with her. But he had to get home to his kid.

So they made out in his car instead. Until one of them pulled away and told the other to go home.

"I'm not here because I want to make out with you," he said, his lip quirking. "I'm here because I like being with you."

"Stop talking like that."

"Why?" He smiled at her, curious.

"Because you're making me fall for you even more."

His throat tightened. He tried not to think too much about the way he was feeling for Cassie. It was complicated and difficult, all mixed up with his need to be a good father, and the guilt he still felt over her being without a mother.

And now he was planning to leave his kid for a couple of days so he could go to this stupid audition.

He was already feeling guilty about that, even though his mom had assured him they'd love to have her while the band headed to New York. And sure, his head told him that everybody would be happy with the arrangement – not least Delilah who'd be the center of attention at his parents' house

But his heart told him she only had one parent. And he was abandoning her, if only for a few days.

And then there was the other guilt. The knowledge that he was doing this as a favor to the rest of them. He was adamant that if the label showed any interest, he'd suggest they find a new singer. There were enough of them around.

Even if the thought of Cassie singing with somebody else made him feel a little dizzy.

But she deserved a break. They all did. They didn't have the ties that he had, and he shouldn't hold them back.

So if the label showed interest, he'd already decided to talk with his dad to see if he had any suggestions about a new singer. He hadn't told Cassie that part. Or any of them.

Cassie reached for his hand, sliding her fingers through

his before squeezing them tight. He squeezed back. When he looked at her, she had the softest expression on her face. Like she knew what he was thinking.

But she couldn't know. If she did, she'd think he was an asshole for wanting them to fail.

And right now, he didn't want her knowing that.

"It'll be fun, going to New York," Cassie promised. "We get two nights alone together."

"Yeah, it will." He nodded, pushing the bad thoughts out of his head. It would all be fine. He'd make sure it was. He was just being stupid, seeing things that weren't there. Worrying about things that hadn't happened.

"Now go home to your daughter." She leaned forward to press her mouth against his. "And call me later."

He kissed her back. "I was planning on it."

CHAPTER
Twenty~Three

"WHAT ARE YOU DOING?" Delilah asked. It was the night before the band was driving to New York and she'd insisted on Cassie coming over for dinner. Cassie was in Presley's living room, using her nail polish remover pads to take off the half-peeled red polish on her nails. She'd need to repaint them before the audition.

"Just taking off my nail polish," she told Delilah. "It got chipped." She held up a nail that she hadn't started on. "See?"

"What are those?" Delilah asked, pointing at the pads.

"They're polish remover pads. You can buy the liquid separately and use it on cotton pads, but I like to carry these around in my bag in case of an emergency."

"Do you always paint your nails?" Delilah asked, tipping her head to the side.

"Most of the time. I like the way it makes my hands look."

"You have pretty hands," Delilah said, reaching out and touching the nail Cassie had just cleaned. "Will you paint them again?"

"Yes, when I get home." Cassie nodded. She'd started taking it off here because she wanted to be able to repaint them as soon as she got home. That way they'd be dry before she crashed for an early night and right now Presley was running Delilah a bath. It was early, but Delilah looked beat.

So did Presley. The poor guy had been working himself to the bone. Cassie was planning on leaving as soon as she'd read Delilah's bedtime story, since the little girl had made her promise to.

"Can you paint my nails?" Delilah asked.

"Sure. I can do it sometime if your dad says it's okay. Not tonight though, because the polish takes a while to dry. And if you touch something while it's wet it gets all smudged and you have to start over."

Delilah nodded, looking serious.

"Why don't you live with us?" she asked.

Cassie blinked at the sudden change in conversation. "What do you mean?" she said, partly to give herself time, but also because she wanted to know where the question was coming from.

"My friend Zoe's mom has a boyfriend. He lives with them."

"Oh, do you mean why am I your daddy's girlfriend but I have a separate house?"

"Yes." Delilah nodded. "Why don't you live here?"

"Bath's ready." Presley walked into the living room, his lips curling into a smile when he saw the two of them so close.

"Daddy, why doesn't Cassie live with us?"

He blinked at the sudden question.

"Her friend Zoe's mom's boyfriend lives with them," Cassie told him, trying to get him up to date.

"Oh, right." Pres swallowed. "Let's go," he said to Delilah.

"But what about Cassie? Can't she come with and give me a bath, too?" Delilah asked.

"You give yourself the bath," Pres reminded her. "I just stay to make sure you don't flood the whole bathroom."

"I don't do that." Delilah frowned.

"Not since I learned not to fill the damn thing to the top," he told her. "Come on, let's get you cleaned."

"But I want Cassie to do it."

Pres pinched the bridge of his nose with his fingers. He was on edge, she could tell that much. He'd been that way all week.

"I'll come up once you're clean," she promised. "I'm reading you a story, remember?"

Delilah's lip pushed out into a pout. "But I want you to bath me."

"Get upstairs," Pres told her, his voice low. "*Now*."

Delilah sniffed, her eyes shining. "No."

Cassie shifted on the sofa, feeling sorry for Pres. Feeling sorry for Delilah, too. She should have refused to come over. They were all exhausted.

"I'm not going to argue with you. If you don't go up now, Cassie won't be reading you a story." His jaw was tight. He wouldn't look her way.

"But Daddy…"

"Get. Up. Stairs."

A tear ran down Delilah's cheek. "You're mean. I hate you. I wish my mommy was here."

Presley's eyes caught Cassie's. She could see the emotion in them, but she felt powerless to help. She lifted a brow, in an attempt to ask if she could do something.

He shook his head imperceptibly, swallowing hard.

"Your mom isn't here, and I'm sorry about that," he said to his daughter. "But you need to get in the bath. Otherwise you'll be going straight to bed. Your choice."

Delilah looked at Cassie. "I wish I lived with you," she told Cassie. "You wouldn't be mean."

Cassie inhaled softly. "I'd still want you to take a bath. Do as Daddy says and I'll come up and read you a story after."

Delilah looked from her to Presley, then back again, as though she was weighing Cassie's words.

"Okay," she said, her voice wobbling. "But I still don't like you," she told Presley.

The way he winced just about broke Cassie's heart.

"Well it's a good thing I love you enough for the both of us," he told her.

———

"I'm sorry about earlier," Presley said, walking into the living room where Cassie was waiting for him. "She isn't usually like that."

She'd read Delilah's story as she'd promised, and then she'd left Presley to do the final good nights, sensing that he needed to be alone with his daughter.

Especially after their argument about bath time.

"I know that. It's been a long day," she said softly. "Or a long few weeks. You're both exhausted. Feelings ran high. It happens."

He collapsed onto the sofa next to her, laying back so his head was on her thighs and his legs were stretched out in front of him on the floor. "What did I do to deserve somebody like you?" he muttered, looking up at her. "Christ, I mess things up sometimes."

"You didn't mess anything up. Kids are kids. You said yourself that it'll get worse when she's a teenager." From this vantage point she could see how dark the shadows were beneath his eyes. She ran her fingers through his hair in a gentle motion, lightly scraping her nails on his scalp.

He closed his eyes. "God that feels good. Just tell me I'm not the worst dad in the world and I'll stop being needy, I promise."

She smiled. "You're a good dad, and I'll keep telling you that. Try having a parent who never calls."

"That's what I'm trying not to be," he muttered. "I want Delilah to know I'll always be here, no matter what. I don't want her to ever worry that she doesn't have me on her side."

"She knows that. She wouldn't have argued with you if she didn't trust you. I never dared to contradict my mom growing up. Because I knew what would happen if I did."

He frowned. "What would happen?"

"She'd take an extended vacation. Either literally or figuratively. If I didn't do what she wanted, she'd learned that ignoring me got the desired result."

She leaned down and softly kissed his brow. He let out a long breath.

"Jade's sister called earlier," he said.

"She did?" Cassie slid her fingers between his. "Is everything okay?" She knew he found it hard to deal with Jade's family. The stupid guilt he still held made everything more difficult.

"Yeah." His eyelids fluttered closed again. "She told me her parents missed Delilah. I've been a little lax in taking her to see them."

"Can't they drive here?" she asked.

"Yeah, I guess. But they never have. They prefer having me drop her off."

"Do they work?"

"Both retired."

"So why do you have to do the driving?" she asked, genuinely curious. "Shouldn't they want to help? The way your mom does."

"I don't know. Maybe they don't want to interfere. I guess I'll call them when we're back from New York."

"That sounds like a good plan," she said softly.

"Sadie had heard about the audition," he told her. "I guess Alex has been spreading the news."

Cassie pulled her lip between her teeth. "What did she say about that?"

"Not a lot. It was a brief conversation." He opened his eyes again and looked at her. "I told her that if we got signed I'd be leaving the band."

Cassie blinked, mostly because he'd never said it out loud before. Sure, he'd voiced his worries that first night. But never more than that.

"You can't leave the band," she told him. "I won't let you."

A ghost of a smile passed his lips. "Yeah, well if tonight's proved anything, it's that my daughter needs consistency. She's not gonna get that if I'm traveling all over the country playing gigs."

"I guess not." She leaned down to kiss him again. This time her mouth caught his. He groaned against her lips.

"Damn, I've missed being in your bed," he told her.

"Well that's one thing to look forward to in New York," she pointed out. "A hotel room. With a lock that Marley and Alex won't be able to open even if they wanted to. I figure this whole thing is an excuse for you and me to spend some quality time together." She paused. "Naked."

This time his smile was big. He reached up to curl his palm around her neck, pulling her back down for another kiss. "Promise?"

"Oh yes. It's pretty much guaranteed," she told him.

"Okay then." His voice was low. Thick. "Bring on the good times."

CHAPTER
Twenty~Four

"LOOK AT THAT," Alex said, as they stood in the center of Times Square. "The New Year ball's real. And the taxis are yellow, just like in the movies."

Pres barely managed to hide his laugh with a cough. Alex had been like this ever since they'd driven through the tunnel into Manhattan. Pointing out the Empire State Building and every other skyscraper like he'd thought they were all make believe.

"Have you really never been to New York City?" Marley asked, frowning. Cassie took a sip from her coffee. It was her first one since they'd arrived in the city and she needed the caffeine hit.

Especially after having to sit in the Beast for hours, listening to Alex talk loudly about whatever subject came to his mind.

"I've seen a lot of shows set in New York." Alex shrugged. "Just never visited."

"But everybody's been to New York City." Marley frowned. "Haven't they?"

"Not everybody was brought up by the king of rock and roll," Alex pointed out.

"Your dad ran a bank. You weren't exactly poor," Marley said. Presley caught Cassie's eye and she grinned at him.

They'd agreed to wander around the city with Marley and Alex, then they'd all have dinner.

And after that? It was on. They hadn't had sex for two weeks. Not when they were both in the same room anyway. With Presley having to work all the hours he could, and spending time with Delilah, there hadn't been the opportunity to be alone.

She was almost certain she was going to explode the minute he touched her. Possibly before.

Hell, if he kept on looking at her like he had been, she might just find heaven on this sidewalk.

It had only been a few months since the city had been her home, yet she felt just as much of a tourist as the others. Maybe it was because she was seeing it through their eyes. Or perhaps because she'd gotten so used to the relative peace and quiet of Hartson's Creek.

"Can we go to Central Park now?" Alex asked. He was desperate to see Strawberry Fields, the memorial to John Lennon.

"Sure." She nodded. "We just need to walk up Seventh Avenue." She inclined her head northward.

"When do we get to see Fifth Avenue?" Alex asked. "Isn't that the good one?"

"You already saw it," she told him. "We walked across it earlier. When you saw Rockefeller Center."

"The one that should have ice skating but doesn't?" Alex asked.

"Yeah, that's the one."

"Oh." He wrinkled his nose. "I thought it'd be bigger."

She looked at him from the corner of her eye. "Are you being serious about all this?" She wasn't sure if he was playing with her or not.

"About what?" he asked, the picture of innocence.

"About not having been here before."

"Serious as a boy scout." He touched his brow with the tips of his fingers. "Pinky swear."

"Well okay then. Let's start walking."

Alex and Marley walked ahead, Pres lingering to slide his arm around her shoulders. "Okay?" he asked, kissing her brow.

"Definitely."

Alex turned around to look at them, then groaned. "Can you two put the PDA on hold, please? We have some serious tourism to do."

Pres smiled against her brow. "Nope, sorry. You're lucky we even left the hotel at all. If it wasn't for Cassie being nice, we'd be naked in the shower right now."

"Eww." Alex wrinkled his nose. "Enough already. Now let's go and pay our respect to John Lennon. Before I barf up that hotdog I just ate."

―――――

"I told you, we're not coming." Pres shook his head. He was standing in the door of their hotel room, blocking Alex from walking in. Cassie was behind him, sniggering as she looked over his shoulder, mostly because Alex looked like a kid who'd just learned that Santa didn't exist.

"Oh come on, man. It's going to be boring if it's just the two of us." Alex pouted.

"Thanks." Marley lifted a brow. "You're making me feel all warm inside."

"Just come to the club for a couple of hours," Alex said. "You know you want to." He'd been sulking ever since Presley had told them over dinner that he and Cassie had other plans tonight. "This is supposed to be the band's trip. Not your chance to have sex with your girlfriend."

"The band's trip?" Presley repeated, amused. "Who said it was a band trip?"

"We're auditioning tomorrow. The band. *Us*." Alex pointed at himself, then at the other three. "We should be bonding. Drinking together. Dancing. Sex, drugs, and rock-'n'roll, isn't that what it's all about?"

"Two out of three ain't bad," Presley told him. "Now have a good night. I hope you have lots of sex. Because that's what I intend to do." He gave them a pointed look then stepped back to close the door.

"Wait!" Alex shouted. "What time should we meet in the morning?"

Pres sighed. "Nine in the lobby. Cass and I are having breakfast in bed."

"Can't we have breakfast together?" Alex asked.

"Jesus, you're worse than Delilah," Pres muttered. He looked at Marley, who looked like he was about to explode with laughter.

His brother didn't give a flying fuck that he and Cassie weren't joining them. He liked music and he liked to dance, and he was planning on doing both.

"Come on," Marley said, pulling at Alex's shoulder. "Let's leave them alone. The first round is on me."

"Why didn't you say so?" Alex turned around, walking down the hallway to the elevators. Marley winked at Pres.

"Have a good evening," Pres told him.

"Likewise," Marley said, grinning. "Though I suspect you both will." He lifted a hand in farewell and followed Alex down the hallway as Pres closed the door.

"Jesus," he said, leaning against it. "He's exhausting."

"You poor baby." Cassie reached for his hand. "Come here, let me make it all better."

She cupped his face and he smiled at her, loving the way she was looking at him. Like he was the king of the fucking world.

He felt it too. Now that it was just the two of them.

"Come here," he muttered, finding it hard to believe this woman was his.

"I'm already here," she whispered.

"I know. But come closer."

"You want me to climb inside your pants?" she asked him and he grinned.

"Wouldn't say no."

She put her palms on his chest, splaying her fingers out over his t-shirt. One of the tips grazed his nipple and he grunted.

"Gotta tell you, this isn't going to be pretty," he said. "It's been too long."

"Two weeks. Way too long." She ran her hands down his chest, as though she was mapping out the muscles on his abdomen, before trailing her fingers along the waistband of his jeans. And of course he was hard.

He always was for this woman.

She smiled at the outline of his cock jutting against his jeans. "So I have a plan," she told him.

"Of course you do."

"You're going to stay right there. And I'm going to put on my leotard. And then I'm going to give you the world's best blow job."

He swallowed.

"It's my birthday," she said.

"No it isn't."

She wrinkled her nose. "Okay, so let's pretend it is. And for my birthday I want you. In my mouth." She pouted those pretty lips. "And what I want, I'm gonna get."

"Have at it," he whispered. "And then I'm in charge." Because he had some plans for her. And all of them included her naked. On the bed, on the floor, against the wall.

In the shower.

Wherever. He just loved that they had hours ahead of them with no interruptions at all.

She grinned, as though she could read his mind. "It's a deal."

———

"We're looking for a very specific vibe," Bryan, the A&R guy told them. "Cool and boho. Your videos made it onto our for you page and we think you could be what we're looking for."

Pres looked at Cassie, his brow raised, and she shrugged. He clearly had no idea what boho was. She'd tell him later.

"Yeah, a lot of people think we have that vibe," Alex said enthusiastically. Or as enthusiastic as he could be with a banging hangover. He'd been the last one to meet them in the lobby. Cassie and Pres had been first.

"You have a good look." Bryan glanced at Cassie. She was in shorts again, with a flowery top. Her hair was in waves down her back. And yeah, if you squinted she probably did have a little bit of the laid back style they wanted. But she definitely hadn't intended it.

"Thanks." She smiled at him.

"And you two…" he pointed at her and Presley. "You're involved?"

Presley shifted in his chair. She could tell how uncomfortable he was. The people sitting at the desk had only wanted to hear them play one song, instead of four. It had taken them longer to set up their instruments than it did for them to actually perform.

She felt like she was in an episode of American Idol. Being judged, and probably falling short.

"Yes," she said, looking over at Presley.

"I guess we could work with that."

Pres tipped his head to the side. "Work with it?" he asked. "What does that mean?"

"I mean we can build a story around it. I don't suppose you're married, are you?"

From the corner of her eye she could see Pres frown. "No."

She reached out to put her hand on his thigh, her palm warm against his skin. She knew he was only here under duress.

Or rather, because he loved his brother and was pretty fond of her. Hell, he was fond of Alex too, but he would never admit it.

"He's a single father," she said.

Bryan blinked. "You have a kid?"

"A daughter," Presley corrected him. "Yes."

"Oh. Okay." Bryan ran the pad of his thumb along his jaw. "Well I guess that's all the questions I have for you. Thanks for coming in. We have a couple more bands to meet with and then we'll be in touch."

"Wait, we're not the only ones?" Alex asked, his voice full of disappointment. "I thought you liked our videos."

Bryan smiled but it didn't reach his eyes. "My assistant said they were great. Thanks again." He stood, making it clear it was time for them to leave. "And have a great day."

Bryan left the room as they started packing away their instruments, his assistant standing awkwardly by the door as they started carrying the boxes onto the carts the label had provided to help them shift their gear.

"You really are good," the assistant told them. "Out of all of them, you're my favorite."

They were on the elevator before any of them spoke.

"Well at least we got a free trip to New York out of it." Marley shrugged. "It could be worse."

"It's not over. He liked what we did," Alex said. "And his assistant loves us. That has to count for something, right?"

Cassie looked at Presley, who'd said nothing. He looked a little annoyed, but that was probably left over from him being asked if he was married. She'd explain the story of the book to him in the car. Then he'd probably understand.

"You should probably have lied about Delilah," Alex said.

"Did you seriously just say that?" Presley frowned. "I'm not going to lie about having a kid."

"He didn't ask you if you had a kid. You volunteered it," Alex continued. "I'm just saying you shouldn't have."

Pres opened his mouth to say something, then closed it again, as though thinking better of it. And when the elevator reached the first floor, he carried his guitar out of there, as she and the others followed behind with the carts.

And to top it all off? It was raining. She groaned as she looked outside. Pres turned to catch her eye.

"It's gonna be fine," he told her. "It'll stop by tomorrow when we have to leave. And anyway, I'm driving."

She nodded. "I know." It was stupid. If he could work himself to the bone to attend an audition for something he never wanted and never intended to do, she could grin and bare it if it rained when they drove home tomorrow.

For five hours.

She exhaled slowly. She trusted him, she really did.

If anybody could get her home safely, Presley Hartson could. He took care of everybody. He'd certainly taken care of her last night, and tonight looked like more of the same.

And she liked that a little too much.

CHAPTER
Twenty~Five

"CAN I BORROW YOU FOR A MINUTE?" Gemma put her head around the door of the studio. Cassie looked up, surrounded by a group of toddlers and their moms. She couldn't hide her surprise. Gemma didn't usually interrupt her during class time.

"Um…"

"It's okay. I'll cover the class."

Her chest tightened. Gemma didn't usually do that either. She walked over to the door, a frown pulling at her lips. "Is everything okay?" she asked in a low voice. They'd been back from New York for a week, and she'd tried to make up for her absence by covering a few of Gemma's classes, too. Which meant she was tired, but it was a good kind of tired.

Everything felt pretty good these days. Even Pres was in a good mood, mostly due to the fact that neither Bryan nor his team had called them. It wasn't a big surprise that the record company didn't want them. They'd made as much clear when they only had them play one song.

Not that she minded. It didn't feel like their trip was wasted, not when she'd gotten to spend two days with Pres.

Her face flushed at the memory.

"Yeah, sorry," Gemma's voice brought her back into the present. "I didn't mean to worry you. It's just that your friend Alex is at the desk and he's insistent you come talk to him right now."

"Alex as in Alex from the band?" Well that was weird. "Why isn't he at work?"

"Your guess is as good as mine. I asked him if it could wait until after class but he insisted. I had a feeling he'd march right in here and pull you out if I didn't."

Oh damn. Was he in a fit again about Presley? She hadn't talked to Alex or Marley this week. They'd decided to take a week off from rehearsals. She'd assumed that was mostly because Alex was still feeling bitter about the audition, but she didn't push it.

To be honest, she needed the break. And she knew that Presley did, too.

She hadn't seen him since they got back, but she'd talked to him on the phone. They'd made arrangements for Saturday night. They were going to take Delilah to the drive in theater. Presley was pretty sure she wouldn't stay awake for the whole movie so he planned to have her in her pajamas and make her a little bed in the flatbed of his truck.

"Alex?"

He looked up as she turned the corner into the reception area. "Finally." He shook his head. "I've been calling you."

"And I've been in class. My phone is in the staff room." She inclined her head at the door next to the reception desk. "What's so urgent?"

"You need to call the record label. Now."

"What? Why?" She pursed her lips, trying to think of a single possible reason that the label would want to talk to her.

Alex grumbled beneath his breath, then pulled his phone out and hit a button. "Just talk to them. You can thank me later."

She looked at the phone he was holding out like it was

some kind of alien artefact. "Did we leave something behind?" she asked him. "Can't it wait? I need to get back to my class."

He huffed and lifted the phone to his ear. "Hi, it's Alex from Altered Reality. Bryan called about half an hour ago. I'm with Cassie Simons. He wanted to talk to her." There was a pause. "Yeah, I'll wait."

"What's going on?" she mouthed at him.

For the first time he smiled. And it was genuine. Well okay then, she'd deal with this then get back to her students.

"Yep, she's here," Alex said, holding the phone out to her again.

This time she took it.

"Hello?"

"Cassie? It's Bryan." She tried not to smile when he didn't give his last name. As though he was the only Bryan in the world.

"Hi Bryan."

"Listen, we really loved the way you sang at the audition, but we decided to go with another group."

"Oh, okay." She shot Alex a look. Had he really dragged her out here so she could hear the rejection first hand. "No problem."

"But I have a proposal for you," he continued.

"What kind of proposal?" she asked him.

Alex lifted a brow, looking smug. She wrinkled her nose at him.

"The band we've gone with is almost there. But they need a female singer. We immediately thought of you. You'd be perfect for them. We've shown them your music and videos and they're very keen on you joining them in New York."

She laughed. "Sorry, what?"

"We want to sign you."

Her eyes met Alex's. "But I'm already in a band."

He started shaking his head.

"What?" she mouthed at him.

He gave a dramatic sigh and she decided to ignore him.

"I understand that. But I've spoken to Alex and he thinks this is a great opportunity for you. He's happy to release you if you're ready to join us."

"I…" She blinked. What did Alex have to do with it? "I don't think I can do that."

Alex practically ripped the phone out of her hand. "What are you doing?" he hissed.

"Did you know about this?"

"Of course I did. It's fucking amazing." His voice was low. "Just… let me handle it."

She felt strange. Like there was ringing in her ears. Alex put the phone to his ear. "Hi Bryan, she's kind of over-whelmed." He laughed. "Yeah, right?" There was a pause. "Oh no, she just needs to sort out some work commitments, but it's all good. Yeah, I'm her manager. Send everything over to me and we'll work it out. Speak later." He hung up before Cassie could even take it in.

"Why are you frowning?" he asked her. "Aren't you happy? I'm happy for you." He gave her a grin. "I mean, I'd be even happier if I was involved too, but this is great. What a fucking opportunity."

Her heart was hammering against her chest. "Alex, did they just offer me a contract?"

"Yes, dummy. They did."

"I can't do it. Not without you all." She shook her head. All she could think about was Presley. She wasn't going to do this. Not without him.

"Of course you can." Alex laughed. "We won't mind. We'll be delighted for you."

"But what about the band?" she asked. But that wasn't what she meant. Not at all.

She just couldn't find the words to express what she was feeling.

"We'll find another keyboardist." He winked at her. "And at least this time it's not my fault you're leaving. Well it is, but at least this is a good thing."

———

"That's amazing," Gemma said, hugging her. "I'm so happy for you."

The class had finished and all the little ones had left the studio with their parents, leaving Cassie and Gemma alone.

"I'm not doing it," she told her. "It's stupid."

Gemma lifted a brow. "A hundred thousand dollars for a few months' work doesn't sound stupid to me."

"It's not about the money. And the initial commitment is only for a few months. There's an option clause that they can invoke." One that could last up to five years if the tour and marketing went well.

Because there was no mistaking the fact that this was going to be a manufactured band. With a lot of record label dollars pumped in behind it.

"I've only just moved here," she told Gemma. "I'm not going back to New York."

"Is this about Presley?" Gemma asked her.

Cassie let out a long breath. She was dreading telling him about this, even though she was planning on turning it down. Mostly because he was already so over the record label thing. The same guy who'd offered her a contract was the one who'd been completely dismissive of him being a father.

She just wanted things to be like they were before they went to New York.

"He'd understand," Gemma told her.

"No he wouldn't. He and Jade were on the verge of breaking up when she died because she wanted to start touring again." There, she'd said it out loud. The thing that was making her stomach feel all twisted up. "He'd do the same thing to me. I'm not even the mother of his child."

"If he broke up with you because you're following your dreams then he's not the man I think he is."

Cassie sighed. "I just… I don't like it. Any of it. It was one thing going with the whole band. That was fun. This just feels…"

"Real?" Gemma asked.

"Yeah, I guess." She shook her head. "It feels off. And I don't like it."

"Maybe you need to talk to Presley," Gemma suggested.

Gemma was right, she knew that. Her friend was right about a lot of things. Which was why she had her life sorted out. A husband, two gorgeous kids. A successful business…

"Remember when we were younger?" Gemma asked her. "You were always the ambitious one. You wanted to be on stage. Wanted to be a star."

Cassie swallowed. "But maybe I've changed."

"Maybe you have." Gemma's voice was soft. "But maybe you pushed it all away because it hurt too much when your dancing career was cut short. What if you don't take this opportunity and you regret it later?"

Hearing those words made Cassie's chest feel tight. Gemma had been her friend since they were kids. They knew each others' hopes and fears.

"What if I want what you have?" Cassie whispered. "A family. Love. Somewhere I belong?"

"The two aren't incompatible," Gemma pointed out.

"They were for you." Gemma had given it all up, after all. "This band, it was just supposed to be fun. A way to meet people."

Gemma's eyes met hers. "And Pres, wasn't he supposed to be a bit of fun, too?"

"Yes. But everything changed."

"A good man would never hold you back from achieving

your dreams," Gemma told her. "You thought you'd lost them. But maybe you haven't. They're just offering themselves to you in a whole different way."

In a way she didn't want. And she wasn't sure how to navigate. That was the problem. She'd finally found her happy and now it felt like it was all being threatened.

Gemma took her hand, squeezing it. "What is it you want?" she asked. "Isn't that the most important question?"

"I want it all," Cassie murmured.

"Sometimes that's not possible. Sometimes we have to choose. The way I did when Riley and I moved here."

"Do you regret it?" Cassie asked her.

"Not for a second. But I'm not you. And you were always better than me."

"Shut up." Cassie rolled her eyes.

"I'm serious. You have a talent. The trifecta." Gemma grinned. "Isn't that what they trained us for. One door closing and another opening? You just need to work it through. That's all."

"I need to talk to Presley," Cassie murmured, because she didn't want to make this decision alone.

"Yeah you do." Gemma nodded, patting her arm. "That's my girl."

———

"Hey." Presley was standing on her doorstep, leaning against the porch wall. "I got your message. Are you okay?"

She opened the door. She'd asked him to stop by before he picked up Delilah. And yeah, she felt guilty about that because she knew that Delilah would have to wait to see her daddy.

But she couldn't have this conversation in front of the little girl. And she couldn't have it on the phone either.

Most of all she didn't trust Alex not to go shooting his

mouth off in town before she had the chance to talk with Presley. She was pretty sure by the weekend everybody would know that she'd been offered a contract with a new band.

"Thanks for coming by," she said softly. "Come in." She stepped aside so he could walk into her hallway. He gave her a confused look then walked in, pulling her into his arms.

Damn, she didn't know how much she needed that. She rested her head against his chest, loving the feel of his strong arms around her. Squeezing her eyes tightly, she inhaled him in.

"I missed you," she murmured.

"Right back at you." He ran his fingers through her hair. "What's up? I was worried when I got your message."

She took a deep breath, looking up at him. "Alex came to see me at the studio today."

He blinked, surprised. "Alex did? Our Alex? Why?"

"The record label wanted to talk to me. They only had his number. So he rushed over so I could talk to them as quickly as possible."

Presley's eyes caught hers. She could see the concern in them, the confusion as well. "Why did they want to talk to you?" he asked her softly.

She hated this. Hated having to tell him. She wished they'd never offered her the stupid contract. Maybe if it had been a bigger town, or if she knew Alex could keep a secret she never would have had to tell Presley.

No, that was wrong. She loved him. Of course she would have told him regardless.

"They found another band," she told him, her chest so tight it was hard to breathe. "And they want me to be part of it."

His eyes were still on hers. And she watched as he slowly blinked, comprehending the words she'd just told him. "They offered you the gig?" he asked, his voice thick.

"I'm going to turn it down." She'd already told Alex that.

And he'd told her she needed to think about it. Let him get the contract and see what the terms were before rejecting it.

And yeah, she probably could have looked up the switchboard number and called Bryan herself. But she was certain, anyway.

"You didn't turn it down already?" His face was expressionless. She wished she knew what he was thinking.

"No. Mostly because Alex has all the details. But they can't do anything without my say so. I just needed to tell you. Because Alex probably will."

"Okay." He nodded, still betraying no emotion. "Congratulations."

"Why?"

"Because they know a good thing when they see it. I always said you were too good for us."

"Don't be silly. And you're the one who's too good," she told him.

"You're not exactly impartial." He lifted a brow.

"And nor are you." She tried to make herself relax. "So that's it. I just wanted you to know, that's all. Now go see Delilah, I bet she's jumping up and down waiting for you."

"I'll call you tonight," he told her, kissing her softly. "And I'm proud of you. I mean it. You're good at everything you do. You deserve to be recognized."

She looped her arms around his neck, hugging him tight. This was where she belonged. In his arms. Grounded.

In love.

She was doing the right thing, turning it down. She didn't want anything but this.

Now she just had to deal with Alex. But that was a job for tomorrow.

CHAPTER
Twenty-Six

PRESLEY WALKED INTO HIS PARENTS' house, trying to keep his expression neutral. His facial muscles were aching from the effort, the same one he'd made when Cassie had told him about the record label's offer.

He was pleased for her, he was. But that feeling of weirdness he'd had ever since they'd got back from New York had increased. It was a strange feeling. Like he couldn't stand still.

Like his thoughts were itchy in his brain.

"Hi." His mom smiled at him. "How was your day?"

"Yeah, good." They were almost at the end of this project. Another couple of weeks and they'd be ready for all the work to be signed off. He already had his next two customers booked in. There was plenty of work for his business, thanks to their reputation of coming in on budget and mostly on time.

"Mine was good too," his mom said pointedly.

"I'm sorry. My mind's a little full." He offered her a smile. "How was your day, Mom?"

"Still good." She nodded. "Delilah has a spelling list to work on. She keeps tripping up on airplane."

"We'll work on it tonight," he told her. "Where is she?"

"At the studio with your dad. I'll let him know that you're here." She went to reach for her phone.

"It's okay, I'll walk out there." He kissed her cheek and turned to head out the door leading to the backyard. Then he turned back to look at her. "Mom?"

"Yes, honey?"

"I appreciate everything you do to help me. You know that, right?"

"Of course I do. And as I keep telling you, it's not a burden, it's a pleasure."

He blew out a mouthful of air. Because a burden was exactly what he was feeling like.

He'd spent the drive here going over Cassie's words in his mind. She'd been as excited as the rest of them, going to New York. And now she'd been offered the role of a lifetime and she was going to turn it down.

And he couldn't help but feel like it was all his fault. Not just for her wanting to stay here in Hartson's Creek, but for the band not getting a chance in the first place.

If it wasn't for him, he had a feeling the result would have been different.

Yeah, burden. That was the perfect word for it.

When he got to the studio, he could see his dad in the mixing room, Delilah next to him talking animatedly. He knocked on the window and she jumped, her face lighting up as she saw him standing there.

"Daddy!"

His dad stood and smiled at him. And for a minute he got a flashback, to the day of Jade's funeral. His dad had stood beside him, holding his hand.

He was a good man. A strong one. He never faltered.

They walked out of the room and Delilah hugged him. He leaned down, inhaling the smell of her strawberry shampoo. "Hey sweetheart." His voice was gruff.

"Daddy, can we call Cassie? I want her to do my hair."

He cleared his throat. "Another day, okay?"

She nodded, as though she could remember the day they argued. And thank god, he didn't think he could cope with another confrontation like that right now.

"I'm going to say bye to Granny," she said. "And get Lola."

"I'll walk you down," his dad said, opening the door of the studio, so Delilah could walk out. She ran ahead as he and his dad walked out of the door. Pres put his hands in his pockets. It was another glorious day. Not a cloud in the sky.

He wished he could appreciate it.

"Everything okay?" his dad asked.

"Yeah, why?"

"You just sighed."

"Did I?" Pres frowned. Was he going mad now? "Just got a few things on my mind."

"Want to talk about them?"

He shook his head. "I don't want Delilah to hear."

That brought his dad up short. "Is it something serious?"

Delilah had made it to the house and was running into the kitchen, while he and his dad were only halfway there.

"Cassie got a call from the record label. They confirmed they don't want the band, but they do want her."

There it was. He'd let it out. But he didn't feel any better.

"As a solo singer?"

Pres shook his head. "To join the band they've chosen."

"Well that's kind of cool," his dad said. "Isn't it?"

"She says she won't go."

His dad said nothing. They'd stopped walking now, the two of them standing in the middle of the yard. Pres' hands were still in his pockets. His dad turned to look at him.

"Why not?"

Pres swallowed hard. "She says she doesn't want to do it without us."

His dad mused on his words. "Is she afraid you'll break up or something?"

"I don't know. We didn't talk much about it. I stopped at hers on the way here."

"Maybe you need to reassure her. Tell her you'll still be here," his dad said. "If that's what you want, I mean."

Pres pulled one hand out of his pocket and ran it through his hair. Truth was, he didn't know what he wanted.

Apart from time to stop.

"Yeah, I'll tell her." But he still didn't feel any better. "Did you ever feel…" he trailed off, mostly because he couldn't put into words what he was feeling right now. Whatever it was, it wasn't good.

He knew that much.

"Feel what?" his dad asked.

"I don't know. Like you've done everything wrong. Like you're holding everybody back. I just think that if it wasn't for me it would all be different."

There was a concerned look on his dad's face. And now he felt more guilty than ever.

"Never mind. It doesn't matter," Pres told him. "I'm just being stupid. I'm tired, it's been a long day. Tomorrow will be better."

"You're not holding anybody back," his dad told him. "You're being you. Being a good dad, a good son." He smiled. "Probably a good boyfriend, though I'd have to ask Cassie about that."

"Thanks." He gave him the tightest of smiles. He wasn't looking for praise. God knew he didn't feel like he deserved it.

He wasn't sure what he was looking for. Maybe some clarity.

Delilah ran out into the backyard, her school bag on her back, Lola in her arms. Behind her, his mom walked out, smiling as she saw him standing with his dad on the grass.

"Do me a favor," Pres said. "Forget I said anything, okay? I know Mom worries about me and she doesn't need to."

His dad nodded. "We both worry about you, but that's what parents do. It's what you'll do with Delilah when you can't bandage up every cut or solve every problem. But I hear you. This is between you and me."

"Thanks, Dad." He forced a smile onto his face because Delilah didn't need her dad to be morose for the evening. "Come on, kid," he called out. "Let's go home and grab some food."

―――――

"Daddy," Delilah said that night, as he sat on the side of her bed, *Goodnight Moon* in his hands.

"Yeah?"

"Do you think Mom is on the moon?"

He blinked at her unexpected question. "What makes you ask that?" he asked.

"Grannie said she was up in the sky."

His throat thickened. "Yeah, I guess she is. Finding a little comfy place to look down on you."

Delilah nodded, turning onto her side. "She loves me."

"Yes she does, sweetheart."

"And you do too."

"Yep." He leaned forward to kiss her cheek. She was still warm from her shower, her skin plump and smooth. "More than anything."

"And Cassie loves me."

He blew out a mouthful of air. "Yeah."

"And we love Cassie."

Okay, he needed this to stop. Because on top of everything else, he didn't need Jade and Cassie in his brain at the same time.

"Good night," he whispered.

"'Night, Daddy."

He stood and walked over to the door, turning the light out. But for a moment he stayed in the doorway of Delilah's room. Just stood and watched her as she curled a little more, clutching onto Lola the Giraffe.

It seemed like a lifetime had passed since she'd lost the damn thing. Since Cassie had brought Lola over and they'd kissed in the hallway.

Maybe he should have stopped it then. Should have known he was too much of a damn weight for her.

He ran his hands through his hair and stepped out of Delilah's bedroom, softly closing the door.

When he got down to the living room he picked up his phone. Because he needed to stop thinking about this. Needed to talk to her. Needed to show her he wasn't a burden.

Needed her to think about herself because he wasn't her burden to carry.

Hey, are you around? – Pres x

He sent the message. His head was hurting. Like somebody was hammering at it from the inside.

Hi. Yeah. Want me to call? – Cassie x

I need to talk to you. To see you. I'm gonna ask Marley if he can come watch Delilah. – Pres x

. . .

You've got me worried now. Are you sure you're okay? –
Cassie x

I'm sure. Don't worry. I just need to see your beautiful face.
Pres x

———

It was half an hour before the Beast's headlights swept across her driveway. She walked to the front door, opening it, a half-smile pulling at her lips.

Pres climbed out of the cab, his long legs striding across the driveway. He hadn't seen her at the front door yet – he was looking at the ground, as though lost in his thoughts.

Then he looked up and her heart missed a beat. Because he looked exhausted. More than exhausted.

"Are you sure you should be driving like that?" she asked him.

He looked up, almost surprised to see her, even though he was at her house. "Hey." He gave her the softest of smiles.

"Come in. Let me make you a coffee." She slid her hand into his. He tightened his fingers around her, like he was afraid she was going to pull away.

They walked together down the hallway, still holding hands. She could feel the bulk of his body behind hers. Could hear the soft cadence of his breath.

"You have to go."

She stopped dead in the doorway to the kitchen and turned around to look at him. "What?"

"To New York. You have to go."

Oh. So this was what it was about. He was worried about her leaving, just like she'd thought he might be. She wasn't sure whether to be relieved or annoyed.

"I'm not going. I told you that. I want to be here."
With you.

He shook his head, his gaze not quite meeting hers. "I don't want you to make a decision you're going to regret."

Cassie frowned. "I'm not going to regret it. I love living here. I love my job. I love the band. I love spending time with you and Delilah." She took a deep breath. "I love you."

It was like her words had knives attached to them. He looked like he was in pain. "Cassie…"

"You don't have to say it," she told him. "I know it's soon. And you've been through so much."

"Of course I can say it." He reached for her, cupping her face. "I love you. I love you with everything I've got. And that's why you have to do this."

She blinked. "I don't understand."

"I can't live life wondering if I'm the one who held you back. Wondering if you're thinking about what could have been. I can't have you resent me."

"I don't resent you," she told him. "I never would."

He blew out a mouthful of air. "I need you to go."

"No." Her bottom lip was wobbling. Damn, she sounded like a child. Like Delilah. "I don't want to. I'm staying here."

"For me. Go for me." His eyes caught hers. "Go and see if it's what you want. If it is, then we'll work through it together. And if it isn't, I'll be here. Waiting for you. I'm not going anywhere."

Her eyes filled with tears. "I can't ask you to wait."

"You're not asking. I'm asking. I'm fucking begging."

"What if I don't want to go?" she asked. A hot tear ran down her cheek. She wiped it away with the back of her hand. "You can't make me."

He stepped forward, wrapping her in his arms. And the tears were flowing more now. Hot and heavy down her cheeks, dripping onto his t-shirt.

"Don't cry," he begged hoarsely. "I don't want you to cry. I want you to have it all. Everything."

And that was how much he loved her.

She could feel it in the way he was holding her, his arms tight, his hands splayed against her back. He was her rock, her anchor.

But she felt like she was the storm.

"I never wanted this," she told him.

"I know. You never asked for it either. And maybe you'll go and hate it." He pressed his lips against her hair. "And that's okay. Because you'll know. For sure."

She lifted her face so she could look at him. He winced at the tears still flowing.

"And if I don't go?"

He squeezed his eyes shut for a moment. And that's when she knew. This wasn't about her, it was about him. About his loss. His fears.

He blamed himself for Jade's death. He felt like he held her back.

That if he'd let her go when she needed to, she'd still be alive.

When he opened his eyes, she could see the strength in them. The certainty.

He'd made his mind up. He needed her to do this.

She loved him so much. The thought of leaving him, potentially forever, felt like a knife to her soul. She wanted this. She wanted him.

But she had no idea how to convince him.

"I'll think about it," she whispered.

"Okay." He nodded. "That's all I ask."

No, he was asking for more than that. He was asking her to accept his sacrifice as well as his love.

And she wasn't sure she could do that.

CHAPTER
Twenty~Seven

"IT SOUNDS like he wants you to have a Rumspringa," Gemma said the next day. She'd taken one look at Cassie's face when she'd arrived and had dragged her out for a coffee. Neither of them had classes until ten, so they had time.

"What's a Rumspringa?" Cassie asked, frowning. She'd told Gemma everything and her friend had listened to every word, her face full of compassion.

"It's an Amish term," Gemma told her. "When the children are in their late teenage years, they're given some leeway to get all those urges and behaviors out of their systems. It's like 'go do what you need to do, kid, and if you want, come back and we'll be waiting for you'."

"I'm not exactly a kid," Cassie pointed out.

"No, but it's the same idea. Through experience they probably learned that it was better than the kids rebelling and leaving the faith forever. This way when they come back they really know that they want this life."

Cassie blew out a mouthful of air. She'd spent most of the night crying after Presley had left. Mostly because she hated the way he'd spoken, the things he'd said.

Maybe even part of her hated that he made some kind of warped sense.

"I love him."

"I know you do."

"He told me he loved me last night." And that made her want to start crying again. It was so bittersweet, hearing him say those words, then urging her to leave him.

"I think it's romantic," Gemma said, shrugging her shoulders. "He'll wait for you as long as it takes."

"He didn't say as long as it takes."

"But I bet that's what he meant. The man has it bad for you. You only have to see him looking at you to know it. Every time you're on the stage together it's like nobody else there."

"I don't want to sing with anybody else," Cassie said. "I don't want to go back to New York."

Gemma gave her the softest of smiles. "I know."

"But if I don't go will he keep wondering? Thinking that I might be settling for him?"

"Maybe," Gemma said. "I guess that's the risk you take."

"You're not helping." Cassie screwed up her face. "I just don't know what to do."

"You could make a pros and cons list," Gemma suggested.

"That's so clinical. Pros – I make Presley happy. Cons – I break my own heart."

"Oh sweetie." Gemma reached for her hand, just as the diner door opened.

Cassie's heart dropped when she saw Maddie walk in. As much as she admired the woman, she didn't need Presley's mom to see her upset like this.

"Hi," Maddie said, smiling as she walked over to them. The smile slipped when she saw the expression on Cassie's face. "Is everything okay?"

Cassie swallowed hard. "Everything is fine."

Maddie looked at her again, pulling her lip between her teeth. "I'll leave you to it."

And now Cassie felt worse. "Sorry. Sit down. We're not staying long. I have a class at ten."

"You sure? I only popped in to get a coffee myself," Maddie told them.

"Of course. Sit." Cassie pointed at the leather covered bench seat next to her. "It's lovely to see you."

"Okay then." She sat and looked at Cassie. "Is it something with Presley? Because he looked like hell yesterday."

Cassie winced. She hated that.

"Want me to tell her?" Gemma asked. Cassie nodded, mostly because she wasn't sure she could say it all again.

Not without crying. And Maddie *really* didn't need to see that.

Gemma looked at Maddie, her voice fast as she explained the call Cassie received yesterday, and Presley's response. Maddie listened quietly, nodding in the right places, her face showing just how worried she was about them both.

"That sounds like my son," she said softly. "He gets the idiocy from his father."

Cassie tried – and failed – to smile.

"He's told you about Jade, right?" Maddie asked her. Cassie nodded. "So I guess you know what a mess he was after she died."

"I have some idea. But I wasn't there. It must have been horrible to watch him go through it."

Maddie nodded. "I barely slept for weeks worrying about him. We did everything we could, but you know Presley. He hates accepting help. He's my son and I love him more than anything, but he's stubborn. Again, just like his dad."

"Like all men," Gemma pointed out.

Maddie nodded. "Never a truer word said." She looked at Cassie again. "What are you going to do?"

"I don't know," Cassie admitted. "I can't see a right decision."

"Sometimes there isn't one. Just a least worst one," Maddie said. "I don't know if it helps, but I can tell you my son loves you. I see it in his eyes every time he talks about you. Every time you're around him."

"See?" Gemma gave Cassie a pointed look. "I just said the same thing. He said he'd wait and he will."

"Are you afraid you'll like being part of the new band?" Maddie asked her. "That you won't want to come back."

"No. Not at all." Cassie shook her head. She'd barely thought about it, to be honest. She was too focused on her own pain. On Presley's.

She dropped her face into her hands. "I don't know what to do," she muttered. She needed to get control of herself. She had a class to teach in thirty minutes. She felt Maddie's soft hand rubbing her back.

Oh how she wished she had a mom like her. Somebody who cared.

Somebody who didn't judge her or demand that she do whatever shone the best light on her like her mom.

"What would you do?" she asked Maddie. "If you were in my position?"

Maddie smiled softly at her. "Honestly?"

Cassie nodded. She needed honesty. She needed insight.

She needed Presley.

"I'd go. Because I know my son. I think he needs this. To sacrifice himself. To give you the opportunity he never gave Jade. And I think it's the only way he'll really know that this isn't history repeating itself."

Cassie's chest tightened. Mostly because the truth in Maddie's words shone through.

"Well, I guess I'll go to New York," she whispered. "Because I love him, and if that's what it takes for me to prove it, then I'll do it. But I'll be back. I promise you that."

Maddie gave her the softest of smiles. "I hope so."

———

"Two days," she told him. "They want me there in two days." She'd already spoken to Gemma, who'd found a teacher from a school a few towns over to sub in for the short term. In the longer term, she'd said she'd recruit somebody full time.

And then Cassie had told her there would be no longer time and she'd cried again.

"Okay." He gave her the sweetest of smiles. "That's good, right? Like ripping the bandage off?"

"Not really." She looked him in the eye. "Just ask me to stay and I will."

He cupped her face, and gave her that sweet smile again. "I know you would. But I can't. You understand why, right?"

"I do." But she didn't like it. Not one bit. "What if I don't want to sing in the band?"

"Then you come home."

"What if I know right now that I don't want to?" This was stupid, she knew it. She was going around in circles. All these things she'd been thinking about when she should be sleeping.

Presley swallowed. He'd stopped over to her place after work again. He could stay longer this time – his mom had called and told him she knew everything. On the plus side, she'd also offered to have Delilah stay for dinner.

Which gave them a few hours. Together.

And they both needed that.

"I don't know," he admitted. "I don't know what I'd do if you said that. And I don't want you to feel like I'm forcing you to go. But I also know that I'd feel guilty if you don't." He reached for her, sliding his fingers into hers. "There's no right answer here. I'm just trying to work out the best thing to do. For us all."

"You're so much like your mom."

He smiled. "Most people say I'm like my dad."

"You're that too. The best of both of them." She squeezed his fingers with hers. "Listen, can you do me one favor?"

"Just say it."

"We have three hours tonight, right?"

"Yeah." He nodded.

"And tomorrow I'm going to have to pack. And I think I'm going to need to do it alone."

"Understood." And dammit he did look like he was understanding. Why did he have to be so sweet?

It was like having your heart broken by a cute puppy. You wanted to be angry with him but you couldn't.

She loved him too much.

"How about you come for dinner with me and Delilah before you start packing?" he asked. "I'll finish early. Pick her up from school."

Her eyes met his. "Are you sure you're okay with me seeing her?"

"Why wouldn't I be?"

"Because I'm leaving. And that could upset her."

He traced her lips with his finger. "I've explained it to her. And she's more annoyed that you won't be teaching her dance class than anything else."

Cassie sniffed. "I'm going to miss her."

"I know. And we're going to miss you. But give it a chance. Throw yourself into it. See if you like it. And don't worry about us, we'll be just fine."

"You know I'm going to call you every night, right?"

He smiled. "I'm good with that."

"And if you change your mind…" she trailed off because that wasn't fair. She'd already asked him what he'd do if she stayed.

She knew he'd welcome her back. That's what he did. But maybe she had something to prove. To him.

She wanted him to know how much she cared. How much she loved him.

"We now have two hours and forty five minutes," she said, because yeah, she was counting. "Can we spend them in bed. Not talking about any of this?"

His eyes crinkled as he nodded. "I can't think of anywhere else I'd rather be."

"Good." She turned and started to run up her stairs. "Catch me if you can."

———

"I don't want you to go," Delilah sobbed as Cassie hugged her goodbye. They'd eaten dinner – pasta, again because he hadn't had much time after picking Delilah up from school – and then Cassie had agreed to give Delilah her bath.

He'd let them be together, despite the fact that he wanted to spend every single moment with her before she caught the plane in the morning.

And now Delilah was in her pajamas, clinging to Cassie's legs, tears running down her face.

Shit. He really thought he'd explained it to her. His eyes caught Cassie's and she looked bereft.

When was he going to stop fucking things up?

"Come here," he murmured, walking over to them. He lifted Delilah in one arm, then put the other around Cassie. And for a moment it was one, long moment of peace.

But as soon as he let them go, it was gone. Replaced by an ache in his chest he didn't know what to do with.

One thing he was sure of, he was doing the right thing. He couldn't look at the woman he loved every day and not know that she'd chosen it with her full heart.

"Wanna come down with me and wave goodbye to Cassie?" he asked his daughter. She nodded, and put her arms tight around his neck.

"I'll be back in a few weeks," Cassie told her. She'd gotten the schedule for rehearsals. Two weeks and then they had a short break before they were traveling to Hawaii to record some songs.

They'd talked about how to deal with Delilah. His only request had been that Cassie didn't make promises she couldn't keep. He trusted her to keep this one.

"Will you call me?" Delilah asked, turning her head against Presley's shoulder.

"Of course."

"Every night."

Cassie's eyes met Presley's. It was time for him to step in.

"Come on now," Presley said. "She can't call you every night."

"Every morning, then," Delilah said stubbornly.

Presley kissed his daughter's head. "She'll call when she can, okay."

His eyes met Cassie's again. "Let's head down, I know you have a lot to do tonight." She nodded, saying nothing, and walked ahead of him down the stairs.

When they got to the bottom, Cassie stopped for a moment. Looking at the hallway wall. Then she looked at him and he knew what she was thinking.

That wall held a lot of memories. The first place they'd kissed. The wall they'd had sex against.

His throat felt tight as he gently lowered Delilah to the floor. She ran at Cassie's legs again, hugging them tight.

"I love you," Delilah whispered against Cassie's jeans.

"Oh sweetie, I love you." Cassie dropped to her haunches, hugging Delilah tight. She whispered in Delilah's ear and she nodded.

When she stood, she looked at him and Pres realized this was it.

And he wasn't sure he could breathe.

This was the right thing to do, he reminded himself. He

wasn't making the same mistakes. He was being a good partner. A good man.

It was the right fucking thing.

So why did every part of him ache?

"Goodbye," she said softly, her lips parting as she stared at him.

And he strode over to her, pulling her close against him. He kissed the top of her head, her cheek, her lips.

Trying to memorize the way she felt. The way she smelled. The way her body molded against his.

Fuck he was being dramatic. She'd be back. Yeah, she would.

Right?

"I'll be right here," he whispered. To her. To him. To Delilah. "Whenever you need me, whatever you need. You call, okay?"

"Okay." Cassie nodded. He could tell she was trying to keep her emotions in control. Dammit he was, too.

"I'm just going to go," she said, her voice low.

"Okay."

She hitched her purse over her shoulder and took one long last look at the both of them, then turned and walked down the hallway, pulling open the door.

And as she stepped through it, Delilah let out a long wail.

Damn if his heart didn't do the same thing.

CHAPTER
Twenty~Eight

"FUCK IT." Presley shook his head, looking up at the gunmetal gray sky. The downpour was showing no signs of stopping, and they'd had to halt their work on the exterior of the house.

And they were so close. If it wasn't for this storm that had been raging all afternoon, they'd have finished by tomorrow.

"It's just some rain," Marley said, his voice even. "It happens."

"I know that." Pres scowled at him. "But it's the fucking summer. Why now?" And why did his heart ache looking at it? If it was any other day, he'd be driving to the dance school and telling Cassie he was taking her home.

But she wasn't here.

"Because the world hates you. There, does that help?" Marley asked him. "Do you feel better now? It's raining because everything is about you."

"Shut the hell up." Presley shook his head. "I'm just trying to make us a profit here."

"No you're not. You're trying to find something – or someone – to blame for your bad mood. When you know you're the one that caused it."

Pres blinked. "What did you say?"

Marley caught his eye. His usually easy-going brother looked angry. Like really angry. "You think you're the only one who's suffered a loss?" Marley asked.

"Where did that come from?"

Marley shook his head. "It doesn't matter. Just go shout at the clouds again."

"Of course it matters," Pres said, more annoyed than anything else. His brother was supposed to be on his side, not making him feel worse. "What loss have you suffered?"

"I said it doesn't matter." Marley's voice was more forceful this time. "And at least I can say I'm not the author of my own fucking misery."

Pres' mouth was dry. He'd spent the last two days wanting to punch something. And right now his brother's face was in the firing line. He turned away, gritting his teeth, because he was a grown man.

And grown men didn't fight.

Plus the way he felt right now, any fight he was involved in would end up with someone in the hospital.

Marley sighed. "Come on, man, you've gotta get out of this funk. You're the one who told her to go to New York."

"I know that." Pres gritted his teeth.

He could hear Marley shuffling his feet. They were in the garage of the house, sheltering from the rain. Trying to see if it was going to stop in time for them to at least finish the work on the roof.

"Have you heard from her?" Marley asked.

"Yep." Pres turned around. Marley was at the entrance to the garage. The overhead door was open, and he was leaning against the wall, looking out at the rain.

"She okay?"

"I think so. She was rushing to another meeting when she called. They're having a lot of them. Trying to get them to bond."

"Did she say if she's staying?"

"Nope."

Marley shook his head. "You're a fucking idiot."

"Thanks, man." Pres let out a low breath.

"I mean it. What was sending her away all about? What kind of stupid mother fucker tells the woman he loves to leave?"

"I didn't tell her to leave," he said. "I just refused to stand in her way."

"Not the way I heard it." Marley shrugged. "From the way Mom tells it, you pretty much said that unless she went to New York you'd never be completely sure about you two."

"I never said that." Pres frowned. "That's definitely not what I said."

"Then what did you say?"

He swallowed. He didn't want to think about this. He didn't want to think about anything. For the past two days he'd lived for messages and voicemails from Cassie. They'd managed one broken conversation last night when she was heading out to a bar to meet the other band members.

"I said she should try it. That's all."

Marley turned his body to look at him head on. "Because nothing says I love you like 'fuck off to another state'."

"You know why I did it." Pres was getting annoyed again. Not that it took much. He felt like a tinder-dry pile of sticks. The merest spark made him want to explode.

"Jade was going to go anyway," Marley said. "You and I both know that. It was never a match made in fucking heaven. You got married because she was pregnant. And she was never the settling down type."

Pres inhaled sharply. "I don't want to talk about her."

"I know you don't want to," Marley said carefully. "But don't you think you should? Because I don't know if anybody else has pointed it out to you yet, but Cassie isn't Jade."

"Don't you think I know that?" Pres shook his head.

"I think you know it here," Marley said, pointing at his own head. "But not here." He pressed his palms against his chest. "Not where it matters. Maybe in here you're thinking that if you play things differently, everything will turn out okay."

"Won't it?" Pres asked, his voice low. It felt like he was being hollowed out. Emptied.

"No. Because Cassie isn't Jade. She doesn't need her freedom or her youth or whatever the fuck Jade was chasing. She needs you. You and Delilah."

"She has us. She knows that. I made sure she knew it." Pres tried to center himself. It felt like his whole world was tipped at an angle. Making him feel dizzy as fuck. "I told her I'm not going anywhere. And I'm not."

"But maybe that's not what she needed," Marley said softly. "Maybe she needed you to fight for her."

His mouth felt dry. "No," he said. "That's not what she needed. I tried that once. A woman ended up dead."

"Your wife died," Marley corrected him. "And not because of you. Because of an idiot who'd been drinking too much and made the stupid decision to get into his truck. It wasn't your fault. You know that." Then he shook his head. "Whatever. Believe what you want. I was right all along, you're a fucking idiot."

"Thanks," Pres said. "It's good to know you're on my side."

———

"Lola's sad," Delilah whispered to him that night as he sat on her bed. She clutched her giraffe tightly to her chest.

"She is?" Pres asked. "Why?"

"Because Cassie wasn't at dance today."

He swallowed hard. "Yeah, I can see why that would make her sad."

"She wants to talk to Cassie," Delilah told him. "Like she promised."

He blew out a mouthful of air. "Cassie's going to call on Saturday. You can both talk to her then."

Delilah clutched Lola tighter. "She can't wait that long."

He gave her the tightest of smiles. "It'll be here before you know it," he said softly.

"But what if she's busy on Saturday? Can we call her now?" Delilah looked at him hopefully.

He frowned, trying to think of the right thing to do here. He didn't want Delilah to start demanding to talk to Cassie whenever she wanted. He knew that Cassie was busy. She sounded tired whenever he spoke to her.

And most evenings this week she had things scheduled.

"I'll see if we can call her tomorrow night," he promised.

"But Daddy…"

"Tomorrow." He caught her eye, trying to send her a subliminal message. Please don't create a scene. He wasn't sure he could cope with it. Not with Marley's accusations from earlier still swirling through his head.

"Okay." Delilah nodded. "Tomorrow."

He leaned forward to kiss her. "Scoot down, I'll tuck you in." And for once, she did as she was told. He kissed her once more and then stood, walking over to turn out her light.

"Daddy?"

"Yes, sweetheart."

"If you left me too, who would look after me?"

His hand froze against the light switch. "I'm not going anywhere."

Delilah said nothing for a minute. "Granny would look after us," she whispered to Lola. "If Daddy is sent away too."

Ah fuck it. He walked back to her bed. "I need you to listen to me. I'm not going *anywhere*." His voice was firm. "I'm right here. With you. And this is where I'll always be."

"Even when I'm grown up?"

He nodded. "Yeah. My mom and dad are still here for me, aren't they? Granny and Gramps I mean."

"Yes." Her voice was small.

He pulled her into his arms, hugging her tight. "Baby, I'm not going anywhere," he promised.

"I miss Cassie," she mumbled against his chest.

"I do too." He stroked her hair. "So much."

"Then why don't you tell her to come home?" Delilah looked up at him, her eyes shining. "Tell her we miss her and that she needs to come home right now."

He opened his mouth to explain it to her. To tell her that they all needed this.

But Delilah didn't. She didn't need this at all. He could tell that from the expression on her face. All she knew was that people kept leaving and she had no idea why.

"Try to get some sleep," he whispered. "It's late."

She nodded against his chest.

He lay her back down, then sat with her until her breathing evened out and she softly descended into oblivion. Her expression was peaceful at last, as he tiptoed out of her bedroom.

He wished it was that easy for him to sleep.

But then maybe it shouldn't be.

Because Marley was right. He was a fucking idiot.

CHAPTER
Twenty~Nine

"DADDY, WHAT'S HAPPENING?" Delilah asked. She frowned as she looked around. "Where am I?"

"You're in the car. Go back to sleep, it's still night time."

She was quiet for a moment, looking round. She was in the backseat of the Beast, in her car seat. He'd carried her out there at four in the morning, covering her with a blanket while she slept.

"Where are we going?" she asked him.

"New York." They were on the highway, about an hour into the trip. He'd packed a bag for Delilah, as well as himself.

The plan had been to leave at first light. But by four AM he was wide awake. Couldn't stop thinking about her.

And yes, this was the stupidest, most idiotic thing he'd ever done. But driving to her felt good, it felt right.

Like he was waking up after a bad dream.

She'd messaged him last night. To tell him she couldn't call because she was in another stupid meeting, but that she missed him.

And that it was raining in New York and she wished he was there to pick her up.

The words had felt like a fist on his chest. But not a painful one. It was like somebody was giving him CPR, trying to make his heart beat again, because he'd thought exactly the same thing yesterday.

It was raining. And she needed him.

And he wasn't there.

He'd sent her back a message, telling her he wished he was there, too. But she hadn't replied before he'd headed to bed.

He'd showered. Put on a pair of shorts and he'd stared at himself in the bathroom mirror.

And that's when he'd realized that he couldn't live one more day without seeing her.

It sounded dramatic. And completely unlike him. That was the stupid part. She didn't know he was coming. And there was a tiny part of his heart that was worrying this would be a mistake. That he'd turn up and she'd tell him that she'd decided to stay with the band. That she wanted that life.

That she'd break his heart – no, that wasn't right. That he'd break his own heart in front of his kid.

But he couldn't leave Delilah behind. Not after last night. He'd promised her that he wouldn't leave her and he couldn't. Not right now, when she was feeling tender about Cassie's departure. If he was going to New York, then Delilah was too.

Yeah, he was an idiot. But at least it was for a good reason this time.

Delilah dozed off again for another hour, only waking up once the sun had fully risen. "Are we there yet?" she asked him.

"Another hour." Maybe more. They were getting closer to the city but the roads were gridlocked. He'd hit rush hour. But luckily Delilah didn't know what an hour was and looked mollified by his answer.

A while later they stopped at a roadside café, and he

ordered them both breakfast. Delilah had wolfed down the pancakes, and he'd managed most of his own, plus two mugs of coffee which had provided enough of a caffeine injection to see him through the next few hours.

After that? Who knew. He'd have to find them a hotel room, that was for sure. And then there was Cassie.

Could he prove that he wanted her with him? That his need to be with her overrode his need for her to prove her love to him.

Because that's what he'd been doing. He could see it clearly now. All those scars he had left over from Jade had turned out to still be wounds. Old, yeah, but never fully healed. And it had only taken this for them to be torn open all over again. Sore and bleeding.

He'd reacted to the pain, then put a little frosting on it to make it look like he was being self sacrificing. But this need for Cassie to go to New York? Marley was right, it was all about *him.*

Redemption didn't come in pretty little ribbons. It came with the hard work, he knew that now. It came with understanding that nobody was perfect. Nobody was blame free. You made mistakes, you tried to atone for them, and you moved on. Hopefully stronger, hopefully wiser.

But you had to move on. He couldn't keep living in a past where he felt guilty for everything. It was no good for him, let alone for Delilah. Or Cassie.

"Okay," he said, putting his now-empty mug down and giving his kid the biggest smile. "Ready to head to New York?"

"Yup." Delilah nodded her head, her eyes lighting up like a Christmas tree. She was loving this adventure. Maybe they needed to do more of this. Be spontaneous. Go out and enjoy life.

He'd spent so long trying to be the perfect parent to her, he'd forgotten about fun.

"Okay, but first we need to go brush our teeth." Okay, maybe somewhere in the fun, he'd add a little bit of responsibility, too.

"Do we have to?" Delilah frowned.

"Do you want people in New York to smell our breath and think we stink?" he asked her.

She tipped her head to the side. "Your breath smells. Mine doesn't."

"That's because you can't smell your own." He leaned forward and breathed in, then made a face. "Damn, that smells like the farts from a dead dog."

Delilah laughed. "It doesn't."

"It won't when they're all clean. Come on, the quicker we do it, the faster we'll make it to the city."

She stood at lightning speed. "What are we waiting for?" she asked. "Come on, let's go brush our teeth."

———

The closer they got to the city, the more his stomach contracted. Why hadn't he spent the time driving thinking about what he was going to say to her?

As they drove through the tunnel and onto Manhattan itself, Delilah had her face pressed against the window, silent as she took in the sights and sounds of New York City.

For a moment she reminded him of Alex and his awe at New York City looking exactly like it did in the movies.

Whatever happened, he promised himself he'd spend a couple of days with her here. Ignoring the fact that the construction site needed him and Delilah should be in school and every other thought that tried to tell him he was being a bad father with this impromptu trip.

They needed this. His daughter needed him. Not as a burden, but as a little girl who loved her daddy.

And damn, he loved her too, so much.

"Where's Cassie?" Delilah asked as they crawled along Fifth Avenue.

"She's staying at a hotel near here. I just need to find somewhere to park."

"Where?" Delilah asked. "Where do you park?"

That was a good question.

"I'll try the hotel lot," he told her. That's where he'd parked last time. And it had been a squeeze because parking spaces in Manhattan weren't built for trucks like the Beast.

Luckily, there was a space. He ignored the large signs telling him he'd be paying fifty dollars for the luxury of having to wriggle his damn body through the smallest gap in his door because he had to park against a Porsche.

By the time he'd managed to get Delilah out, he'd broken a sweat. He caught a glimpse of himself in the side mirror and winced. Damn, he needed a shower. And a good night's sleep.

Cassie would probably take one look at him and run away.

He clicked the lock on his keys and reached for Delilah's hand.

"You don't let go, okay? It's real busy here and there are a lot of people. We stick together."

"Like glue." She nodded.

"Exactly." Even walking across the lot was a lesson in dodging injury. They narrowly avoided being flattened by a Toyota, then had to jump out of the way of a motorcycle that looked like it was trying to break the land speed record.

Pres sighed and lifted Delilah into his arms. He could be quicker this way. They walked through the rotating door into the hotel lobby, and Delilah was twisting in his arms to try to take everything in. In the end he put her back down on the floor as holding her was too much like trying to wrangle a wet alligator.

"Is she here?" Delilah asked, pulling at his hand. "Where is she?"

"I don't know. I'll ask at the desk." He swallowed hard. "Listen, she's not expecting us, so I'll need to explain a few things."

"Like what?"

Like what an idiot I've been. "I don't know. She might be surprised is all."

"But she'll be happy too, right?"

"Yeah. I hope so." Fuck, he really hoped so. Was he making another mistake? He had a feeling that only time would tell him the answer to that.

"Can I help you?" the receptionist asked when they'd finally made it to the front of a long line of guests trying to check out.

"Uh yeah. I'm looking for Cassie Simons. Room seven eight one. Could you call up and let her know I'm here?" He'd thought about calling her himself, but he wanted to give her time to compose herself.

"Sure. One moment." The receptionist lifted the phone receiver to her ear and pressed some buttons. A minute later she gave him an apologetic smile. "I'm afraid she's not there."

"Do you know where she is?" What a stupid fucking question. This hotel had at least five hundred guests. They didn't exactly put trackers on people.

"I'm afraid not. Would you like to leave a message?"

"No, it's fine. I'll call her. Thank you."

"Where is she?" Delilah asked, as they walked away from the desk.

"I don't know. Maybe she already left for the day."

"To where? A dance school?"

"She's not at a dance school, remember?" he told her. "She's singing."

"But not with you."

"No." He gave her a tight smile.

"But she likes singing with you, doesn't she?"

"Yeah, she does. Why don't you sit here and I'll call her." He pointed at an empty leather bucket seat. Delilah jumped into it, twisting herself around until she was sitting upright, her legs dangling only halfway to the floor.

Pres hit Cassie's number and waited for the call to connect. And of course it went to voicemail.

Damn. Was he doing the right thing? He hoped so – there was no way he was driving back to Hartson's Creek now.

Then his phone pinged with a message from her and his heart did a leap.

Sorry – just setting up to try out a new song. Can I call you in a few minutes? Love you – C xx

No problem. Just wanted to wish you a good day. Love you more. – Presley xx

"Didn't she answer?" Delilah asked, her eyes catching his. His breath caught at the trust in them. She believed he could make everything right.

"No, but I know where she is. Let's go find her."

"Okay!" Delilah grinned. "I love this adventure."

———

"Cassie?" Cho, Bryan's assistant whispered to her. "There's a little problem in the lobby."

Cassie looked at Cho. She really liked the woman. Bryan, not so much, but you had to take the rough with the smooth.

"Can it wait?" Cassie asked. "I just need to make a phone call." She was desperate to talk to Presley. Yes, they'd spoken last night, but when he'd told her about Delilah missing her and wanting to talk it had made her heart clench.

Was it possible to feel this desperately homesick for a place that's only been your home for a few months? She hadn't thought so, but then she hadn't lived in Hartson's Creek before.

Home hadn't had Presley and Delilah in it before, either. She had a little framed photo of them beside her hotel room bed. Gemma had given it to her. She'd taken it one day without Presley knowing. He was holding Delilah in his arms and Delilah was holding a bag of rainbow colored cotton candy she'd fallen in love with. And they both had their head tipped back as they laughed uproariously at something.

She couldn't remember what they were laughing at, but the photograph brought her such joy. Peace, too.

Like her anchor was still there. Just in another state, waiting for her.

"Five minutes and we're going again," Bryan shouted out. Every day so far had been like this. Rehearsals in the morning, meetings in the afternoon and evening. They'd been styled to within an inch of their lives, and they'd already had a photoshoot of 'the band', even though they didn't feel like one.

And all through it, she was just going through the motions. For him.

Because Presley needed this. And she'd do whatever it took.

Cho gave her a tight smile. "I'll tell them to come back later."

"Who is it?" Cassie asked.

Cho glanced at Bryan then leaned forward, keeping her voice low enough for only Cassie to hear. "It's one of the people from the band you used to be in."

"Did he give you a name?" she asked, pushing down the

feeling of excitement. Because there was a ninety-nine point nine percent chance it was Alex, trying to get in on things.

"No, but he has a little girl with him."

Her heart just about stopped. "Does she look about six?" Cassie asked.

"I don't know. It's a kid." Cho wrinkled her nose. "I don't have any. I'm bad at ages."

But Cassie didn't need the answer. She knew. And her heart knew, too. "I'm going now," she said. "If Bryan comes looking for me, tell him I'm taking a bathroom break."

Cho glanced from the corner of her eye to where Bryan and the bassist were having a heated discussion. "Um, he wants you to start again in five minutes."

"I know. But this can't wait."

Cassie's heart was hammering against her chest as she ran down the hallway, punching her finger impatiently against the elevator button. He was here. Presley was here. And so was Delilah. She needed to get down there now.

When the elevator arrived she stepped inside, her heart dropping when she realized it was going up, not down. People pushed past her as they exited on the next floor, and she leaned forward to press the ground floor button.

And still it went up.

"Dammit."

An elderly woman lifted a brow at her. "Is there a problem?"

Cassie swallowed hard. This building had about thirty floors. And the elevators were constantly busy. Should she get out and hope another elevator came along that happened to be going down? Or just stay in this one and hope for the best.

"My boyfriend's downstairs waiting for me," Cassie said. "I haven't seen him in a week."

The woman smiled. "I remember my husband being away in the Army for years."

Cassie grimaced. "I'm sorry. That must've been hard. I know a week isn't anything but…"

"But you're in love with him."

Cassie nodded. She was trying not to cry.

"Okay, everybody get out," the woman said, producing a little key from her pocket. "Penthouse owner's perks," she told Cassie. "We're heading right down to the lobby."

There was some grumbling as the elevator doors opened, but everybody did as the woman said. She slotted the key into the lock that Cassie hadn't even noticed above the buttons and pressed the button for the lobby.

And to her amazement, the elevator went straight down.

"I'm only supposed to use it in emergencies," the woman confessed. "But I figure love is always an emergency."

"Thank you." Cassie leaned forward and hugged her. "Thank you for helping me."

"To be honest," the woman told her, "it's made my day."

As soon as the doors to the lobby opened, Cassie ran onto the marble tiled floor, scanning the lobby for the two people that mattered most to her.

And then she saw them. Standing by an oversized plant. Delilah was pointing at something in the plant pot and Presley was nodding.

As though he could sense her standing there, he slowly looked up. His eyes caught hers, and even though she was twenty feet away from him, she could see the crinkles form next to them.

She felt breathless. Giddy.

And then she ran.

She didn't care that she was in a swanky lobby in the center of Manhattan. Or that everybody was looking at her as she almost skidded to a stop when she reached them.

Or that as soon as she did, Presley swung her into his arms and squeezed his eyes shut, as though she was the most precious, beautiful thing he'd ever held.

"Lift me too!" Delilah shouted, pulling at Presley's arm.

He put Cassie down, his eyes still on hers. And swung Delilah up so her face was at the same height as Cassie's.

"We came in a taxi!" Delilah told her. "It was bright yellow. And Daddy swore because he couldn't download the Boober app."

She smiled at him, loving Delilah's mispronunciations. Damn she'd missed them both. He grinned back.

"What..." She shook her head. It didn't matter what he was doing here. The fact he was here was everything.

He shifted Delilah onto his hip, then reached out for Cassie, his hand cupping her face like he couldn't believe she was there.

"I'm an idiot."

"No, you're not." She shook her head. "Nobody calls my man an idiot."

"Is that what I am?" he asked her.

"Always."

He exhaled heavily, leaning forward to brush his lips against hers. "That's good. Because I've come to take you home."

———

"I think I just got fired." Cassie grinned at him as he tiptoed out of the hotel bedroom. Delilah was fast asleep.

"Did Bryan call?"

"No, his assistant did. She wanted to know if I'd be back tomorrow because we have an interview with a magazine."

"What did you tell them?"

"That I'd be in Hartson's Creek by then. With the people I love."

"That sounds more like you quit than got fired," he said softly. He walked toward her, pulling her close. Damn, he'd missed this. The softness, the talking, the being with her.

It had only been a week, but it felt like a lifetime.

They'd spent the rest of the day taking Delilah around New York. They'd gone up the Empire State Building, visited the zoo at Central Park, and then they'd gone to a diner where Delilah had gotten the biggest burger she'd ever seen.

By seven she was exhausted. So they'd put her in the bath of the suite that Presley had paid for – mostly because it had two bedrooms – and then he'd let her watch some TV in bed before she finally fell asleep.

And now it was just the two of them. "Want me to order some room service?" he asked.

"That sounds good. I'd love a burger. I've been jonesing for one ever since Delilah scarfed hers in the diner." She grinned.

"I'd take you out if I could but…" he glanced over at the door to Delilah's bedroom.

"You don't get it, do you?" She smiled at him, wrapping her arms around his waist. "I like room service. I like staying at home and watching television with you. I like putting Delilah to bed and knowing she's safe while we get to spend some time together. I don't need you to take me out to know you love me. I fell in love with the package deal."

He swallowed. He still couldn't believe he was here. Nor could anybody else. His phone had been ringing most of the afternoon after he'd let Marley know where he was.

His mom, who'd pretty much sobbed when she called. His dad who'd given him a gruff verbal slap on the back for going to win the girl.

His clients who wanted to know when he'd be back to finish up the work and meet the deadline.

And finally Alex, who'd blown up at Pres for going to New York and possibly ruining Cassie's chances. She'd stolen the phone from him as Alex lambasted him, and carefully told him that she'd decided to invoke the break clause of the contract.

Which meant as her self-appointed manager, Alex wasn't going to get the nice bonus he'd been offered.

As Delilah had run ahead of them in Central Park, they'd taken a few stolen moments to talk. He'd filled her in about his four am decision, and his drive to New York. And she'd held him tightly, as though she was afraid he'd disappear if she let go.

They'd planned to stay for another day in New York, but Delilah had been firm that she wanted to go home. She wanted to see her grandparents, her school friends. And Pres, suspected, most of all she wanted to make sure Cassie came back to Hartson's Creek.

Not that Cassie was upset about that. She agreed with Delilah, it was time to go home. And he was so damn excited about that. Every time the guilt threatened to rise he pushed it firmly back down.

She wanted to come home. She'd made that clear.

And he wanted nothing more than to be the one to drive her there. He'd made her leave and he'd be the one bringing her back. There was a symmetry to it that felt right.

He rang down to room service, ordering them both a burger. When he turned around, Cassie was curled up on the sofa, hugging her legs to her chest. She'd changed into a pair of yoga pants and a sweater that fell over her shoulder. He'd never seen her looking more beautiful.

"Are you sure?" he said, his voice thick.

"About the burger?" She gave him a confused smile.

He shook his head. "About this. About us." He gestured around the living area of the suite, which was full of Delilah's things. Shoes by the door, coloring on the table. She'd even left her socks on the floor.

"I've never been more certain of anything," she told him.

The tightness in his chest felt different this time. Not painful. More like something in there was being mended. Fused.

Coming together, the way it was supposed to. He had another person in his heart now.

And she was there to stay.

He walked over and dropped to his knees in front of where she was sitting, pulling her forward until their lips met. "I've missed you so damn much."

"Then stop sending me away," she murmured.

"I've stopped," he promised. "It's not happening again."

And then words disappeared because they needed this kiss. It was more than a reconnection, it was a promise.

I promise I won't be an idiot again.

I promise I won't listen to you if you are.

They didn't need words, when their mouths connected like this.

He pushed the hair from her face, kissing her jaw, her cheek, her brow. "It's not going to be easy, you know that?"

"I've been dating you for a while. Long enough to know you're not an easy man." Her gaze was soft. "But nothing worth fighting for is ever easy. I love you and I love Delilah. That's all that matters. Everything else will have to wait."

His breath caught. "We love you so much."

"Then come here," she whispered, pulling his mouth back to hers.

So he did. And it was heaven.

CHAPTER
Thirty

"OH MY GOD, that man sure does clean up well," Gemma whispered to her, as the two of them watched Presley climb out of the Beast and walk over to the dance hall.

Cassie's heart pounded against her chest. It had been two weeks since she'd come home, and they'd spent most of their free time together – with Delilah. On Sunday they'd gone to church together and then to dinner with his family, and Delilah had been her little shadow.

They'd agreed that they should still live apart for a while. Get Delilah used to having Cassie around before they decided what to do next. But it felt like they were traveling the journey together – one that would end with them all living together.

It was exciting and comforting all at once. She loved it.

"Hi." He smiled at them both as he walked through the door. "You ready?"

"Yes. But where are we going?" she asked him. He'd asked if he could pick her up right from work, since it was her late night. She'd managed to finish her class and jump in the shower before he'd arrived.

He'd told her to dress casually, but that was such a man-type instruction. What did that mean anyway? Jeans? Sweats? In the end, she'd chosen a little dress embroidered with flowers, plus some cowboy boots and a denim jacket.

And now she was glad she'd made an effort, because her man was looking *fine*. He must have stopped at home from the new renovation he was working on over in the next town, because he'd changed out of his work jeans and engineer boots into a pair of dark navy pants and a blue shirt, that brought out the color of his eyes. His hair, like hers, was damp.

They both worked jobs that required energy. And a shower in the evening. She liked that he'd dressed up for her.

"Yeah, where are you going?" Gemma asked, grinning at him. "We've been trying to guess all day."

"What did you come up with?"

"Well, if it was me I'd be suggesting you go straight home to Cassie's and christen every room. But you two have the patience of a saint."

His eyes met Cassie's and he grinned, because alone time was a precious commodity. That was one of the things about being a single dad. You came as a package.

One she loved desperately.

But this alone time together, they both needed it. Date night. They'd agreed to do it once a week starting tonight.

"Tempting as that sounds, I'd like to feed her first," he smiled. "I'm not a complete animal."

"Just a partial one," Cassie said, biting down a smile. Because there was that one time last week when things got the better of them, and they'd slipped outside and some things got done when Delilah was asleep.

Specifically her. She got done. So good her thighs were still clenching thinking about it.

In some ways, it was like she'd never left for New York. Gemma had welcomed her back with open arms, and after a couple of days she'd rediscovered her groove with her classes, much to the pleasure of her students.

And she'd called Alex. Who'd begrudgingly said that she'd done the right thing in coming home. They were due to play at a bar in a couple of weeks, but everybody was clear that this was all the band would ever be.

Just a bit of fun. A hobby. Marley had laughed and told them he didn't want it any other way. Alex had asked if he could keep posting TikToks.

And yeah, they were all okay with that.

She'd even called her mom. Told her where she was living now. And yes, her mom hadn't seemed very interested but for the first time in her life it hadn't hurt when she hung up with her. There was an acceptance there. Her mom would never be involved in her life.

But she'd found her family. Her home. With the Hartson's. Maddie was as excited to have a new woman in the family as Cassie was to be there. They'd already made a date to go to a spa in a few weeks time.

She smiled at the thought of it.

"What's got you grinning?" Presley asked.

"Just thinking about your mom."

Gemma laughed out loud. "Is that the most unromantic sentence in history, or what?"

"Shut up. I like Presley's mom." Cassie shook her head, grinning.

"Yeah, but try not to think about her tonight, okay?"

Presley groaned. "Can we stop talking about my mom, please?"

"You started it," Cassie pointed out. "You're the one who asked what I was smiling about."

"I take it back," he said, deadpan. "Let's not think of any family members tonight.

"We can try," she agreed.

They said goodbye to Gemma, and then they walked over

to the Beast. Pres had promised to drive her to work in the morning, since she wouldn't have her car at home.

And of course he opened the door for her, because he was definitely half-gentleman half-animal.

Like a minotaur. But better looking.

She smiled to herself again.

"I'm not asking this time," he said, climbing into the driver's seat.

"You can ask. No family members are involved."

He tipped his head to the side. "What are you thinking about?"

"That you're an enigma. A gentleman when clothed and a beast in bed."

He blew out a mouthful of air, his face flushing. "Okay then."

She grinned. "You *did* ask."

———

"I love that movie," Cassie said, smiling, as Presley pulled out of the drive-in theater. They'd had a prime spot on the parking lot, mostly because his uncle and aunt owned the theater and he'd called ahead to reserve it.

He'd made a picnic for them that they'd eaten on the flatbed of the truck while they waited for the movie to start. And of course half the town had walked over to say hi to them, in an attempt to get all the gossip on her being back in Hartson's Creek.

She'd half-expected Presley to be annoyed about it, but he'd actually been smiling at people, laughing and joking.

She felt like she'd found yet another side to this man who seemed to have a thousand facets. The friendly, laid-back side. She hadn't seen it before. But some of the people who'd known him for years hadn't been fazed at all.

She wondered if he'd hidden that side after Jade died.

Whatever it was, she liked it almost as much as the gentleman and the animal.

Though she'd always have the softest spot for the animal.

The credits were rolling, and Pres leaned forward to switch off the digital radio station they'd tuned to for the movie audio. Her heart did a little clench because only Presley Hartson would have noticed that as part of an eighties revival festival, *Flashdance* was playing at the drive-in.

He'd never seen it before. And yeah, it was cheesy and so very old-fashioned with the steel mill and the welding, but he'd held her tight while they watched it.

And reminded her that he still wanted to rip a leotard off her.

Next date night, she was going to make that happen.

"Where are we going?" she asked, when he took a left instead of a right out of the theater.

"We've got one more hour before curfew," he told her. "I promised Delilah I'd be home by midnight."

One of his neighbors' teenagers was babysitting. It was another first, him being able to trust somebody other than family with his daughter.

Not that he hadn't been checking his phone every half an hour. But she liked that.

Liked that he'd always put his daughter first.

"We could go back to my place," she suggested. Because she did have a leotard in mind.

"We could. Or we could go here. He turned up a dirt path. The Beast's suspension started to rise and fall with the dips in the dirt, making her lift up and down with it.

"What's here?"

"Nothing," he grunted. "That's the point."

They'd reached the end of the road. Ahead of them was a gate that led to a forest. She assumed it was an access road.

"Did you just bring me to the local make out spot?" she asked him.

He gave her a wicked grin. "Very possibly."

"Even though we're both grown adults and we have our own homes where we could get undressed without half the local wildlife watching?"

"We can't go to my place, and it'd take too long to get to yours," he told her.

"It takes ten minutes."

His eyes met hers. "As I said, too long. Now are you coming here or what?"

She looked at the space between him and the steering wheel. "It looks kind of cozy."

"That's the plan." He was still looking at her as he reached his arm down and sprung the seat backward. Then he was helping her scramble on top of him until she was straddling his long, muscled legs, her arms wrapped around his neck.

"Hi," she said softly.

"Hi." He brushed his lips against hers. "Have I told you how beautiful you look tonight?"

"Yes, but I'm happy for you to do it again."

His lips curled. "You're the most gorgeous woman I've ever seen."

"Actions speak louder than words," she told him.

And it was like she'd said the magic words. Because he was kissing her like his life depended on it, his hands feathering over her body, his fingers tracing the soft skin of her thighs, then moving up to her hips, pulling her down on him.

Leaving her in no doubt of how gorgeous he thought she was.

Their kiss deepened, and she realized how much she needed this. The animal in him.

Her beast.

He tipped her head back, grazing his teeth across her

throat, then dipped his head to the top of her chest, kissing it, before reaching around to unzip it at the back.

"Bet you're glad I wore a dress now," she said breathlessly, as he cupped the weight of her breasts through her bra.

"Very, very glad."

"Note to Presley. Don't say casual when you mean fuckable."

He grinned at her. "Noted."

"Thank you."

Her bra was next to come off. His mouth captured her nipple and the pleasure of it made her body arch. Too far, because she hit the horn on the steering wheel making them both jump.

"Jesus." He shook his head. "You want to wake everybody up?"

"There's nobody here." She looked around. "Is there?"

He laughed. "No, luckily for us. How often have you made out in a car anyway?"

"I grew up in New York City. Nobody had a car."

He lifted a brow.

"In that case, welcome to your first lesson in being a small town girlfriend."

The next few moments were a scramble of mouths and fingers. Unfastening jeans, pulling down panties. And when he finally lifted her over him his eyes were shining.

He was smiling.

And yeah, she was smiling too.

Because it didn't get much better than this. Making out with your guy in the cab of his truck because you couldn't wait until you got home.

And then she slid down on him, a groan escaping his lips as he was engulfed by her. He let her get settled for a moment. Accustomed to being full. Before he curled his fingers around her hips and braced his biceps to lift her up before slamming her back down. He buried his face in her breasts, kissing and worshipping, then he moved a hand down between them to make sure she came first.

There he was. The gentleman. Blending perfectly with the animal.

He was her beast.

And she would never get enough of him.

Epilogue

"SHE'S HERE, Daddy, she's here." Delilah was bouncing up and down as she stared out of the window, watching as Cassie parked her car in the driveway. As Cassie climbed out of the car, her long legs stretching out as her feet hit the blacktop, Delilah turned to look at Pres.

"I can see that." He winked at her as she started racing for the door. "Hey," he called out. "This isn't your house, you're not supposed to be the one welcoming people."

It was Thanksgiving morning and the whole family was spending it at his parents' house. Mostly because it was the biggest, but also because his mom and dad loved to entertain.

The whole place smelled of the turkey that his mom had gotten up to put in the oven at some stupid time in the morning. Cranberries were cooking in a pan on the stovetop, their ruby red skins splitting as they bubbled away. His mom had already put a Christmas playlist on — following a long discussion with his dad about when exactly it was acceptable to have Mariah's voice blasting out of the speakers.

His dad lost that argument. But he got a kiss out of it, so he looked happy enough.

Delilah opened the door, completely ignoring Pres' warning and Cassie walked inside, hugging her tightly.

"Look at you," Cassie said." What a pretty dress."

"I'm Belle," Delilah told her, doing a twirl in her golden dress, the metallic threads catching the light as she turned. "From *Beauty and the Beast*."

"I can see that," Cassie said, indulging her even though she'd seen Delilah's outfit before. At Halloween, and then pretty much every day since, because he could barely prise his daughter out of it.

She'd insisted on wearing it for Thanksgiving, and Pres couldn't see any reason why that was a problem. He hadn't been able to give her ringlets the way she wanted, but she was beaming anyway.

Stepping back, Cassie's hands rested on her shoulders as she smiled at his little girl. And when she looked up, her eyes caught Pres'.

His eyes searched her face. Damn, she was beautiful.

"Everything okay with Gemma?" he asked. Cassie had called to say she'd be a little late, because Gemma was having contractions.

"Yep. Just a false alarm."

"Another one?"

Cassie smiled. "I think she's going for the trifecta."

Gemma was pregnant with her third — and according to her last — baby. She was almost nine months now, and hating every moment of her last trimester. Cassie had stopped by to help her with some Thanksgiving preparations before coming to meet him here.

"You look good," she murmured, walking over to hug him. He'd put on a pair of dress pants and a pale blue shirt. "Ooh, you smell good too."

"So do you." His eyes glanced down at the knit brown dress she was wearing. It clung to her every curve, making his mouth dry and his body ache. She'd teamed it with some brown leather boots and was wearing her hair down, the way he loved it.

"Come with me," Delilah urged impatiently, pulling at Cassie's hand. "I want to show you something."

Cassie laughed, allowing Delilah to lead her away. Pres watched as they disappeared around the corner, their laughter echoing back to him.

Taking a deep breath, he walked over to the kitchen where his mom was stirring a pot of gravy.

"Hey, sweetheart," she said, looking up at him. "Cassie get here okay?"

"Yeah. She'll be in in a minute to say hi. Delilah just dragged her off. I think she wants to show Cassie her *Beauty and the Beast* dance."

"She has a dance already?"

"She has a dance for everything," Pres said. "You know that." She never walked when she could dance. Right now her dream job was to be a ballerina when she grew up. Or it was, until he'd told her she may have to move to a big city to work.

"Can't I be a ballerina in Hartson's Creek?" she'd asked frowning.

"Probably." That conversation was for another day. The kid was only seven, after all.

Pres walked around the breakfast bar to where his mom was standing, the wooden spoon she was using to stir the gravy still in her hand. Her hips were swaying softly, as Elvis crooned that he was having a blue Christmas.

"Can I do something to help?" Pres asked for the third time that morning.

And once again his mom shook her head. "No. We've got this. Your dad is just sharpening his knives."

Another Thanksgiving tradition. His dad's carving knives were his babies. If anybody else touched them he'd have a fit. And Pres knew better than to try.

"So, how's work? You started on a new job, didn't you?" his mom asked, stirring the gravy again.

"Yep. A commercial building. It's good. Busy, but good." He paused, taking a deep breath. "Actually, Mom, there's something I want to talk to you about. While nobody else is around."

His mom turned off the burner, sensing the seriousness in his voice. "What is it?"

"I'm planning to propose to Cassie today."

His mom's eyes widened, a smile spreading across her face. "Oh, Pres. That's wonderful news!"

He grinned because it really was. He and Cassie had talked about this. About marriage and family and babies. And they'd agreed they'd know when the time was right.

Last week they'd gone shopping for some outfits for Gemma's new baby – a boy – and it felt like something had changed. They probably weren't ready for children yet, but they would be.

And if they wanted that someday, he was going to be married to the woman.

"Thanks," he said softly. "I just wanted to ask your advice on something."

"What is it?" She tipped her head to the side. "If it's my blessing you want, you know you've got it. Not that you need it, you're both grown adults." She gave him a soft smile. "You've done everything right, honey. You've taken it slow. Made sure Delilah is happy. But you deserve this for yourself."

Yeah, they'd taken it slow over the past year and a bit. Cassie was still living in her house, and he in his. But it was getting harder and harder to say goodnight to her without having her in his bed.

He was ready for the next step. He hoped she was too.

But that wasn't what was bothering him.

"I'm wondering about Delilah. Should I talk to her before I

propose? After?" He lifted a brow. "I googled it and there was no consensus." Damn the internet. Where was it when you needed some black and white advice?

His mom thought for a moment, her soft gaze on him. Her brows pulled together as she finally responded. "You know what? I think you should talk to her first. She's a smart girl. She'll understand what's going on. And if there's something she hates, it's not being included in things."

Wasn't that the truth? She'd gotten used to him and Cassie disappearing on date night, but she preferred it when he and Cassie spent time with her.

And they did it a lot.

Cassie hadn't been lying when she said she loved his daughter. Watching the two of them bond over the past year had been one of the most beautiful experiences of his life.

It was like they both needed each other. Cassie needed to be a better mom than her own, and Delilah needed somebody to love her like a mom.

"And you know," his mom continued. "If Cassie says no, then she'll be able to help you explain it to Delilah. She loves that little girl so much."

He blinked, shocked by her words. "You think she'll say no?" His stomach tightened.

Something about his expression made his mom laugh.

"No, I don't. But I can imagine you're thinking the worst. So I thought I'd add that in there." She walked over to check on the turkey.

"By the way, Cassie told me her mom called last week," his mom said when she'd checked the temperature of the turkey and put it back in the oven. Her eyes were soft. She knew how difficult Cassie's relationship with her mom was. He was proud of his mom for stepping in there and being supportive. Being the mom Cassie never had.

Pres got the distinct impression that his mom was as

supportive of Cassie as she was of her own kids. And he liked that a lot.

He let out a long breath. "Yeah, she called asking if she could come down for Thanksgiving. Apparently she found out who Dad was. And suddenly wanted to come and visit."

His mom winced. "Ouch. I'm guessing she said no."

"She did." And he was damn proud of that, too. "She told her she wasn't interested in having a relationship with somebody who wasn't there for her at her lowest. And then she hung up."

His mom caught his gaze. "That was brave of her."

"It was." He nodded. She'd cried afterward though. But it had been a good kind of cry. The type that cleansed, not hurt.

It felt like another step forward. They were making them together, every day. Making their lives better with every stride.

The timer on the stove started ringing, letting his mom know that the potatoes were ready."

"Good. I'm glad she stood up for herself." His mom checked the potatoes. "Now I need to get everything ready for dinner. Go spend some time with your girls. And don't forget, you, Marley, and Hendrix will be cleaning up later."

———

"They're like animals," Maddie said to Cassie as she watched her boys fight over who had to clean the pots. "I tried to bring them up to be polite. I swear I did. But..." she trailed off as Hendrix threw a handful of water at Marley. "Boys! No water fights."

"Can I join in the water fight?" Delilah asked hopefully.

"No." Maddie shook her head firmly. "Water fights are for the summer."

Hendrix sniggered as Marley shook his now-wet hair at him. "You look like a dog," he said. "But uglier."

"Shut up." Marley rolled his eyes.

Delilah walked over to Cassie and sat on her lap. "I know a secret," she told her, turning her head to look at Cassie. She was beaming. "But I can't tell you what it is."

Maddie clucked her tongue. "You're not supposed to tell people that you know secrets."

Delilah looked at her, wide eyed, as though Maddie was telling her the sky was green. "Why not?"

"Because then they're going to try to guess what it is. And spoil the surprise."

"Do you know what the surprise is, Granny?" Delilah whispered loudly. "Did Daddy tell you too?"

"No." Maddie shook her head, but there was a smile on her face. One that made Cassie suspect she was lying.

"I do, I know." Delilah sang, looking extremely happy about that. "It's such a good secret, too." She turned to Cassie, a huge smile on her face. "You're going to love it."

Maddie glanced at Delilah, then looked over her shoulder at Pres. "Why don't you go talk to Daddy about the secret?" she suggested.

"Because we already talked about it." Delilah rolled her eyes. "Silly."

Cassie was trying not to laugh. She had a little inkling of what was going on. And it made her heart beat way too fast. "Maybe we should talk about something else," she suggested, mostly because Delilah looked like she was about to burst.

"Like what?" the little girl asked, tipping her head to the side as though she was trying to think of anything that was more exciting than her secret.

"I don't know. How about you show me your dance again?" Cassie pointed at the rug in front of the sofa where the three of them were sitting.

Delilah shook her head. "But I don't want to dance. I want Daddy to..."

"Honey, hush," Maddie said quickly. Then she quickly got

up and strode over to the kitchen were Pres and Marley were talking softly. She whispered something in his ear.

Pres rolled his eyes and nodded. For a moment he looked so much like Delilah that Cassie's heart clenched.

With a determined expression on his face, he put the dishcloth down in the sink and strode over to the living area, picking Delilah up. "Are you trying to spoil my surprise?" he asked her, tickling her sides until she started to giggle.

"When are you going to ask her, Daddy?" Delilah squealed.

"I guess right now." He put her down, sliding his hand into his pocket to bring out a velvet box.

Before Delilah could say anything else, Pres knelt down in front of Cassie, taking her hands in his.

"You're the best thing that's ever happened to me," he said, his voice soft but full of emotion. "From the first moment I saw you, something inside of me knew you were the one. And every moment we've spent together since, I've become more certain. You're the most beautiful, funny, kind person I've met."

Delilah was jumping up and down. "Ask her! Show her the ring."

Pres' shoulders started to shake with laughter. "I'm trying, kid. Give me a break here."

"It's green," Delilah told Cassie, clearly getting impatient with Presley's proposal.

"Honey..." Pres lifted a brow at her.

Delilah frowned, then leaned forward, whispering loudly, "And it has diamonds," she told Cassie. "Big sparkly ones. And there are carrots. But I don't know where because I didn't see them."

Cassie started to laugh, because this was just too perfect. Delilah looked at her strangely. "Why are you laughing?"

"I don't know," she told her. "I'm just emotional."

Delilah ignored her. "But you only get to wear it if you say yes. That's what Daddy said."

Cassie's eyes met Presley's. He was laughing too now.

"I'm sorry," he said. "This was all planned out."

"And he told me," Delilah said proudly. "It was our secret." She looked at Presley. On his knees, his face was at the same height as hers. "Give her the ring, Dad."

He blew out a mouthful of air. "Cassie Simons, will you do me the honor of becoming my wife?" He said it quickly, as though afraid Delilah would interrupt again.

Cassie was still laughing. And Nodding. "Yes," she told him, tears filling her eyes. "Yes, I will."

"She said yes!" Delilah did a fist bump. "And now you just won a ring."

"She didn't win it," Maddie whispered. "It's a gift."

"Is it? I thought it was a prize."

"You know what?" Maddie said to Delilah. "There's something in my bedroom I want to show you. Shall we leave Daddy and Cassie to it?"

"Is it a secret?" Delilah asked, clearly on a roll.

"Yes. A big one."

"Hoo boy!" Delilah clapped her hands together. "Then let's go."

Marley and Hendrix had conveniently escaped, too. No doubt they'd gone down to join their dad in the den, to watch the pregame warm up.

She knew they'd congratulate them in a bit. But right now it was just her and Presley.

And the ring he was holding out.

"I'm sorry," he said again. "It was going to be more romantic."

She shook her head. "It was perfect. Exactly what I wanted." Presley and their daughter asking her together. Because Delilah really felt like hers.

They'd talked about her adopting Delilah one day. When

the time was right. With their engagement, they were getting a step closer.

Pres stood and pulled her into his arms, the velvet box still in his hand. Cassie felt the cool metal of the ring as he slipped it on her finger.

"I love you," he whispered in her ear.

"I love you too," she replied, feeling the weight of the ring on her finger. She lifted it up, turned her hand left and right, watching as the light caught the stones.

It was beautiful. Like him. Like the life he was giving her.

"Thank you for my prize," she whispered. And he started to laugh again.

"I feel like I'm the winner here." He brushed his lips against hers, sending a shiver down her spine. "Thank you for being mine."

"I always was." Her eyes caught his and her chest felt full. She was finally home. And there was no place else she wanted to be.

The End

Dear Reader

Thank you so much for reading THAT ONE TOUCH. If you enjoyed it and you get a chance, I'd be so grateful if you can leave a review. And don't forget to check out the free bonus epilogue which you can download here: https://dl. bookfunnel.com/u98wcdmehp

The next book in the series is Marley's story. Find out what happens when he falls for single mom Kate in THAT ONE HEARTBREAK

WANT TO KEEP UP TO DATE ON ALL MY NEWS?

Join me on my exclusive mailing list, where you'll be the first to hear about new releases, sales, and other book-related news.

To sign up just put the following address into your phone browser:
https://www.subscribepage.com/carrieelksas

I can't wait to share more stories with you.

Yours,

Carrie xx

Also by Carrie Elks

THE HEARTBREAK BROTHERS NEXT GENERATION SERIES

THE HEARTBREAK BROTHERS SERIES

A gorgeous small town series about four brothers and the women who capture their hearts.

THE SALINGER BROTHERS SERIES

A swoony romantic comedy series featuring six brothers and the strong and smart women who tame them.

THE WINTERVILLE SERIES

A gorgeously wintery small town romance series, featuring six cousins who fight to save the town their grandmother built.

Hearts In Winter

Leave Me Breathless

Memories Of Mistletoe

Every Shade Of Winter

Mine For The Winter

ANGEL SANDS SERIES

A heartwarming small town beach series, full of best friends, hot guys and happily-ever-afters.

Let Me Burn

She's Like the Wind

Sweet Little Lies

Just A Kiss

Baby I'm Yours

Pieces Of Us

Chasing The Sun

Heart And Soul

Lost In Him

THE SHAKESPEARE SISTERS SERIES

An epic series about four strong yet vulnerable sisters, and the alpha men who steal their hearts.

Summer's Lease

A Winter's Tale

Absent in the Spring

By Virtue Fall

THE LOVE IN LONDON SERIES

Three books about strong and sassy women finding love in the big city.

Coming Down

Broken Chords

Canada Square

STANDALONE

Fix You

An epic romance that spans the decades. Breathtaking and angsty and all the things in between.

If you'd like to get an email when I release a new book, please sign up here:

CARRIE ELKS' NEWSLETTER

About the Author

Carrie Elks writes contemporary romance with a sizzling edge. Her first book, *Fix You*, has been translated into eight languages and made a surprise appearance on *Big Brother* in Brazil. Luckily for her, it wasn't voted out.

Carrie lives with her husband, two lovely children and a larger-than-life black pug called Plato. When she isn't writing or reading, she can be found baking, drinking an occasional (!) glass of wine, or chatting on social media.

You can find Carrie in all these places
www.carrieelks.com
carrie.elks@mail.com

Printed in Great Britain
by Amazon

41858956R00178